THE WAY TO THE SUN

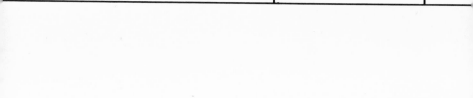

THE WAY TO THE SUN

BY ROBERT BEYLEN

TRANSLATED FROM THE FRENCH BY LEN ORTZEN

LITTLE, BROWN AND COMPANY   BOSTON   TORONTO

FOREWORD

At the end of 1940, the United States, Russia and Japan had not yet entered World War Two. The Free French Forces had just been constituted and Britain and Germany were fighting at sea and in the air. But the sole land fighting armies were the British and Italians in North Africa.

These opposing forces in Libya and Egypt were not only numerically unequal—Graziani had nearly a quarter of a million men under his command against Wavell's thirty-six thousand—but the British had insufficient artillery, supplies, armoured vehicles and the means of transportation in general; a severe disadvantage in a country where distance was a weapon of war.

But this small British army was comprised of first-rate soldiers, whether English—such as those of the Seventh Armoured Division (the famous 'Desert Rats', as they came to be called)—Indians, New Zealanders or Australians. Plus, the commanding officers were intelligent and keen, open to new ideas and prepared for bold action.

The terrain—the vacuous and arid desert—forced these combat troops to carry with them all that was needed in order to live, travel and fight. It was the ideal situation for military strategists to play out a 'war game' with real vehicles and real men.

In September 1940, Graziani had gone over to the attack. It was a timid advance; after four days of cautious probing, his invading Italians reached Sidi Barrani and began digging in. Rome claimed a great victory and triumphantly announced that 'the trams were running again in the streets of Sidi Barrani'.

This communiqué was somewhat surprising since at that time Sidi Barrani could claim little more than a few huts of baked mud and a landing-strip pompously called 'the aerodrome'.

Meanwhile, Wavell had completed the planning of 'Operation Compass', which when submitted to Churchill for approval had made him 'purr like half-a-dozen cats'. This offensive operation was put under the command of General Richard O'Connor. With his slight lisp and shy manner, this small man was very different from the piratical-looking Wavell and had nothing of the conqueror or Empire-builder about him. But O'Connor's understanding of the terrain and its possibilities resembled that of Wellington or Rommel.

On 6 December 1940 the small British army began moving up towards the assembly area—nicknamed 'Piccadilly Circus' in mock British fashion. On 9 December the Italian fortified camp at Nibeiua, held by a division commanded by General Maletti, was attacked and taken by a Scottish and an Indian battalion supported by two squadrons of Matilda tanks. General Maletti was killed as he stepped from his shelter and that evening the nearby fort at Tommar was also captured by the British.

Thus a brilliant offensive began which, planned as a five-day raid into enemy territory, continued without halt for two months. By then, O'Connor's little army had advanced 500 miles, destroyed 10 Italian divisions, taken 130,000 prisoners, and captured 850 trucks, 400 tanks and thousands of vehicles. All for a loss of 1,774 men killed, wounded or missing.

On 10 February 1941 British advance units reached El Agheila on the border of Tripolitania and halted to allow time for re-formation. A hundred miles to the west, the remnants of the Italian army were hurriedly digging in around Sirte. The events in this novel are not set in the coastal areas where this fighting took place nor are they concerned with staff conferences. Its chief characters are not drawn from those officers and men who fought so courageously.

Neither Basil Ferguson, François Mattei nor Lorena Dalloz was inclined towards heroism. But subtle events and violent circumstances after February 10, 1941 were to take control and decide the future of these three—so disparate in background and lifestyle yet dependent on one another in their fight for survival.

PART ONE

'Every chance meeting is really an appointment.'
                                    J.-L. Borges

I

Basil Ferguson sat with his back against the fuselage, his hands on hunched-up knees. The wind—the fresh, rarefied air—penetrated his thin, unsuitable clothing.

Two legs dangled from the turret where Skinny sat leaning forward on his Vickers machine-gun. To his right loomed Calloway's broad back; the Australian pilot had a black silk stocking tied loosely around his neck, a shoulder-holster housing a heavy revolver and a ridiculous Anzac hat hanging from the back of his seat.

Skinny turned and bent towards him, held up a forefinger and drew the other across it. 'Half an hour,' he mouthed.

The din of the engines made his voice inaudible but Basil smiled in understanding.

He wanted to stretch his legs but it was impossible. The hold of the Beaufighter was filled with crates and cases with only a small space made available for him when he had clambered aboard at Gibraltar. He envied the two airmen who could talk to one another over the intercom. His mouth dry from lack of conversation, he tried to remember the last words he had uttered before take-off, before the engines had burst into a deep, steady roar—except when Calloway had jettisoned the extra fuel-tanks and the engines had momentarily raced. But he could not remember.

He wanted to be with Calloway in the protruding cockpit where he'd be able to see the other Beaufighters flying in formation. It would be reassuring.

But he was forbidden to budge. His cramped legs were numb now and his back ached.

Why had he asked for a place aboard this uncomfortable aircraft anyhow? He could have been waiting quietly now at Gibraltar while repairs were made on the ship which had brought him from England. Had he felt guilty for being at the War Office in London where the greatest danger was the possibility of being knocked down by fire-engines roaring through the streets? But it could not be that, for Cairo H.Q., to which he had been posted, was much less vulnerable than London—apart from the risk of cirrhosis of the liver. An impulsive act, then? God save you from any others! Then the memory of the explosion of a munition ship not far from his troopship chilled him. Again, he saw the flaming debris hurtling through the air, the huge cloud of lurid black smoke belching up, and that horrible thing that had fallen on the deck, the flabby, bloody, armless trunk of a man.

Perhaps it was due to fear then? You acted from fear. Fear of shrieking like those seamen you saw struggling in the water, their eyes bulging with horror. If this Beaufighter is shot down, at least death will come quickly. At three hundred miles an hour, he thought with gloomy relish, there'd be no one to witness your dying.

But then he knew he had not acted from fear, nor from scruples, nor from impulsiveness. He had never done anything for such reasons. Often he did not do what he wanted; in fact, sometimes he did just the opposite, which led him into confused situations. He remembered the day—it was two years ago now—that he had persuaded the editor of *Punch* to take a weekly cartoon from him. That done, he was perplexed and annoyed by having to think one up. However, he had acquired a reputation as a humorist and when the war broke out, he was given a commission and posted to the map section at the War Office.

His parents were surprised at his transfer to Cairo.

'Whatever you do,' his father had said, 'don't start taking yourself for another Lawrence of Arabia. I wouldn't reproach you for uniting the Arabs, but for writing indecent books.'

'How lucky you are, Basil,' his mother, who could not adjust to the wartime rationing, had exclaimed. 'You'll be able to get some decent tea and much else besides!'

He felt the aircraft drop into an air-pocket and the engines seemed to falter. Above his head, Skinny was banging his boots together. The gunner must be cold too. Basil thrust his hands under his armpits, shivered and yawned.

You'll see the sun again, he told himself, and thought back to that summer in 1936 when he, Tommy Greenhouse and Al had set off in Tommy's old car and driven across France from Calais to Perpignan. He remembered the sandy coast—somewhere near Montpellier, wasn't it?—with those ugly chalets, salt lakes smelling of mud, and lukewarm sea. They had taken long lazy walks in the sun, and drunk a dry pink wine that had nearly knocked them out. Then they had driven along the Pyrenees but were not permitted to cross the frontier into Spain. Watching Irun burning, they were unaware that the war would ever concern them. The columns of smoke rose high in the warm air and the refugees poured across the international bridge. It was there on the beach at Hendaye that he had made love at three in the morning, after a night of drinking. The girl said it was the first time she had tasted whisky, and he had admitted that it was the first time he had made love on a beach. Another evening he and Al had gotten into a fight in front of this girl—what was her name? Marie-Lou, that was it—and she had thought they were fighting over her. Al left by train the next day, but Tommy had stayed with him until their money ran out. And now Al was dead, killed at St. Valery-en-Caux during the retreat in 1940, and Tommy was waiting for him in Cairo. ('This is going to be a long war,' Tommy had written a few months before, 'so it's best to go through it with your friends.') That had been the one and only mention of the war in his letters. It would be good to see him again—maybe even this evening.

Basil looked up and saw Skinny beckoning him to come up into the turret.

He rose heavily and shook his legs. Clambering over some crates of beer, he hoisted himself up to Skinny by gripping the shiny machine-gun.

The five other Beaufighters were swaying gently in formation. Skinny pointed to something in the distance below. It looked like an oval table-top, grey and green, placed on white cliffs standing in a sea of marvellous blue, with a tiny island on either side.

'Malta!' Skinny yelled.

Just then, the formation slowly and gracefully broke up, and the details of the island gradually became distinct—the wide jagged bay of Marsa Xlokh, the long inlet to Valletta harbour and the town of flat roofs, the fields and their network of stone walls and hedges.

The Beaufighter banked into a turn, almost throwing Basil off balance. He grazed his hand on something and steadied himself by clutching Skinny's shoulder. The sergeant with his sunburnt face and red woollen bonnet drawn down over his forehead reminded him of peacetime ski-slopes, not war in the air.

'Coo-ee!' Calloway gave his native Australian cry in a voice so high-pitched that it could be heard above the engines, and Basil felt the aircraft sway as the pilot put the nose down.

The Beaufighter came to a stop at the end of the runway, just missing some soldiers and civilians who were busily filling a bomb-crater with gravel.

Calloway shut off the engines and the sudden hush was almost painful. Basil felt immobile. Calloway, however, took his wide-brimmed hat from the back of his seat, dented the crown with the side of his hand, and put it on. Unbuckling himself, he slid from his seat.

'How did you like the trip?' he asked Basil.

Without waiting for a reply, he opened the trap-door and started down the iron ladder. Basil sat and watched him, and caught the smell of earth and warm oil.

Calloway, stopping halfway down the ladder, his head and shoulders still inside the aircraft, said kindly : 'Come and stretch your legs. We'll be off again in an hour.'

He disappeared from view.

'Here we go,' said Skinny, jumping down from his turret and helping Basil to his feet.

As he followed Skinny down the ladder, he sighed with pleasure. The sun was high, the air wonderfully mild, and the tarmac warm to his feet.

'Much better down here, eh?' said Skinny, rubbing his hands.

'Yes,' agreed Basil.

'Well, how did you like the trip?' Calloway asked again. 'It was a good one, wasn't it?'

'Not bad,' Calloway admitted, his chiselled features breaking into a smile while his grey eyes remained cold. 'This the first time you've flown in a kite like that?'

Basil nodded.

'We flew low because of you. But don't worry, we'll get you to Cairo this evening,' said Calloway, taking off his fur gloves and tucking them into his flying-jacket. 'And I'm ready for a night on the town!'

Basil returned the pilot's smile.

An old Austin came speeding across the airfield. Basil, recognising it as a London taxi painted khaki, watched the crews of two of the other aircraft climb in and wave to Calloway as they passed.

'I'll come back for you!' the driver called in a Lancashire accent.

Calloway took out a pack of cigarettes, offering one to Basil and Skinny.

'How about walking it?' Basil suggested.

Calloway shook his head as he noticed a tanker approaching with two mechanics on the running-board.

'You go ahead, I'll stay here while they fill her up with gas. Every glassful counts on our next hop.'

'Shall I stay with you?' said Skinny.

'No need. You go with the lieutenant.'

'See you later then,' said Basil. 'I'll order you a whisky.'

Calloway grinned. 'Make it a double.'

Skinny and Basil started walking down the cracked runway, an ancient parchment stretching into the distance. Here and there small clumps of dry grass with tiny, violet-like flowers poked their way up through the cracks.

'It's a queer country, sir,' said Skinny.

'Here, you mean?'

'Everywhere.'

'What made you leave Australia?' Basil asked.

'It was Cab,' said Skinny with a smile. 'He had nothing but debts, with his automobile business. One morning he says to me, "Skinny, I'm pulling out. I've had enough of these lawyers always after me. Tell them I've gone for good." "I'm not telling them," I says, "I'm going with you." In my case, it wasn't lawyers but a girl. Ethel was her name, a lovely bit. But she wanted to get married and I wasn't about to set up on my own account and all that. Cab and me, we arrived in England in September '39, just after the outbreak of war, and we volunteered for the RAF.'

And I enlisted, Basil thought, because Julia said I'd look well in khaki. Guess that's how history is made. He chuckled to himself.

'Do you know Australia?' Skinny asked.

'No. I've been to France and Holland. And to Italy, especially Italy . . .'

That's quite close, he told himself. In clear weather, Sicily is probably visible from some parts of this island. Sicily, with its monuments the colour of sulphur and its burnt earth, and that sea which is not equalled anywhere in the world.

'What are the Italians like?' asked Skinny.

'They hate war and they dislike working.'

Skinny laughed. He had big, prominent teeth, and his face crinkled up when he smiled, making him look much older. 'Yes, it's a queer country all right.'

The warmth in the air and the smell of the sea made Basil feel on top of the world. This evening he'd be in Cairo, and would phone Tommy and say 'Guess who's here'. And Tommy would give a shout of joy and reel off the names of all their friends who were out there, and with whom they'd spend the evening.

'Listen!' said Skinny, stopping in his stride.

The air was throbbing with sound that grew louder every moment.

'Bombers,' said Basil.

The two were halfway down the runway. They looked up at the dazzling sky of unvarying blue but saw nothing.

Then Skinny suddenly cried, pointing, 'There they are!' Turning towards the aircraft he shouted, 'Look sharp, Cab! At three o'clock!'

Calloway, who was chatting with the mechanics, looked up and then started running towards the edge of the airfield. The loud throbbing suddenly turned to a high-pitched whistling sound. Three fighters came screeching down towards the runway. The tarmac began to sizzle, the air to hum and the ground to heave, throwing up fine particles of dust that stung Basil's face. Skinny had already plunged flat on the ground. The three Macchis pulled out of their dive and swept low over the airfield. Basil caught a glimpse of their blue underbellies and the Fascist markings on their wings. Then he saw small black dots tumbling down.

'Quick!' yelled Skinny, heaving himself to his feet.

He was already ten yards ahead when Basil started to run. At that moment the first bombs exploded, throwing up great geysers of sand, earth and flame that drew frighteningly near in a mad, zigzagging rush. Basil ran as never before. He felt he would be unable to stop himself when he reached the Austin, which was now standing outside the building a few yards ahead of him. The passengers were getting out of it in rapid succession. One slipped and fell, another plunged head first behind a heap of gravel. Basil heard a loud whistle rising to a terrifying shriek. 'This is it,' he thought. Swerving round the Austin as if avoiding a bull and passing Skinny, he pushed open the door of the building, tripped over a step but had the presence of mind to swing himself round and fall against the opposite wall. There was a blinding flash, and a cloud of dust and earth enveloped him. Bomb-splinters zoomed over his head and chunks of plaster fell down. Curses, shouts, and bouts of coughing erupted around him. Someone's legs were entwined with his. He was choking, and for a few moments he lay still. The danger seemed to be receding. As the dust began to settle, he saw Skinny's white face in the pallid light on his left and a plump major in khaki shorts and sandals, head covered with plaster, lying near him on his right.

The major sat up in a dignified way and looked at Basil and Skinny.

'I was on my way to the shelter,' he said with some annoyance.

Basil looked around and realised they were in the entrance hall to the building. The door had been blown in by the blast and the floor was littered with broken glass. To his left, concrete steps descended into darkness.

The major picked his hat up from the floor and rose to his feet with effort. Basil and Skinny stood up on trembling legs.

Basil felt a certain astonishment. Although his legs were shaking, he felt quite calm. 'It's over for the moment,' he said to himself.

Someone outside was shouting, 'Any casualties?'

The major was vigorously brushing his hat and looking from Basil to Skinny and back again. In the distance a Maltese voice, distinguishable by the Italian intonation, was giving thanks to the Madonna and cursing the heavens above.

'I must point out to you,' the major said to Skinny, putting on his hat, 'that this building is for officers only . . .'

He turned to Basil as though Skinny no longer existed. 'By the way, would you care to make a fourth at bridge?'

The air-raid shelter in the basement of the concrete building was roughly rectangular in shape. A bar took up one end. The bottles and posters along the wall made Basil feel for a moment like he was back in London. Iron tables and chairs were spread out over most of the floor and several narrow passages, strongly buttressed, led out to the ack-ack positions.

Major Thickeridge was guiding Basil to one of the tables when the second wave of bombers began to drop their load. But the bombs seemed to be falling on the other side of the airfield, although the ground above them shook and a fine white powder drifted down onto the shoulders of the officers. None of them, however, seemed to be aware of it. There were RAF pilots in blue shirts and shorts, army officers in khaki, and a few gold-ringed haughty-looking Navy representatives. Even a turbaned Sikh major with his beard carefully rolled up under his chin was playing darts with a captain in the Coldstreams.

Two subalterns stood up as Major Thickeridge approached their table.

'I didn't quite catch your name,' the major said to Basil.

'I didn't have time to introduce myself, sir, I'm afraid. Basil Ferguson.'

Under the electric light, the major looked rosier and plumper than before.

'Any relation to Lady Gwendoline?' he asked.

'I'm her son.'

'The archaeologist?'

'No, that's Geoffrey, my elder brother.'

The major introduced him to the two subalterns. 'Albert Lommer, Richard Feather.'

Basil shook hands with them. Neither was much older than himself.

The cards had already been dealt. 'Are you in the middle of a rubber?' Basil asked, sitting down with the others.

'We play during air-raids,' said Lommer, who was as short as Feather was tall.

'That's dummy's hand you have there,' the latter pointed out somewhat unnecessarily. 'Our fourth was killed.'

'Oh really?' said Basil uneasily.

'Rotten luck,' sighed Lommer. 'He was the best bridge-player in Malta.'

'Poor Ted,' said the major, sorting out his cards.

A heavy explosion sounded overhead. The room shook under the impact; the lights flickered and more falling plaster.

'Was your friend killed during an air-raid?' asked Basil, wondering what had happened to Skinny and Calloway.

The major looked shocked. 'He'd never have taken such a silly risk. No, he was killed while defusing an unexploded bomb.'

'He was in the Engineers like us,' Lommer explained.

'He went about it the wrong way, did he?'

'Not at all. He put his finger at once on what had gone wrong,' said Lommer, hesitating between playing a spade or a diamond, 'and it blew up instantly.'

Another series of heavy thuds overhead.

'Albert,' said the major, 'did you really mean to lead clubs?'

'Sorry, sir. My mind was elsewhere.'

'People don't play bridge the way they used to in my young days,' sighed the major. 'And these iron tables are far from comfortable.'

'They're good for protection if the ceiling collapses,' said Feather.

'Can you see me on all fours under one of them?'

'I hope never to see you in such a posture, sir.'

Again the ceiling was shaken by an explosion. The lights went out, then came on again. Dust swirled about, then began to settle.

'Do you expect to be stationed here for long?' Lommer asked Basil.

'I ought to have been on my way again by now. I've been posted to Cairo.'

The dusty, smoky atmosphere made him drowsy, and he looked around for Calloway. 'If his Beaufighter has been damaged,' he said to himself, 'it looks like I'll be spending the rest of the war playing bridge in Malta.'

'Are you looking for someone?' Lommer asked.

'My pilot. I don't know what's happened to him.'

'You have your own aircraft . . . ?' queried the major with a startled expression.

'I was in a hurry to get to Cairo, sir. There was this squadron of Beaufighters about to leave Gib, so I charmed one of the pilots.'

Things had not happened quite like that, but Basil always liked to keep up his reputation as a lucky devil and an irresponsible charmer.

'What were you doing at Gib?' asked Feather.

'My ship was torpedoed.'

'Oh? Badly?'

'No, we didn't even sink. Still, there was a big hole in the bow —so I was told. I didn't see . . .'

Three bombs fell, the last quite close. The bulbs swayed but stayed lit; more dust. The Sikh major and the captain started another game of darts.

'I wonder what the Eyeties think they're up to,' said Lommer.

'It's impossible to make war with them,' the major commented. 'They're never there when we attack them, and they always come over just when we've something else to do. It's the first real raid for a week,' he added, turning to Basil. 'All this dust is giving me a thirst. How about you?'

'A little, yes.'

'Would someone go and ask the barman for my bottle of Scotch and four glasses. Anyone take soda with it?'

'Yes please, sir,' said Lommer.

'People don't drink now as in my young days,' sighed the major, and began making an impressive number of tricks.

Feather's face fell.

'I'll go, sir,' said Basil, pushing back his chair. As he made his way between the tables to the bar he noticed an officer smoking a pipe and reading Gibbon's *Decline and Fall*.

'I thought you'd been smashed to pieces,' came a voice from behind him.

'And I thought you had,' said Basil, turning and smiling at Calloway. 'How did you land in here?'

'That's exactly what I did. I think I've sprained my wrist.'

'How's your kite?'

'It was still intact after the first wave had gone over. Seen Skinny?'

'We were together. But apparently this place is for officers only.'

'These pommies,' grunted Calloway, massaging his wrist. 'I'm sure I've sprained it.'

Basil leaned on the counter and beckoned to the barman. The shelves along the wall were filled with bottles of all shapes and sizes—Burgundy, Malaga, Champagne, straw-covered Chianti. He could see the entire room from there, the clouds of white dust and bluish tobacco-smoke swirling about, and the naked light-bulbs swaying and jumping. The barking of the Bofors and the booming of the ack-ack batteries were very distinct.

Am I frightened? Basil thought. Everyone else seems so calm. Too calm. As if this cool, reserved attitude is part of the game. Is that officer with *Decline and Fall* really reading?

'Yes, sir?' said the barman.

'Major Thickeridge's bottle, please, and four glasses.'

'Right away, sir.'

The barman hurried off. Basil leaned towards Calloway, who was listening curiously to three Guards officers talking shop.

'What book,' Basil whispered, 'would you like to read during an air-raid?'

Calloway looked at him in surprise.

'What . . .' he began.

Basil suddenly felt himself go deaf; as if two heavy hands had smacked his ears. The floor shook beneath his feet. Fiery flames and smoke burst into the shelter, and he felt a gust of red-hot air plucking at him. As in a slow-motion film, he saw tables rise and buckle and knock together in a deathly silence, men float towards the ceiling with arms and legs flapping like fins, the Sikh's turban flutter in the air, the lights flicker out and come on again, hats whirl through the smoke, and the pages of a book skip over by themselves. Then the counter collapsed behind him. All the lights went out. I'm going to die, he said to himself. But it's really not at all unpleasant.

2

François Mattei sat in his shaky old deckchair by the wheelhouse, sweat pouring from his forehead and shoulders. In front of him the two Arabs, Achmed and Amidou, mended the nets. Now and then a warm gust of wind brought from the galley the smell of food frying where Mahmoud was cooking on his small spirit-stove.

Mattei leaned over and splashed some water on his face and shoulders from a canvas bucket and snorted with pleasure. The water dried quickly, leaving salty lines on his stocky brown chest.

'Keeping on course?' he called out suddenly.

'Don't worry,' came Skoda's voice with a Slav accent.

'I didn't worry last time, and you took us straight under the battery at Fort Balbo. Four six-inch guns trained on a small boat like this—it's infanticide!'

Skoda laughed and, although not understanding why, Achmed and Amidou laughed too.

Mattei looked at the triangle of the bow rail and listened to the chug-chug of the venerable engine and the swish of the water against the sides of the *Santa Clara*. He liked the name. It inspired confidence; such a humble saint would never be suspected of trafficking.

Getting to his feet, he hitched up his canvas trousers and shuffled into the wheelhouse to avoid the direct rays of the sun. Mattei was a strong, broad-chested, swarthy man and he was beginning to bulge at the waist.

'Another two hours,' said Skoda.

'We've made fast time.'

'Too fast. We'll have to heave-to later.'

'I don't mind,' said Mattei, taking a cigarette from his trouser pocket. He lit it and inhaled deeply. Skoda with his sharp features and thick black hair that came low over a prematurely wrinkled forehead was looking ahead intently, his hands on the small, shining brass wheel. That's the only thing more or less clean on this old tub, thought Mattei.

'Hey, you've brought this bloody thing along with you again,' said Mattei patting an ancient revolver with a curved butt stuck in Skoda's belt.

'Well, if we run into trouble . . .' Skoda began evasively.

'The trouble would come from you having that,' said Mattei, looking wryly at the weapon.

'You never know, with what we've got on board . . .'

'Look—I'm not at war with anyone. I buy and I sell. It's a trade.'

'Yes, but you buy and sell stolen weapons,' Skoda replied.

'Well, in the first place, I don't know who they're stolen from. Secondly, I don't know who benefits from them.'

'I think they go back over the frontier into Tripolitania,' said Skoda thoughtfully. 'They go to the Senussi tribes who are in revolt against the Italians.'

'In any case,' said Mattei, 'stolen is just one way of looking at it. I might have found these weapons.'

'Like you found your boots,' laughed Skoda.

It was an old joke. Mattei laughed too.

'Yes, like my boots.'

That was how he had started in this business—with army boots, seventy-five thousand pairs of them left in a warehouse after the retreat from Dunkirk. By November 1940, he had sold the lot and was on his way towards Tunisia with false identity papers and well-lined pockets, to the island of Djerba, to be exact, just in time to take over from Petrides, who was crippled with rheumatism and getting too old for smuggling.

Petrides' set-up was still intact—the contacts in Tripolitania, the boat and the buyers. Mattei simply had to win over his 'correspondents' who had all backed out except Colombani— Sergeant Colombani, lately of the French Foreign Legion, the Rif campaign and then the Fascists. Now he was in the Italian police at Tripoli.

'If we were caught . . .' began Skoda again.

'If we were caught, that thing you've got there wouldn't exactly help matters.'

'You know what they do to their prisoners?'

'I know. You've told me before.'

'A bullet in the mouth is the better way,' said Skoda. 'After that, they can do what they like to me.'

'I don't like firearms,' said Mattei.

Skoda gave a shrug.

'I sell them,' Mattei went on, 'but I don't like them.'

Mahmoud's head appeared at deck level. 'It's ready,' he said.

'What I like about Mahmoud,' said Mattie, 'is that he's as filthy as a pig, is stupid and a liar, and added to that his cooking is revolting.'

Mattei said that on every trip. It was a sort of ritual, as if the success of their voyage depended on its utterance.

'Off you go,' he said to Skoda. 'I'll take over.'

He took the wheel, the brass was warm to the touch, and watched his companion splash water over his face and then go below.

He liked to be alone, Mattei thought, as he gazed at the water shimmering around him. No one else had ever really mattered to him. No one. Certainly no woman.

The boat lifted gently then fell with a sharp smack, and Mattei felt the helm stiffen slightly. Probably a shift in the wind. He drew the high stool towards him and sat down, resting his feet on its rail. 'Old age coming on,' he said to himself. 'Apart from that, never a day's illness.' He'd inherited good health from his parents. His mother would be seventy in March and once again he would not be with her on her birthday. Maybe next year? If things continued going well, he would return to Cannes with a bulging wallet and show them he'd made good. He'd take a room at the 'Martinez', but only for a few weeks. His future was in Tunis. Besides, he wasn't keen on being too near the old folks. Make life easier for them, yes; but put himself under their thumb again, no, never! That was fine for Marcel, his elder brother who worked at the post office in Nice, and even for Jeannine, his sister. But not for him. His father had made enough trouble when he'd left home even though he hadn't known the whole story—about the seventy-five thousand pairs of army boots, for instance.

Yes, he'd have a bedroom with a balcony and a view of the sea at the 'Martinez'. He'd invite his father for aperitifs at the bar and have a different girl every night. He'd wear silk shirts, hand-sewn shoes with thick soles and a grey pearl tie-pin. And he'd buy his mother an electric sewing-machine, his father a plot of land, his sister jewellery and clothes and Marcel—nothing. He'd never gotten along with Marcel. Never. Not even when he'd won the heavyweight championship and had his photo in *Le Petit Marseillais* and *La Dépêche de Nice,* and some of his glory had rubbed off onto Marcel. Perhaps it was because of that . . .

What a good time I had then, thought Mattei. Fast money, girls, life was easy. Then came that trouble.

But after all . . .

He liked to see the sun sparkling on the water. If there hadn't been that trouble, what would he be doing now? Probably not this. But then again he was independent and got a kick out of trafficking. Actually, he'd never felt so alive. Perhaps it was because he was forty. Maybe because he really had chosen this way of life.

He remembered the gloom that had hung over the warehouse as he approached it alone and hungry. Two days before he had left behind his steel helmet and army jacket because of the heat, and also his rifle because he'd been unable to get a round of ammunition into the breech.

He had found a dead man inside the door of the warehouse which had been blasted by machine-gun bullets. He relived the fierce joy that had come over him while he searched that corpse. He found more than ten thousand francs in brand-new bank-notes, identity papers in the name of Jerome Bertrand, shop-keeper, and a certificate excusing him from military service due to a heart condition, and also eighteen 20-dollar gold coins in a canvas body-belt.

Mattei's heart had raced.

'This is my lucky chance,' he had thought. 'As never before. Not even when my left landed on Salvatore Anneotti's jaw and I knew I'd finished him and heard the crowd cheering. Not even then. Here's my chance.'

'Did you hear them last night?' said Skoda with his mouth full.

'I sleep at night,' retorted Mattei, annoyed at the interruption.

Skoda leaned against the wheelhouse door and gave a shrug. 'Planes going over.'

'That's nothing unusual.'

'A lot of planes,' said Skoda, looking at his slice of bread.

'Italians, returning from a raid on Malta.'

'No, their bases are at Catania. They were going like that . . .' Skoda swept his arm from north-west to south-east.

'Don't know then. What's to eat?'

'Fried sardines.' Skoda swallowed the rest of his bread. 'And this *pâté*. The beer is foul. Like asses' piss.'

'Have you drunk it often?'

'What?'

'Asses' piss.'

'Never!' exclaimed Skoda indignantly. Then he laughed. 'I'll take over.'

'See that you stay on course. The wind's freshening and night's coming on.'

Mattei slipped into his shabby sandals and went below. There was a mess-tin full of fried sardines on a corner of the table.

Mahmoud had a sweat-rag round his neck and he used it frequently to wipe his face. He loathed Mattei, as was obvious from his look.

One of these days he'll try and do me in, thought Mattei as he began to skin the sardines. I'll have my back turned just a second too long and he'll stab me with his carving-knife. Not for money. Not from greed. Just hatred. And on impulse.

'These are fine,' said Mattei, savouring the sardines which Mahmoud had seasoned perfectly.

He drank some beer and found that Skoda was right. He grimaced as he swallowed the warm flat liquid.

'One of these days,' said Mattei, 'we'll buy a small ice-box.'

'With ice in it?' asked Mahmoud.

'Among other things.'

He ate hastily, with his elbows on the sticky table. Just a routine trip, he thought. He tried to recollect how many trips he'd made since arriving at Djerba. Two a month, on the average, except in January, when he'd made three. About ten altogether. 'As many again,' he said to himself, 'and then I'd better find something else to do. I can always come back to this later.' Colombani had once talked to him about some Italian

24

gasoline dumps somewhere between Tripoli and the Tunisian frontier. But that was a very different affair.

'I'll show you how to make *aïoli*, Mahmoud,' he said, swallowing the last of his lunch.

Astern, the many-hued traces of gasoline had almost dispersed. Mattei slipped the strap of his binoculars around his neck and, leaning on the rail, scanned the horizon.

He could just make out the thin yellow coastline.

Skoda shading his eyes and looking in the same direction asked, 'Can you see it?'

'Yes,' said Mattei.

He picked out the dismantled watch-tower which was no bigger than a matchstick, then the slot of the rocky inlet and the white rim of the waves breaking over the reefs.

'Do we go in?' asked Skoda.

'No. We'll wait till it's dark.'

'I hope Colombani will be waiting for us.'

Mattei shrugged his shoulders. 'He always is. He's a punctual guy.'

'You never know ...'

'Of course you never know,' snapped Mattei. 'What's wrong with you? Getting pessimistic, heh?' Mattei let the binoculars dangle on his chest.

'Maybe.'

'But business is booming.'

'Yes booming. And everybody around us is at each other's throat.'

'Exactly. That's why business is booming. Does that worry you?'

'A bit,' said Skoda.

'Ah well, in that case ...' Mattei glanced towards the distant shore and then added: 'As far as I'm concerned, war and talk about patriotism and glory and all that—to hell with it. If you want to chuck this, chuck it, I can't stop you. Everyone's free to do as he likes ...'

'I know, I was once in the French army,' said Skoda pensively.

'So was I. So what?'

'Nothing.' Skoda looked stubborn. 'Did you like being trampled on? Did you like the Germans invading France?'

'You only had to slip across to England if you wanted another go at them.'

'That's why I came to Tunisia,' said Skoda.

'And then you changed your mind.'

'No, I didn't change my mind.' Skoda was looking at the play of light on the water. 'But you can't always do what you want.'

'I can,' said Mattei. 'Why did you leave your own country?'

'I was anti-royalist,' was Skoda's dignified reply.

'You were a militant?'

'No. But I had friends who were, and I helped them because I thought they were right. They were my friends, understand?'

'Yes, that's the sort of thing I understand.'

'They were fighting for a cause, you see,' said Skoda. 'It's hard to explain. I envy them.'

'Where are they now?'

'Some are in prison. Others escaped to France with me. One of them got killed on the Aisne.'

'And you envy him?'

'If I have to get killed, I'd rather be killed like him than for smuggling stolen arms. Know what I mean?'

'As I see things, some people kick others in the ass and some people get kicked in the ass and I don't want to be among the second lot. I'm working for myself. When I take risks, it's my choice. If I get killed, it'll be my own fault. As for anything else . . .'

'You like seeing Italian soldiers in Cannes, strolling along the Croisette?'

'No, I don't like it. But it doesn't keep me awake nights either. It's no more selfish to do what I'm doing than to stay at home with the old woman and the kids and live on turnips, sitting back and waiting for the Jerries and the Wops to clear out. And anyway, I'm risking my life for something I believe in—dough.'

Mattei straightened up and stretched himself. A breeze had risen and the sea was darker, with a slight swell. 'If you ever want to chuck it, let me know in good time, won't you?'

'Don't worry.'

They fell silent.

Finally Skoda whispered, 'Listen.'

Mattei straightened up.

'A plane.'

Skoda scanned the sky.

'Hey, you lot!' Mattei shouted to the Arabs. 'Look like you're fishing!'

'It's over there, I think,' said Skoda, pointing.

A twin-engined plane appeared skimming over the water, so low that it seemed about to touch the crests of the waves. It was swaying slightly; and Mattei, through his binoculars, saw that the starboard propeller was motionless. Smoke was streaming from one side, stopped for a moment, then belched forth again.

'It's a Beaufighter,' shouted Skoda.

Then two Italian fighters came into view and dived swiftly upon the Beaufighter, easily spotted by its trail of smoke. The sea just ahead of the Beaufighter became a cauldron, raked by bullets.

'Missed!' shouted Skoda.

The Italian fighters, spitting fire, plummeted down a second time. Again the waters were raked, in the rear of the Beaufighter this time. Then the crippled plane suddenly banked steeply and swooped towards the boat. The Italian planes broke off and zoomed skywards.

Mattei still had his binoculars on the Beaufighter as it careened towards him, increasing in size at a tremendous rate. He saw distinctly the shining circle of the port engine and the three idle blades of the starboard propeller. The undercarriage was hanging down, apparently damaged.

Amidou and Achmed plunged below and Skoda dived behind the wheelhouse as the Beaufighter skipped over the boat. Mattei could feel the hot breath of gasoline and his eyes watered from the acrid black smoke that swept the deck.

The hanging undercarriage furrowed the water. Then the Italian planes returned. The final act was short and sharp. A sheet of flame lit up the sea. Then night fell abruptly.

3

When the two Macchis attacked the Beaufighter, Basil was planning the details of his arrival in Cairo. He'd phone Tommy from the airfield and ask him to come and pick him up. It would be foolish to report to Army Headquarters immediately since no one was expecting him so soon. He'd take a room at some hotel in town for the night. But for some reason, these thoughts made him uneasy. Maybe it was due to recent events.

He thought back to Malta and pictured himself standing casually at the bar talking to Calloway when the underground shelter had received a direct hit. He was now amused by his reaction to what then seemed impending death. 'Is this all it is?' 'How easy . . .'

But then his ears had popped and he had heard someone saying most politely, 'Would you kindly take your feet off my face?'

The lights had come on again and Basil had slowly risen to his feet, wiping the dust and grit from his eyes and face.

'Nothing broken?' Calloway had called. The blast had blown the Australian behind the bar, and his uniform was covered with beery froth.

'No, everything seems fine.'

Through the smoke and swirling dust he had made out other figures groping among overturned tables, broken glass, plaster and a few bodies.

He had then staggered across the room bumping against a gunner officer who had raised his glass triumphantly and exclaimed, 'And I never spilt a drop . . .'

Basil finally reached the table where he had been playing

bridge. A number of officers were grouped around it and he stared at the sight on the floor.

'Rotten luck, eh?' said Calloway, who had followed him.

Basil had looked at the ceiling overhead where the bomb had torn a large hole, and then at the bodies covered with blood and plaster. Then the long high-pitched note of the 'All Clear' had come over the loudspeaker.

It was Skinny who saw them first, and Basil did not respond at once. He saw Calloway look round and make a face and felt the plane's speed increase as the engines roared more loudly. Calloway put her nose down towards the sea which looked like a sheet of metal four thousand feet below.

Basil straightened up and put a hand on Skinny's dangling leg. The gunner held up two fingers and articulated, 'Eyeties at five o'clock.'

Basil watched Skinny's feet as they worked the pedals which made the turret swivel. Smoking cartridge-cases hurtled around him, bouncing off the fuselage in a quick succession of sparks. Basil's heart tightened.

Skinny had told him what to do under such circumstances and he dropped on all fours and reached towards the ammunition-boxes. A rapid series of sharp shocks hit the side of the plane and five or six small holes appeared just behind him. He felt the icy air whistling in.

Opening a box he pulled out a heavy, folded belt of ammunition, and waited to pass it to Skinny. The gunner's face was tense as he followed the tactics of the Italian fighter-planes like a watchful goalkeeper, crouched over his machine-gun, thumbs on the triggers and his eye in the line of sight.

Basil saw tracer-bullets coming towards them with amazing slowness, then suddenly swerving away as though some magical force protected the Beaufighter.

Then the air was rent by deadly whistlings. The lid of a crate of beer splintered and thick white froth spurted forth. There were two neat holes in the turret; Skinny stopped firing. He pointed downwards, and Basil understood that the danger was now below them.

Skinny opened the breech-block of his Vickers and Basil, his hands trembling, helped him insert a belt of ammunition. Skinny slammed the breech back and another burst of bullets whipped between Basil's legs and smacked furiously against the metal casing. Skinny gave a wild start, and a red hole opened under his jaw. Blood gushed from his nostrils and flowed over his mouth and chin. His body suddenly stiffened, then collapsed like a sack, held only by the seat-belt. Basil quickly unfastened it. Skinny's mouth opened and his body folded up and fell onto the crates below as Basil hoisted himself into the gunner's seat.

He spotted two Italian planes swaying slightly, like scorpions before making their sudden deadly dart. Trying to keep the closer of the two in his sights, he pressed the steel triggers. The Vickers jumped with a wide, smooth movement and the quick-firing made his ears sing. He saw tracers making sharp dotted lines in the quivering sky, then vanish beneath the belly of the enemy fighter which made a half-roll and disappeared from view.

The other at once appeared, flashing fire. The Beaufighter lurched as Basil fired, the Italian plane banked gracefully and dropped out of sight.

Suddenly Basil was thrown from his seat, knocking his head against the turret. One of the engines coughed, hesitated, then picked up again. Basil heard a furious twanging over the inter-com—it was Calloway swearing to himself as he bent over the controls. The starboard engine stopped and the Beaufighter lost speed so quickly that Basil thought they were going into a spin.

The enemy fighters were nowhere in sight. The sea was coming up at a dizzy speed, but Calloway still seemed to have control. Basil could see only his back and strands of wet brown hair on his neck. The plane pitched heavily and he saw black smoke pouring out on his right before being whisked away by the wind.

Christ, he thought, seeing the waves so near, cresting up towards him. What happens now? They would hit the sea with a tremendous impact. Death is not as pleasing when it is foreseen. He tried to avoid thinking about it. He looked at Skinny, lying in utter abandon below him, his head resting on his chest, and a lattice-work of dark blood on his face. A letter stuck out of a pocket on his jacket, and Basil could read some of the writing: '. . . for the fridge, John has asked Frankie to change the thermostat, but it's had to be ord . . .'

'Fire!' came Calloway's yell above the throbbing of the engine. 'Fire, you blasted idiot!'

The two Macchis were diving at them again like birds of prey, almost vertically.

Coming in for the kill, thought Basil turning back to his gun. Press these triggers and drown your fright in the noise of the bursts.

Again the tracers zoomed through the air like fiery darts.

'You won't even have the satisfaction of hitting one of them,' he said to himself. Calloway was shouting something but he could not understand. 'You'll never be more than a lousy amateur.'

He saw the trail of smoke on his right thicken and become a long brown scarf. The empty cartridges were flying past him, capering joyfully; the air was shattered by explosions, he fired aimlessly. The Beaufighter suddenly bucked. Basil had a glimpse of a small dark vessel below with a few indistinct figures busy on deck. Then he was thrown forward, instinctively he put his hands out to protect himself, and received a hard blow on the chest from the machine-gun. An explosion filled the air and a curved section of sheet-metal spun slowly on his right.

Calloway gave an inarticulate cry.

Basil fell from his seat, and in one vivid flash saw some crates tumbling towards him and Skinny's body flopping about like a dummy, then the sea burst around him. In a sort of greenish mist he had a vision of Calloway struggling wildly, appealingly, in the foam.

Basil choked and read his fate. Basil Ferguson, age twenty-eight, died at sea.

He was dragged down by the swirling water and a frightening roar filled his head.

Something hit his shoulder and held him. He struggled wildly to free himself. Then he was floating free, rising with nightmare slowness.

His head and body broke the surface and the air scorched his throat and lungs.

The Beaufighter had struck the sea about five hundred yards from the boat and had sunk almost immediately. In the last rays of the setting sun one wing stuck up for a moment like an appeal for help, then slid beneath the waves.

One of the Macchis swept over the iridescent swirl of water then banked to fly low over the boat. The pilot made a sign with his gloved hand.

Mattei raised his arm in reply. 'Dirty bastard,' he said.

Skoda was leaning over the rail and staring at the spot where the plane had disappeared. Debris floated among large opalescent patches. 'They've sunk,' he said.

'Okay, they've sunk,' answered Mattei matter of factly. 'Now we can make for the coast.'

Skoda said nothing. He moved reluctantly from the side of the boat and went to start the engine. The bow swung round and the boat began making headway. Mattei joined Skoda at the wheel.

'That was a lousy business,' said the Serb.

Mattei gave a shrug. 'So what?' He noticed they were drifting to starboard. 'Where are you going?'

'I want to see . . .'

'Right the helm.'

'I want to take a look,' said Skoda calmly. 'We've enough time.'

'Go on then,' grunted Mattei.

The waves were bigger now, and the spray smacked against the bows. The three Arabs were muttering among themselves as they peered into the growing darkness.

Mattei was the first to sight the swimmer—his face rising and falling with the waves. He swam slowly towards the boat barely drawing his arms above water.

'Hey!' he called. But there was nothing despairing or anguished about his shout.

'We're coming!' Mattei shouted back. 'Can you climb aboard by yourself?'

'I don't know,' came the man's calm voice, also speaking in French, but with a marked English accent.

If you were alone . . . , Mattei thought. Then he corrected himself: if you were alone, you'd have picked him up. But he was not entirely convinced.

'Is one of them alive?' Skoda called excitedly.

'Yes. Stop the engine.' Mattei turned to Amidou. 'Throw him a line with a slip-knot in it.'

The end splashed down near the swimmer, who grabbed it and slipped the loop around him.

'Okay,' said the swimmer. 'Pull me in.'

Amidou and Mahmoud hauled in the rope while Achmed stood with one leg over the rail, ready to help the man aboard. The rope tightened and he came alongside, half out of the water. He tried to help himself up, but his strength was gone and Achmed grasped him under the armpit and hoisted him into the boat. He lay gasping on the deck while Amidou unfastened the rope.

He coughed with difficulty and then looked up with a distorted smile. 'I guess I've been lucky.'

'I guess you have,' said Mattei.

The Englishman peered at him in the half-light. 'Are you French?'

'Yes. Fishermen from Tunisia.'

'The devil's own luck,' said the Englishman. 'But thanks very much—all of you.'

'We thought you'd all gone down,' said Skoda.

'The others—yes, they're gone. The gunner was killed during the fight, and Calloway . . . he couldn't free himself . . .'

He tried to stand up, but his legs were useless. 'I think I'll stay here for a bit . . .'

His teeth started to chatter and he began fumbling in his pockets.

'Achmed, fetch a blanket and the bottle of brandy,' said Skoda, kneeling down to take off the Englishman's shoes and socks. Mattei stood looking on.

'No cigarettes left,' the Englishman said in a broken voice.

'We've some,' said Skoda. 'But let's get you dry first.'

He was shivering all over now uncontrollably.

'It's the shock,' Skoda smiled at him.

He nodded. 'I think I'm going to be sick . . .' He gave a deep hiccup, struggled to his feet and staggered to the rail. 'Sorry, gentlemen.'

When Mattei went below he found the Englishman lying in Skoda's bunk covered with a grey blanket. The lantern dangling from the cabin roof sprayed shadows on his face; with his tousled fair hair and dark rings under blue eyes, he looked like some romantic young invalid. His clothes were scattered about to dry.

'Hallo,' he greeted Mattei, raising the half-full glass in his hand. 'This stuff is strong. I'm afraid it's making me drunk.'

'It's calvados,' said Mattei. 'Apple brandy.'

'You're sure I'm really alive? I can't believe it.'

'Yeah, you're okay.'

The Englishman smiled. 'It would have suited you if I hadn't survived the crash, wouldn't it?'

'Yes,' said Mattei. He was leaning against the door with his arms folded.

'I thought so. What are you going to do with me?'

'Put you ashore.' Mattei pulled out a stool and sat down, took out a pack of *Gauloises* and offered one to the Englishman, who put it between his swollen lips. Mattei gave him a light.

'In Tunisia?' he asked.

'No, Tripolitania.'

'Oh, I see.' He inhaled thoughtfully, and the strong cigarette made him cough. 'I suppose I must consider myself fortunate. You don't want to take me back with you, is that it?'

'I can't,' said Mattei.

The Englishman made a dismissive gesture. 'It doesn't matter.'

Mattei wondered at this impassiveness but then thought it was probably a pose.

'You've been lucky,' said Mattei. 'It's up to you to make the most of it.'

The other looked at him questioningly. 'Are you going to Tripolitania because of me?'

'No.'

'Ah . . .'

'I could've left you in the drink.'

'The whole of Neptune's vast ocean,' the Englishman muttered to himself.

'In your opinion,' he said, 'what should I do when I get to Tripolitania?'

Mattei sniffed. 'You'll be about five hundred miles from the British lines.'

'Really? That many?'

'Perhaps a little more. There's only one thing I ask if you're captured—don't say a word about us.'

The Englishman laughed lightly. 'Oh, so you think I'll be captured . . .'

'If you want to be, it's easy enough.'

The Englishman laughed louder. 'Sorry—I must be drunk.'

'All right, you're drunk,' said Mattei. 'You've every reason to be drunk. Only don't say anything about us.'

'Square dinkum,' he replied gravely, raising one hand.

'Pardon?'

'It's Australian slang, meaning something like "word of honour".'

'You're an Australian?'

'No, but the two chaps in the Beaufighter were. And you, I don't think we've introduced ourselves.'

'It's not necessary.'

'As you please.' He lifted his glass. 'To your good health.' He emptied the glass and poured himself another. 'I shall be the most drunken British prisoner of the whole war.'

'Where did you learn French?' Mattei asked.

'In France. And at college. I'm very fond of France—the land of the arts, arms, and laws.'

The chugging of the engine suddenly stopped.

'Are we there?' asked the Englishman.

'Not yet.'

'You'll have to lend me a shirt and trousers.'

'If you're picked up in civvies, the Italians will take you for a spy and at best shoot you. In a damp uniform you might catch pneumonia, but at least you'd survive that.'

The Englishman nodded. 'I hadn't thought of that. It's a good suggestion.'

'I'm not leaving you any choice,' said Mattei. He'd had enough of this. He felt the damp clothes. 'The best thing you can do is put these on now. They'll dry as you move about.'

'Thanks for your kind suggestions.'

Mattei started up the companion-way, feeling the Englishman's eyes boring into his back.

4

Basil ran his hand through his hair, it was dry.

'The skipper's right,' he told himself. 'Get dressed and there'll still be time to finish the bottle and maybe get your clothes dry.'

He threw off the blanket and sat on the edge of the bunk touching a large bruise on his chest where the butt of the Vickers had struck him. His right knee was swollen, very painful in fact.

'That's annoying, you won't be able to walk. Sleep—that's all you want. Yes, sleep and drink. Not even sex. Hell no,' he said aloud, looking at his limp penis. 'You're drunk. But that's no excuse. You've got to get dressed. Come on. Must prepare for your departure from this tub.'

He put on his socks which Mahmoud had draped over the spirit-stove. They were now warm but smelled stale. He felt his trousers, still wet.

He heard someone walking across the deck, and a murmur of voices. He finished dressing, wrapped himself in the warm blanket and picked up the bottle of calvados, taking a long swig. The fiery liquid trickled down his throat and burned his stomach; tears came to his eyes and he coughed. His head began to swim with the vision of the Beaufighter strangled by its heavy scarf of smoke.

'Here's to Calloway,' he said aloud, raising the bottle of calvados and taking another gulp.

He moved across the room and his head hit the lantern. Do ghosts take revenge? No, only memories. He alone was left to remember the crash and Calloway's helpless and tortured face.

He felt his heart beating and then suddenly: 'My God, I'm alive.'

It was dark on deck. There was no moon.

'He won't be much longer,' Basil heard the skipper say as he groped towards the two shadowy figures.

The taller of the two men looked closely at his watch. 'He ought to be there by now.'

'He is,' said the other, pointing.

Basil saw a light flashing in the distance—two short, one long.

'Let's go,' said the skipper.

The tall man hurried aft and started up the engine.

'Steady!' shouted the skipper.

The chugging took on an even, gentle rhythm, and Basil felt the deck quivering.

'What, you here?' said the skipper, turning around.

'I was fed up down there,' said Basil.

'Not too cold?'

'No. I'm feeling better.'

'Can you smell it?' said the skipper. 'That's the land.'

'Never noticed that before,' said Basil. 'I'll remember the smell.'

'We'll be ashore in about fifteen minutes,' said the skipper.

Soon a dark shape loomed up on the port side, a rocky promontory, and the boat slipped slowly along it.

Mattei put a leg over the side and dropped into the water, wading to the beach where a figure stood waiting.

'Is that you?' came Colombani's voice.

'And supposing it wasn't?'

He groped for Colombani's hand in the dark and shook it. The palm was hard and calloused, and the fingers were thick. A real peasant, thought Mattei, stout and stocky, slow in mind and body but reliable.

'How are you?' said Colombani. 'You're looking well.'

'You always say that,' retorted Mattei. 'But you've only seen me in the dark. You wouldn't recognise me in daylight.'

'Oh, I'd know you by your voice,' said Colombani. 'It's like a file grating on metal.'

Skoda joined them, followed by the Englishman carrying his army blouse over his arm like a tourist. Colombani stared at him.

'Who's this guy?'

'An Englishman,' said Mattei. 'We fished him out of the sea.'

'Good God!' exclaimed Colombani. 'And what the hell was he doing there?'

'I was drowning,' the Englishman said in an ironic tone.

'His plane was shot down,' Skoda explained.

'Ah, so that's what I heard,' said Colombani. 'What you going to do with him?'

'You're the cop, it's up to you.' Mattei turned to Basil. 'My friend's a cop.'

'Oh? Does he want to arrest me?'

'Do you want to arrest him?' Mattei asked Colombani.

'Are you mad? Where would I put him?'

'In prison. You could put me in prison,' suggested the Englishman. 'I suppose you've got one? In any case, I promise I won't try to escape. Are you really a policeman?'

Colombani replied crossly, 'Can't you see my uniform?'

Basil turned to Mattei. 'You've got very good connections.'

'Why did you bring him here?' asked Colombani.

'Well, I couldn't leave him to drown,' said Mattei.

Silence followed as Colombani fingered his chin.

'Well, we could take him in the Fiat,' he finally suggested.

'No thanks, I think I'll wait here till daylight,' said the Englishman. 'Is it far to a town or village?'

Colombani pointed into the night. 'Zwara's along there.' He seemed reassured.

'How many miles?'

'Ten kilometers,' said Colombani. 'More or less.'

'I think I can manage that. Is it in the direction of the Tunisian frontier?'

'Yes. Why? Don't you want to escape?'

'I hadn't thought about it. In fact I haven't thought about anything. I'm drunk . . .'

Basil could now make out Colombani's stocky figure clothed in the beige linen uniform of the *carabinieri*, a sun-helmet with green braid, and a white leather cartridge-belt strapped across his broad chest.

'Well, what are we going to do?' said Skoda as if nothing had been settled.

'Skoda wants to take the Englishman along with us,' Mattei

said to himself, 'and he'll grumble all the way if we don't. Well, he'll have to grumble, that's all.'

'Let's go,' he said. Turning to the Englishman he held out his hand. 'Good-bye and good luck!'

''Bye-bye, old chap,' said Basil. His hand was icy cold. 'And thanks again.'

'You're welcome. Don't forget what you promised.'

'Square dinkum,' said Basil.

Skoda went and shook hands with Basil. 'I kept these for you,' he said, bringing out some Weekend cigarettes and a box of matches. He hesitated then added, looking Basil straight in the eye:

'You're sure you don't want some food and water?'

Basil envisioned himself hobbling along with a swollen knee and carrying a bulky pack on the endless desert.

'No, thanks. It's very kind of you.'

He felt embarrassed by this show of heroism, but it brought no response.

'Right, let's go,' said Mattei.

Colombani was about to say something but turned and plodded off along the beach. Skoda and Mattei followed.

As they reached the path that led up the rocky promontory to the dismantled watch-tower, Mattei looked back and saw the Englishman sitting with his hands clasped round his knees and gazing at the water like a contented tourist. He was watching the boat which Achmed was taking out to sea. The gentle chugging of the engine flowed distinctly across the calm waters of the inlet, and the phosphorescent wake spread out evenly in oblique ripples.

Skoda stopped too.

'Hey, are you two coming?' called Colombani, who was already fifty yards ahead.

'Yeah.' Stones slipped from under their feet as they climbed the rocky path.

'You told them to be back tomorrow night?' Mattei asked Skoda.

'Yes, at eight o'clock.'

'Good.'

'Amidou noticed a shoal of sardines this afternoon.'

'Fine, that'll keep them occupied. It's Mahmoud I don't trust.'

They were bent double, climbing swiftly when Mattei began to drop behind.

'Wait a minute,' he gasped, and stopped to get his breath. They were some hundred and fifty feet above the sea now. The boat was a black silhouette on the iron-grey waters and was rounding the small rocky headland commanding the entrance to the inlet.

The Englishman was still in the same spot but judging from his dim shape he was now lying down, probably with his ankles crossed and one hand behind his head, for Mattei could see the red dot of a lighted cigarette in the other. Just like on the bunk, Mattei recalled.

'I think we could've at least put him on his road,' said Skoda sulkily.

'What road?' said Mattei with a shrug. 'And suppose we were caught with him?'

'I liked him,' said Skoda slowly.

'Sure, sure.'

'Where are you two?' came Colombani's voice, his figure appearing at the top of the path.

'We're coming,' called Mattei. He slapped Skoda on the shoulder and pushed him forward. 'Don't worry about him. He's no bloody concern of ours.'

'You don't understand,' said Skoda in a dignified way.

'You're right, I don't understand.'

5

Basil's head throbbed. The air-raid shelter full of noise and smoke, the hazardous take-off of the Beaufighter from a runway pitted with bomb-craters, and Calloway struggling in the treacherous sea kept coming back to him. He had difficulty breathing deeply and his knee and shoulder were stiff and burning. His whole body ached whenever he moved.

He was tempted to spend the night on the beach. If he were found by the Italians—well, so much the better. He'd had enough. They'd take him to a POW camp but he'd probably be freed by the British advance in a few weeks, maybe even a few days. It might even be an amusing experience.

'That's it,' he told himself, 'you've found the right word— amusing. You're just a comic soldier and you know it.'

He felt himself dropping off to sleep and made no attempt to rouse himself. He saw Skinny with both hands at his throat spewing up dark bloody mush, and the sea was coming up to meet him like an impenetrable wall. He jerked and came out of the nightmare. But had he really been asleep? He could still hear the chugging of the boat.

'All right,' he said to himself, getting to his feet and gasping as a sharp pain shot down his back, 'you've got to move on. And if you meet a patrol, you'll give yourself up. A British prisoner would be a rare bird at this point. And a staff officer, nonetheless!'

He unbuckled his webbed belt, took the heavy revolver out of the holster and weighed it in his hand. He'd used it only once at target practice. In any case, he'd never be able to hit a tank at ten yards with this piece of armoury.

This is not at all patriotic, he thought as he threw the revolver in the air. It fell into the water with a dull plop and pain shot up his arm.

'That's gone,' he said aloud.

He dropped the revolver-belt on the sand and as he bent down to lace up his damp shoes all the muscles in his body protested and he vowed to make no unnecessary movements in the future. Then he started up the beach without a backward glance. His knee was very painful, and when he began climbing the mule track he realised that he wouldn't get very far.

'And what's more, you're soft,' he told himself with a note of despair.

When Basil reached level ground he felt absurdly disappointed. Only a straight road, soon swallowed up by the night, lay before him on the flat harsh desert.

What did you expect? he asked himself. An empty automobile to be waiting?

He began walking in the direction indicated by Colombani but his leg felt as if it might bend the wrong way any moment. Moreover, he was cold.

'Is it really impossible for you to walk any farther? Or are you just too lazy?' He found it difficult to compare his present state with any physical fatigue in the past. He had done some running at Oxford and had completed his military training with little feeling of exhaustion, only deep boredom. But that was the extent of his physical feats. His greatest weariness had come the morning after a night of drinking and women, but that bore no resemblance to his present condition. What would Julia say if she could see him now? Poor darling, very likely. 'You poor darling,' she'd coo in that airy unconcerned voice. 'Poor Basil' she'd say whether he was dead, a prisoner-of-war or unhappy with the climate in Cairo.

It was that same neutral tone Major Thickeridge had used when saying 'Poor Ted' about the bridge-player who had been killed while defusing an unexploded bomb.

'Poor darling,' he said aloud.

He wondered about the correct procedure when taken prisoner. Should he salute? But he had lost his hat. Give up his sidearm with dignity? But he'd thrown it into the sea. Raise his hands in the air and cry 'Kamerad' like the German soldiers during the Great War? But these attitudes did not seem to fit his nature. What he must not do, in any event, was run. But he couldn't do that even if he tried. What then?

'Improvise,' he told himself. 'You've always been good at that.' He looked at his watch which had stopped at ten past five; probably the time the Beaufighter crashed.

'I'll remember that,' he mused, and pictured himself at the bar in the Dolphin Club with a glass of Scotch in his hand, '. . . and I was shot down at ten past five exactly.' Or telling Tommy about it, and when Tommy asked what he had felt, he'd reply, 'Nothing at all. I was too busy. All I can remember is that it was ten past five . . .'

If he had not been conscious of having walked some distance, he could easily have believed himself in the same spot. The road stretched before and behind him and the desert remained unchanged; flat, severe and unending. There was one comfort, however, he was less cold. But his damp shoes were painful.

He sat down, yawning, on one of the heaps of gravel placed at intervals by the roadside. He took off his shoes and socks and gently massaged his feet. As he sighed with relief, he suddenly realised that he was hungry. It was rather ridiculous to be hungry and cold in the midst of the Libyan desert.

Why had he refused the food that chap with a Slav accent had offered him? Maybe to ensure against his setting off on some mad scheme. He was on his guard against those sudden impulses—few and far between, admittedly—but he tried to temper them these days.

Zwara, the Italian policeman had said, was six or seven miles away. Less than six now. There was bound to be a prison at Zwara and they'd give him a plateful of spaghetti.

'So let's get going,' he said to himself. But he did not move. He continued to rub his feet and then he heard faint voices in the distance. As they drew nearer, he made out four cyclists idly zigzagging along the road. A cycle patrol, thought Basil, as he caught sight of their army caps and rifles slung across their backs.

He picked up his shoes and socks and dived behind the heap of gravel. What are you doing? Thought you wanted to be arrested, he said to himself. But he did not relish the idea of being shot in his bare feet by a cyclist firing blindly. That would be such a common death.

They were very near now and Basil lay flat behind the gravel.

He heard a burst of laughter which seemed directly above him. Had they spotted him? He turned his head slightly and looked up expecting to see the hulk of a man with white teeth smiling down at him. But there was only darkness.

He held his breath and his fingers gripped the ground tightly until the voices began to fade. Then he raised himself on his elbows and watched the wavering shadows melt into the night.

6

Six bulbs hung from the ceiling and shed a pallid light on the figures in the large room. The walls, which had once been white when the *dopo-lavoro* had been a proper place for workmen and minor officials of El Atsitia and not a low dive for soldiers, were now grey and covered with patriotic slogans in large lettering and lewd scribbles.

Renata Vanucci was washing glasses behind the bar with her eyes always on her customers. Near the door sat Corporal Bertolucci and his little group finishing a game of cards beneath the huge, framed photos of the Duce and Victor-Emmanuel. By the window Sergeants Collo and Malabranca talked in low tones, their elbows on the table and heads almost touching, their tepid glasses of beer still nearly full. Their interminable mutterings stopped only when someone came near their table.

The liveliest group was nearest the bar, half-a-dozen boisterous soldiers who were spending their pay on red wine and salami; one of them was Gino, whom Renata had slept with on one occasion out of despair and loneliness.

Generally Renata avoided sleeping with enlisted men because they then thought they could invade her café at all hours of the day and night, drink and eat without paying and become jealous over nothing. But there were very few officers at El Atsitia and they were usually old and tired.

Things had been very different with Franco Sveno. When he left for the front, Renata had been despondent. Franco was slim and elegant and wore soft leather boots that always shone brilliantly. He had first appeared one morning in July 1940, having disembarked with his unit which was on its way to the Egyptian front. He had stayed for nearly a month. Although officers generally avoided the *dopo-lavoro,* he had begun frequenting the place, coming in and sitting by the window (in fact at the table now occupied by the two sergeants) and drinking tea—Renata had never before served tea to anyone—while writing long letters on pale blue notepaper or reading a thick book with small print. Renata thought at first that it was the Bible, considering its size, until one evening, probably five or six days after his arrival, she saw that the title was *Ulysses.* As she leaned over his shoulder to pour the tea (she had been to Tripoli and bought a proper teacup especially for him) Franco had looked up and seemed to acknowledge her for the first time. He smiled.

'That's a big book,' she had said.

'Yes, it will last me the whole war.'

'Ulysses. Is that the name of the hero?'

She didn't really care but wanted to talk to someone and no one else was in the café that evening. Her father had been dead only three weeks and she wanted to postpone the loneliness of going upstairs to the large first-floor bedroom—her parents'—into which she had moved.

'Yes,' he had said. 'That's the hero.'

'What's it about?'

'It's an itinerary. A rather special sort of story . . .'

She had thought he was referring to dirty stories told in great detail, and had given a throaty laugh. But his eyes told her differently and she had felt uneasy.

'A sort of transposition of the voyages of Ulysses, the Greek hero, to present-day Ireland.'

She had failed to see what connection there could possibly be between Ireland, which she had heard about and knew was somewhere in England, and Greece. The only Greek she knew was old Petrides who lived on Djerba and came once a month with smuggled goods for her father—French-made fancy goods and toys which Giuseppe Vanucci disposed of to nomad tribes or at the Tripoli market, 'Parisian' lingerie which was bought by the wives of officials living in Tripoli, and even hardware which had become very scarce in wartime.

She did not understand the story that Franco had told her, but she listened intently, heedful of the inflections in his voice, of his gestures, the cut of his light hair, and the faint yet penetrating smell of lavender which exhaled refinement and luxury.

Before he left he had asked her about herself and she told him with no hesitation about coming to Tripolitania with her parents in 1930, the State farm which had not been very successful, her father taking this *dopo-lavoro* after her mother had died from cancer, and his recent death. He then rose and started towards the door. Suddenly stopping, he turned, very stiff and straight in his jacket, and looked at her intensely. 'I want you, Renata.'

She had lifted her eyes questioningly but only met a cold unwavering look. Her mouth began to tremble and her breasts stiffened under her blouse.

'And you?' he had said. 'Do you want me?'

She had breathed a 'yes' as she lowered her eyes.

The polished boots had advanced towards her. Lifting her head to receive a kiss, she had watched him walk around her, put his book on the counter, and start up the stairs to her bedroom.

Automatically, she had locked and bolted the street door and followed him.

She'd never be able to forget that night nor the following nights when Franco was free to be with her. She had never known a lover so stern yet so passionate and tender. He had taught her everything—making love with the lights on and looking into each other's eyes (previously she had known only furtive, hurried and mechanical embraces), adoring the flesh and body of another to the point of sobbing, and giving and loving in ways she had never known. Every evening she had waited for Franco, anxious when he was late, aching with impatience and never knowing what he would demand of her but ready to consent to anything from him and for him.

Then he had come to the café early one morning to tell her his regiment was leaving for the Egyptian frontier at midday. Tears filled her eyes but she was unable to reach out to him, to hold him in the midst of the café full of soldiers drinking and singing. 'I'll come back, I promise you,' he had said. Renata could say nothing but she saw a look of tenderness in his clear, cold eyes for the first time.

In the weeks that followed she had often wept all night, racked by desire and anxiety, tossing and turning in a bed that had become too large and where she could still smell a scent of lavender.

He had written three times, brief letters that she read with difficulty and did not understand. Then silence. When she went to Tripoli she inquired after his unit but no one knew of a Lieutenant Franco Svevo.

François Mattei had then come into her life. In the beginning she had given herself to him from physical desire more than anything else; especially since he made little if any effort to be pleasant to her. He was blunt and adamant in their business deals, reducing her cut—for she carried out her father's role as receiver of his stolen goods. Although devoid of any show of tenderness, he was a fairly satisfactory substitute for Franco. He lacked the lieutenant's refinements but did have the other's passionate violence. And it was she—once the early diffidence was overcome—who had taught him how to be an accomplished lover.

Corporal Bertolucci's group broke up and the corporal himself came and put the dirty, dog-eared pack of cards on the counter. '*Arrivederci,* Renata.'

'*Arrivederla,* Giuseppe,' she said.

It was ten o'clock. Mattei, Colombani and Skoda would soon arrive. Her thoughts were not of rifles and ammunition stored in the outhouse on the other side of the courtyard, nor of the talking and arguing that always took place, but of Mattei and his tough, hard body pressing on her, his rigid hard flesh penetrating her during the night and the long day to follow.

'Hurry up, it's closing time,' she called. 'I don't want to get into trouble with the military police.'

'Just one more glass, Renata,' pleaded Gino.

'One more and that's the lot,' she granted, going round the counter to fill their glasses. Then she went across to the table where the two sergeants were sitting; they fell silent as she approached.

'We're going,' Collo said to her. 'We're on our way, my beauty.'

'I'm not your beauty, and besides you owe me fifteen *lire* from the day before yesterday.'

'Malabranca will settle up. He's had a money-order from his family.'

'Yes, I'll pay,' said Malabranca.

As she went back to the counter, Gino caught her by the wrist. 'You smell good to me,' he said.

48

She broke away from him unsmilingly. 'Where d'you think you are? In one of the Tripoli brothels?'

'There's a Renata in Tripoli too,' Gino said with a laugh. 'But her real name is Marcelina.'

'Go back to her then.'

She thought back to when she had been in Tripoli two days ago getting supplies. She had heard that things were becoming disastrous and had watched as many wounded soldiers were taken on board a ship. Hundreds of them in bloodstained bandages, maddened by the sand and the flies and their officers, trying to board with bulging suitcases but being pushed back by *carabinieri*. And she had seen soldiers without their weapons, barefoot and unshaven, struggling along the roadside and shouting insults at any staff-car that passed. What would happen if the English got here? She thought of Lieutenant Svevo. Where was he now? Dead, or a prisoner? Supposing he came back? She smiled to herself: 'I'd tell Mattei to go and sleep in the outhouse.'

The two sergeants, still mumbling to each other, were just leaving the café when she heard the little Fiat chugging into the courtyard—Colombani always revved up the engine as he came to a stop—and then the doors banged.

'Get along, I'm closing,' she called to the last dawdling customers.

She stepped into the courtyard where Colombani's Fiat was parked and went across to a large shed or outhouse with a galvanised iron roof. The wooden double-door stood ajar and she could see light from the hurricane-lamp.

She stood with her back against the door-post, both hands behind her, one knee slightly bent. The three men had not heard her approach.

Mattei had climbed onto the old open truck and was examining a rifle, sliding the bolt up and down with sharp, competent motions. Skoda stood at his side, holding up the lamp while Colombani sat smoking a cigarette, knees apart and leaning forward, his sun-helmet pushed to the back of his head.

Mattei put the rifle back in the crate and picked up another, weighed it on the palm of his hand, worked the bolt-lever, looked down the barrel, and felt the hammer with his thumb to make sure it had not been filed down. Renata could not help smiling. She knew nothing whatever about firearms, but she liked watching Mattei, the strength and decision in his gestures.

'You going to check them all like that?' said Colombani, smothering a yawn. 'They're not playthings, you know.'

'Where did you get them from?' asked Mattei, who had already selected another rifle to examine.

'It's a consignment that the Quartermaster's office hasn't asked about.'

'How's that?'

Colombani drew on his cigarette. 'The fellow who made out the order for them to be returned as unserviceable is a buddy of mine. He handed the order over to me.'

'For nothing?' said Mattei with a smile but still intent on his job.

'What d'you think?' Colombani rubbed his thumb and fore-finger together in a universal gesture. 'I dropped him a little something. They're in good condition, aren't they?'

'They're all right,' Mattei conceded. 'Better than the last lot. Three of those had faulty hammers, one a bent barrel, and I don't know how many with breeches that stuck. What else is here?'

His head thrown back, Colombani reeled off the items between puffs on his cigarette.

'One crate of hand-grenades. Ten pounds of dynamite. Fifteen Berettas with fifty rounds each. Four batteries for Fiat trucks. Some coils of brass wire. A typewriter, as good as new. Twenty-five bottles of White Horse whisky.'

'Good stuff, White Horse.' Just then Mattei noticed Renata. '*Ciaou*,' he greeted her.

'*Ciaou*,' she replied without changing her position.

'Hullo, Renata,' said Skoda.

'*Ciaou*, Skoda.'

'The White Horse is worth having,' said Mattei.

'Spoils of war,' Colombani explained. 'From a British cargo-ship that went ashore at Misurata. There are two cartons of Players cigarettes too. They're at the back—the things in silver wrappings.'

'Pretty,' said Mattei.

He seemed to have forgotten Renata but she was not offended. She knew his mind was too busy with addition, so much for Colombani, so much for Renata, and how much he could make for himself—what price he could get for a pack of Players and a bottle of White Horse in the cafés at Gabes and Sfax. It might even be worth while to make a trip to Tunis, where black-market prices were so much higher.

Renata looked him slowly up and down, her gaze lingering on the square, unshaven jaw, the ears that stuck out a bit, the arched eyebrows and hard mouth which broke into an ironic twist when he smiled. She could almost feel the hardness of his bulky body between her open thighs. She wondered if he had a woman at Djerba—that Zorah for instance, who kept house for him—or whether she was his only lover. She had once questioned him on the subject. 'A woman at Djerba?' he had replied. 'What for?'

He stood up as if satisfied with his shipment, wiped his hands on his trousers and jumped down from the truck.

He walked towards Renata unhurriedly, feet slightly turned inwards and balanced on his toes, chin held in.

'*Ciaou*,' he greeted her again, but more pleasantly this time, and stroked her cheek with the back of his fist, a familiar gesture.

'Coming in?' he said to her, then turned to Skoda. 'I'll leave you to check the rest.'

The three sat in the empty *dopo-lavoro*, at the table where Corporal Bertolucci and his companions had been playing cards. Renata had drawn the thick cotton curtains across the windows and had set a bottle of Chianti and some slices of salami before the two men.

Mattei drew a folded sheet of paper from his pocket, opened it and handed it to Colombani. The police sergeant pulled a pair of steel-framed spectacles from his uniform jacket and put them on.

'It's the statement of your account at the Bank of Tunisia after the last trip,' said Mattei. 'Check it over.'

Colombani's thick lips began moving slowly and the light from the kerosene-lamp hanging from above shone on his bald head.

'That's the bank's charges,' explained Mattei, pointing to some figures on the sheet of paper.

'I see. How much have I got now then?'

'One hundred and seventy-five thousand seven hundred and twenty-two francs and twenty-one centimes,' said Mattei.

Colombani sighed with satisfaction. 'That's fine,' he said. 'And this debit—what's that for?'

'It's the local residential tax.' Mattei smiled at him. 'Whenever you want to go and live at Sfax, everything's in order. You're legally domiciled there. No problem.'

'Fine.' Colombani nodded his heavy head approvingly. He copied the final amount into a small, dog-eared, black leather notebook, then put a match to the paper that Mattei had given him, watching it burn between his fingers.

'I'll let you have this present load for forty-two thousand,' Colombani said. 'That's not counting the whisky, the cigarettes, the batteries and the typewriter, which I got for nothing. You can give me fifty per cent of what you sell them for.'

'Forty-five per cent,' said Mattei. 'And thirty-eight thousand for the load.'

'Ah no, that's not good enough. I want . . .'

'God above!' Renata said to herself. 'Here they go and it's already eleven o'clock! It'll be midnight before we get to bed. To the devil with their haggling!'

Renata's bedroom had whitewashed walls and the huge bed could only have been conceived by Italians, who still cling to the elaborate love-making of Renaissance times and the rigid principles of Christian procreation. Sleep was not the main object between the great black bedposts carved with bunches of grapes, vine-leaves and garlands. Renata felt secure and protected with a man beside her. On the opposite wall hung the wedding photograph of her parents, he in a dark suit with a white wing collar up to his ears and a handlebar moustache, she in a white lace dress with her eyes modestly lowered and her ample bosom bulging. There was also a photograph of her father in his Great War uniform, his tin-hat tipped jauntily over one ear and wearing his bayonet in its scabbard.

She lifted her gaze to the zigzag crack in the ceiling and the yellowish patches scattered along it. Each bend in the crack seemed to correspond with the pulsing of the blood in her veins. She was lying naked with her legs still apart, and her sweating body felt bruised by Mattei's hard hands; he was lying on his stomach with his head resting on bended arms.

'All right?' came his muffled voice.

'Yes,' she said.

She still had the feel of his flesh within her. She looked from the ceiling to the photographs and then at her parted thighs. She turned her head towards Mattei, his sturdy, hairy legs, his loins; and she wanted him again. She turned on her side and put her arm across his chest.

'My man,' she said.

Mattei's dark eyes glittered and he turned towards her.

His lips touched her neck, her eyes, then her lips. She thrust her knees against his thigh and he rolled on top of her. Her hands gripped his back as he buried himself in her.

'Yes, François, oh yes,' she whispered, her voice coming from deep within her throat. She felt the movement within her and her body rose to his to make the penetration deeper.

'François,' she said again.

'Yes, I'm here. I'm here. Can you feel me?'

'Oh yes, I can feel you. It's good. It's so good.'

They clung together tightly and she began to moan, softly at first then louder and louder as his rhythmic movement increased —faster, faster. Then halting for a moment, he lifted his head to look at her and continued his penetration slowly until she was gasping and twisting below him. She gripped him with her heels, and he clutched her round the neck and waist, bringing her to a release of joy. She gasped at the first contractions. His body responded and his arms tightened around her. They were drowning together in mutual pleasure. She cried out, then fell back on the crumpled sheets. Mattei, exhausted, turned onto his side, still with one arm round her. They lay in silence.

7

It was about ten the following morning when Basil was made prisoner. His capture consisted of none of the drama or excitement he had imagined during the long previous night. In fact, the Italian soldiers he had surrendered to were not immediately aware of who their captive was. While being taken to 'prison' by the courteous Italians, Basil had the impression of being in the midst of a group of hospitable and joyful peasants like those he had often talked and drunk wine with during his youthful travels through the hills around Florence.

Since Basil had finally concluded that he would have to rely only on himself to reach the British position, he had decided to definitely give himself up at Zwara. But even that decision seemed fruitless because of the mounting pain in his knee. Moreover, he was thirsty and feverish.

Then he spotted the Italians sitting by the roadside and having what appeared to be a leisurely meal. There were three of them settled comfortably on a heap of gravel, their bicycles lying on the ground nearby. They had lit a 'desert fire'—a tin pierced with holes and full of sand soaked with gasoline—and were heating up sausages and beans in a mess-tin. As Basil approached, one of the soldiers, a short, plump man wearing rope-soled sandals and the side-cap of the *bersaglieri,* was pouring wine into three mugs.

As he placed the bottle beside him he noticed Basil and looked up, shading his eyes from the sun with the air of languid curiosity.

Basil raised his hand in greeting. *'Buon giorno,'* he said.

'Buon giorno, signore,' the other replied.

His two companions looked up and squinted. Maybe they can't see my uniform and I am only a dark form against the light, thought Ba '. They remained speechless and surprised when he stood directly in front of them : 'I'm thirsty, may I?' he said in Italian.

He bent forward, pointing at a water-bottle. 'May I?' he repeated.

The three looked at him uncomprehendingly.

My pronunciation must be bad, he thought. He put out his hand and picked up the water-bottle, uncorked it and lifted it to his lips. 'To blazes with them, anyway,' he said to himself. The tepid water tasted rusty but it soothed his throat.

'You were dying of thirst,' he told himself. 'No, it really wasn't that bad. You'd just had enough of discomfort, a little pain and unpleasantness. Just like women. You've never ended a relationship because you didn't love her any more, whatever love is, but because it became too much trouble. Like Kathleen. Nice girl but it was a nuisance to take the train to Eastborough every Friday evening.'

The water-bottle was empty. He handed it to the plump soldier and smiled. *'Grazie,'* he said. *'Grazie tanto.'*

The soldier took the water-bottle and shook it. 'You had a. hell of a thirst,' he said, and then added, 'Who are you?'

'Ah yes, of course. I'm English.' He repeated distinctly *'Inglese'*, and awaited the immediate snatching up of guns. But the plump soldier merely said *'Inglese,* eh?' as if this were not only odd but rather comic. He appealed to the other two, and they repeated with an air of astonishment, *'Inglese?'*

'In fact,' said Basil, 'I'm a British officer.'

One of the soldiers nudged the man next to him. 'Take the sausages off, Ettore, can't you see they're ready?'

'Are you alone?' asked the plump one.

'Yes,' said Basil. 'The others are dead.'

He could not think of the words in Italian, so he made a twisting, diving motion through the air with his hand and ended with 'Crash!'

'Poor fellows,' sighed the plump soldier. 'But that's life . . .' and he gave a shrug.

Basil, overcome by the rich, appetising smell of the sausages and beans, looked longingly at the three soldiers who were now talking much too fast for him to understand.

'*Va bene,*' the plump soldier then said to Basil. 'You must be the Englishman we're all looking for. They found your revolver belt on the beach early this morning. A patrol searches the beaches every night after midnight. Do you agree to give yourself up?'

'Yes,' said Basil, looking at the sausages.

The other gave a wide smile. 'Then sit down, *Tenente.* Here, next to me. You'll eat with us.'

'And drink,' said Ettore, holding up the wine bottle. 'Are you tired, *Tenente*?'

'A bit,' Basil said. 'Is it still some way to Zwara?'

'Four miles. We'll take you to the billet there.' The soldier who had answered held out a greasy hand. 'My name is Gianni. Angelo Gianni. He's Ettore Pascalino.'

'And I'm Ercole Panni,' said the plump one.

Basil shook hands ceremoniously saying 'Ferguson' each time. Then he added : 'So I'm your prisoner then?'

'Don't let it worry you, *Tenente,*' said Panni.

Gianni looked at him kindly. 'War's a rotten business, eh, *Tenente*?'

'Most of the time,' said Basil.

'When d'you think it'll end?'

'I've no idea.' Basil could only think of food and would have been happy to spend the rest of the war sitting by the roadside with these three worthy peasants. 'Soon, perhaps,' he added.

'I come from Chioggia,' said Gianni, 'and he's from Bologna and Panni's from Brindisi.'

'Near Brindisi,' Panni corrected him. 'I'm a shoemaker.' Pointing to his rope-soled sandals, he laughed. 'Shoemakers are always the worst shod, aren't they, *Tenente*?'

Basil smiled in reply.

Panni wiped his fork on his trousers and handed it to Basil. 'Dig in,' he said, handing him the mess-tin full of steaming sausages and beans.

Basil ate greedily. The beans were delicious, with a strong taste of garlic, and the sausages were crisp and firm.

They finished the wine and while Pascalino and Gianni went to clean the mess-tins with sand, Basil and Panni stretched out and smoked a Weekend.

'You won't say anything about finding us sitting here, eh, *Tenente*?'

56

'No, I promise,' replied Basil, reminded of the similar promise he had made to the French 'fisherman'.

'Our orders were to patrol,' Panni went on gaily, 'and not to sit and eat.'

'I understand,' said Basil. 'I'll say you captured me.' Panni gave him a questioning look. 'I'll say that I started to run when you spotted me but you caught me.'

Panni laughed. When the other two returned with cleaned mess-tins, Panni said, 'Let's get going.'

'Here, I'll take you on my cross-bar, *Tenente*,' said Pascalino.

'Won't that be too awkward?'

'Not at all,' replied Pascalino, picking up his bicycle. 'I always took my brother to church on Sunday on the cross-bar. He was a lot heavier than you and there aren't any hills here.'

'Let's go,' said Panni.

And so he made his entrance into Zwara perched on the cross-bar of an old bicycle with his arm around the neck of an Italian soldier.

'If Tommy could see me now . . .'

Skoda was lying between the crates in the back of the truck, using his roll-neck sweater as a pillow.

He had checked all the rifles and even unpacked some rounds of ammunition. It had been a pleasure to feel the metal in his hands and work the bolt and catch the round as it was ejected.

There were several possible ways of getting back into the war, he thought. He could hire a boat at Tunis and try to reach Malta; or he could find the leading British troops, who were said to be at El Agheila; or he could wait for them here. But he was sick of waiting. He was on edge these days.

He was reaching in his pocket for a cigarette when he heard voices and studded boots scraping over the ground. He sat up.

He threw the blanket off his legs as the voices approached the courtyard. The gate creaked as someone said in Italian: 'Shall we look in here?'

'Better call Renata first,' came another voice.

'Yeh. It'll be a good sight. She sleeps naked.'

'How do you know?'

'Oh . . . I just know.'

'*Mama mia!*' exclaimed a third person. 'Gino, you call her . . .'

Skoda slipped silently to the door of the building and put his eye to a crack. He could see four soldiers standing in the yard with rifles slung on their shoulders and a fifth one looking up at the windows.

'Leave her in peace,' said one. 'She might empty a chamber-pot on us, I wouldn't put it past her.'

'D'you want to see her buds or not?' Gino asked.

'Oh Renata!' he shouted. Silence. Then he shouted again. 'Renata! Come to the window for a moment!'

Skoda heard Renata's voice ask 'What is it?' but he could not see her. 'What do you want?'

Gino took off his cap and swept the ground with it in a deep bow. 'We've come to offer you our nocturnal respects.'

'Are you crazy or what?'

'Come forward a bit, so that we can see you better, my little moonbeam.'

'Drunken lot!' screeched Renata.

And an appreciative gasp of 'Ah!' went up from the soldiers.

'No kidding, Renata,' said Gino, his head raised. 'This is serious business. An official visit.'

'And my ass? Is that official too?' retorted Renata.

The soldiers burst out laughing.

'Come on, Gino, let's be off,' cried one. 'Renata is too shameless for us.'

'What about the search?' asked Gino in an ironic voice. Looking up again he called, 'We've come to make a search, Renata.'

'Search for what?'

'An Englishman. A patrol found his revolver belt on the beach earlier. He must have survived a plane crash. See if he's under your bed.'

Skoda heard Renata laugh. 'I wouldn't put an Englishman under my bed, you Abruzzi pig, but in it!'

There was another burst of laughter. 'Renata, how about giving us a drink?' Gino suggested.

'Go to hell,' she retorted.

'Where d'you hide your wine? We'll help ourselves.'

Skoda saw one of the soldiers look towards the shed and his heart pounded.

'In the shed over there, Renata?' came Gino's cheerful voice. 'Is that where you keep your best bottles?'

'Leave my shed alone,' said Renata. 'You'll disturb my

chickens and then I shan't have any more fresh eggs . . .'

'Then give us a drink.'

There was a short silence, then 'All right, wait a minute and I'll come and let you in.'

'Thank God,' whispered Skoda.

'Don't give them too much to drink,' Mattei warned as he watched Renata slipping on her dress. 'One of them might get the idea of coming up to bed with you,' he added lightly, trying to relax the tenseness that had invaded his body.

'D'you think I bring them up here just like that!' exclaimed Renata, stepping into her shoes.

Mattei put his finger to his mouth. 'Ssh.' He needed a cigarette. *That blasted Englishman. I should never have picked him up.*

As Renata opened the door, they heard a loud voice that rang with authority.

'Are you in there, Bertolucci?'

'Yes, *Tenente,*' replied one of the soldiers.

Renata froze, and Mattei sat up in bed.

'We're going to search Renata's place, *Tenente,*' came another voice.

'You're a lot of idiots! D'you think he's in her bed? If someone survived that crash he's hiding somewhere. All you can think of is wine and pinching this girl's bottom.'

'But, *Tenente* . . .'

Mattei laughed to himself. *The officer was going to get rid of these soldiers.* But then he heard:

'That shed over there—that's a hiding-place, isn't it?'

A short silence followed, then the officer added: 'You! Open that door.'

Mattei froze and beckoned to Renata. 'How can we get out of here?'

'We're trapped,' she said with no trace of panic in her voice. Then she said, 'Over the roof.'

'That's where she keeps her chickens, *Tenente,*' Bertolucci protested feebly.

'To hell with her chickens!' the officer yelled. 'Open that door!'

He crossed the yard, striding directly towards the shed door. Skoda instinctively moved back to the truck, snatched his ancient revolver from under his sweater and crouched behind the vehicle. The door opened with a prolonged metallic squeak.

A circle of light from an electric torch swept into the shed and rested on the truck. Skoda saw the soldiers gather around their officer. A white hen ran cackling across the floor, flapping its wings and shedding feathers.

Skoda could feel the coldness of the mudguard against his body. Suddenly he saw that he had left one of the crates of rifles open. 'No chance,' he thought.

'What's all that?' said the officer.

Stepping towards the truck, his boots scraping over the ground, 'Here, hold this,' he ordered, handing the torch to a soldier.

Skoda saw the shadow of a soldier extending towards him. I've had it, he thought, as he slowly drew back the catch on his revolver. But I'll give Mattei a little time.

Then he watched as the shadow became fuller. He looked up and the soldier, holding his rifle across his chest, exclaimed 'Hey . . . !'

Skoda lifted his revolver. He could not miss at this distance, and squeezed the trigger. An orange flame spurted forth and the revolver jumped in his hand. The soldier bounded backwards, his arms flung wide, then fell to the ground.

Skoda sprang forward and fired twice. The stupefied soldiers scampered out into the courtyard. The torch rolled along the ground and Skoda sent it after them with a kick.

Renata and Mattei had reached the other side of the flat roof, overlooking the narrow street. There were more than a dozen soldiers now below them who stood about like a hesitant herd, waiting for orders from their officer.

Mattei put a hand on the rusty drain-pipe.

'Can you get down?' he whispered to Renata. 'It's not much more than a dozen feet to the ground. If the pipe comes away from the wall, jump . . .'

Skoda banged the shed-door and fired through the crack. One of the soldiers fired back.

'Scatter! Take cover!' yelled the officer.

Two more shots rang out and a soldier stumbled and fell in the middle of the courtyard.

'Now's the moment,' murmured Mattei.

.'You go,' said Renata. 'I'll never make it. Go on,' she said calmly.

Her tone seemed to mean 'It's better for both of us.'

Mattei felt the same. He'd rather be alone. It was going to be difficult enough without the added responsibility of a woman. But he said, 'You're sure?'

'Yes, sure.'

He put one leg over the edge, feeling for the wall, and gripped the drain-pipe.

Just as Mattei began to draw his other leg slowly over the edge, one of the soldiers appeared in the street below. He was about six feet from the bottom of the drain-pipe, as far as possible from the shed and the rifle-fire.

Skoda tore open the crate of hand-grenades, thrust two into his pockets and another on his belt. Then he grabbed a Beretta machine-pistol, put a clip in it and another in his shirt-pocket.

'Fire!' the officer shouted.

The door of the shed was forced open by the volley. The side of the truck rang long and loud from the impact of the bullets.

'Surrender!' the officer called in English.

Skoda's face was distorted. He had thrown himself against the wall of the shed, the Beretta in one hand and a grenade in the other.

'Surrender!' the officer called again.

'Go to hell, you bastard!' Skoda replied.

He pulled the pin out of the grenade with his teeth, counted to seven, then swung round and hurled the grenade through the doorway. He watched it roll along the ground before he flung himself back against the wall.

'We'll see if these bloody things work . . .' he said to himself.

The explosion blinded him. Red and green lights danced before his eyes. Now, he thought, now is the moment . . .

When the grenade exploded, the soldier below dropped flat. Mattei, without a word or gesture to Renata, gripped the drain-pipe and began to let himself down the wall.

The pipe came away almost at once but he had gained three or four feet. He jumped. The ground rose towards him, and he landed hard on his feet, his knees bent and trembling. 'Nothing broken,' he told himself.

The soldier had disappeared, but just as he straightened up he saw another man dash from the courtyard. Mattei moved into the shadow of a doorway.

The Serb bounded past him, firing as he went. A group of soldiers were now in the narrow street, on either side of Mattei, firing at Skoda's fleeing figure. They did not notice Mattei flattened in the doorway, so intent were they on the man who, fifty yards down the street, had just reached towards the wall for support, dropped to his knees and then dragged himself to an angle in the wall.

Skoda tried to raise himself but the pain in his right side was too sharp. He fell to his knees again, his features contorted.

The sound of running feet snatched him from his pain for a moment. He propped himself against a small boundary-stone, putting his left elbow on it to support the Beretta he still carried in his right hand. 'There must still be four or five rounds in it. Perhaps only three.' He felt a warm sticky liquid ooze from his hip and run down his thigh. The gate to the courtyard was no more than fifty yards away.

'I can see him.'

Skoda looked around but could only see the narrow street and the dark sky above the buildings. He tried to take one of the grenades from his pockets but he had no strength.

'Surrender!' shouted the officer.

Skoda felt his head falling forward. 'Surrender? What's he mean?'

'Can you see him?' someone called.

'Yes.'

Skoda jerked his head back and fired. The spurt of flame dazzled him. Then a hard blow racked his chest and toppled him backwards. As he fell, his fingers pressed the trigger and he saw the ground smoking in front of him. A dry earthy smell penetrated his nostrils.

'That's got him,' came a shout.

Skoda opened his eyes. He saw his outstretched arm with its hand in the dust, and several pairs of legs coming slowly towards him.

Something hard and round was pressing against his stomach. The grenades, he thought. But he couldn't move.

'He's dead,' he heard from above.

'No, he's still moving.'

Then a pair of boots stood in front of his eyes. He watched as one of the boots kicked aside the black shape of the Beretta. His chest was numb and the pain in his side had vanished; when he drew a breath he heard a gentle wheezing and gurgling.

'I'm a Serb,' he wanted to say.

Suddenly his eyes shot open and he saw a dazzling light, like a huge sun. He coughed and lukewarm fluid surged up his throat and flowed from his lips.

The dazzling light was still there; but it was fading, vanishing quickly.

The army truck moved slowly along the narrow street, passing Mattei, and stopped by the soldiers gathered around Skoda.

As the soldiers moved aside, Mattei could see Skoda's body, bathed in the blinding light of the headlamps. The light made his face masklike, with only slots for eyes.

Mattei could feel the warmth of the wall against his shoulder, and on the other side of the nail-studded door he heard voices from the Arabs woken by the firing.

Move from here. He had to move away. Or should he knock on the door and seek refuge with the Arabs? No, their fear of the Italians far outweighed their hatred. They'd hand him over immediately.

Mattei peered around him. On one side stood the group of soldiers above Skoda's body; on the other, two soldiers by the entrance to Renata's courtyard.

There was nothing to do but wait.

Wait for the truck to take away Skoda's body, for the soldiers to return to their billets. There was one chance in a hundred that he would not be seen. Then he'd have to get out of this maze of streets and reach the desert; in four or five hours he could be at the inlet . . .

Just then, the two soldiers outside the courtyard began walking slowly up the street towards Mattei. He shrank back into the doorway. If they passed without noticing him, he was safe. For the time being, at least.

Only six feet away. Three feet now.

Suddenly one of the soldiers came to a stop, gazing in surprise. 'What . . .'

Mattei remained motionless for perhaps two or three seconds.

After what's happened, he thought, they're likely to be trigger-happy. He put his hands up.

The two soldiers seemed stunned, then one levelled his rifle at Mattei.

The other soldier ordered him forward. '*Avanti,*' he said quietly.

Mattei walked with his arms held high towards the group still gathered around Skoda's body.

8

Basil stepped outside the army post. It was still cool, and he felt renewed after his rest. A covered army truck stood before him and the driver, a big man with close-cropped hair, looked up at Basil and smiled. 'Are you my passenger, *Tenente*?'

'Yes,' said Basil, returning the smile. 'Am I the only one?'

'For the present, yes. But I think we're going to El Atsitia to pick up two others.'

'Two other prisoners?'

'Yes. Don't know who they are, though.'

Basil climbed into the back of the truck where two soldiers sat dozing. Looking at them as the truck started to move, he imagined himself in one of those jolting, rattling buses that wander through the Italian countryside picking up a farmer or two in one village, putting down a cheapjack in another, never full and never quite empty, with each new passenger showing a polite indifference to those already in the bus. Basil wondered if he were to step between the two soldiers and jump casually from the slowly moving truck whether they would move or merely gaze at him and gloomily nod: *'Arrivederci, Inglese.'—'Arrivederla.'*

Basil unbuttoned the top pocket of his army blouse and took out the pack of Weekends. There were still eight cigarettes left. The sizzle of his match made one of the soldiers look up. He smiled.

Basil held up the pack. 'Want one?'

The man shook his head. 'You keep them, *Tenente*. A cigarette is a prisoner's only pleasure.'

'Exactly,' said Basil. 'So I'd better start going without them now. Here, take one.'

The soldier got up.

'Take one for your buddy too,' said Basil.

'Thank you, *Tenente*,' said the other soldier, 'but I don't smoke.'

Basil drew on the cigarette and leaned back.

What would Julia be doing just now? It must be about ten o'clock in England. If there was no air-raid last night, Julia would be wandering about Chelsea looking in all the antique shops, her face pressed against the musty windows. Then she'd go in and finger the gilded cherubs she adores and the snuff-boxes. Julia with her aristocratic manner and her silly endless telephone conversations, and her passion for watches which she wore on long chains around her neck. Or she might be asleep, or perhaps a bomb had converted her body into light and heat. Or perhaps . . . well, she'd be within her rights, thought Basil, but she behaves so ridiculously that she might remain faithful for years.

The driver was singing operatic arias and the two soldiers were looking out of the back of the truck at the road slipping away in the dust, at the sparse tufts of grass, and an occasional white farmhouse with a few emaciated sheep grazing nearby under the care of a Biblical-looking shepherd with a crook.

'El Atsitia!' shouted the driver. 'Empty your bladders and fill up with water.'

The truck ground to a stop in a small square in front of an army post almost identical to the one in Zwara.

The two soldiers let the tailboard down and jumped heavily to the ground.

'Are you coming, *Tenente*?'

He followed them and stretched his legs. There was only a dull ache in his knee now.

He leaned against the truck and suddenly saw the skipper of the fishing-boat being brought handcuffed out of the army post.

He started forward, about to say, 'Well, fancy meeting you . . .' but stopped and drew on his cigarette.

The skipper's face was swollen and bruised and he passed Basil without any sign of recognition.

A young handcuffed woman followed. She was tall and dark and wore a light grey skirt and a man's torn shirt.

'Put them in the truck,' an officer shouted.

Basil got in and sat opposite the two prisoners and looked intently at the skipper as if waiting for him to speak.

Finally, he whispered, 'I was caught yesterday.'

'At night?'

'No, yesterday morning. Where's your friend?'

'Dead,' said the man. 'They thought he was you.' There was a silence. Then he nodded towards the girl. 'She's Renata. My name's Mattei.'

'Everybody there?' called the driver, looking in the back of the truck.

'Yes,' said Basil.

The two soldiers climbed in.

Mattei stretched his legs and put his head back, his eyes closed.

There are two here and two in front, he thought. The driver is the most dangerous. He's singing now but he'd shoot me without hesitation. I could topple the tall one over the tailboard and the other one probably would just stand there. You could do that handcuffed.

He opened his eyes and looked at Basil leaning back in a repose of complete unconcern. Is he likely to help me?

'You wouldn't have a cigarette?' he asked, leaning towards Basil.

'Of course.'

Basil brought out a pack and put a cigarette between Mattei's split lips.

'I'm going to ask them for a light,' Mattei said in French.

'All right,' said Basil, slipping the matches back in his pocket.

Mattei got to his feet and faced a rifle.

'Stay where you are,' said the soldier.

'I only want a light.'

'The Englishman will give you one.' The soldier smiled at Basil. 'Would you mind giving a light to this maffioso, *Tenente*?'

'Not at all,' said Basil.

Mattei sat down again. 'No go.'

Basil smiled as he held out a lighted match. Mattei inhaled deeply and felt dizzy. It had been twenty-four hours since his last cigarette and much longer since he had eaten.

'Where are we going?' Mattei asked.

'Tripoli,' said one of the soldiers.

'The longest way around,' commented Basil, smiling.

He takes things too easy for my liking, thought Mattei. In fact he seems pleased at his present role as prisoner.

Mattei leaned towards Renata and put his head on her shoulder.

'Do you know where we are?' Mattei murmured.

'We're getting near Tarhouna,' she muttered.

'What's that?'

'A small town just before Tripoli.'

'Do we go through it?'

'I think so.'

'If I make a bolt for it,' he whispered, 'will you follow?'

'Yes,' she replied. 'If I can.'

At the back of the truck the two soldiers nodded sleepily.

The truck slowed and the driver began blowing his horn and hurling curses out of the window. The road was filled with fruit-laden barrows hauled by ragged Arabs and donkeys.

'This is Tarhouna,' said the tall soldier. 'We drop the sergeant here.'

Basil stood up and looked through the window in the back of the driver's cabin.

The truck slowly wound its way up a street lined with low houses and stalls where biscuits, cakes and tooled leather goods were sold. The air smelled of frying-oil and rotting rubbish.

This is the East, thought Basil.

As he sat down he saw Mattei looking quickly from him to the soldiers and then to the street.

Then he watched Mattei rise slowly to his feet and take two strides to the back of the truck.

He slashed one of the soldiers with his handcuffed fists and caught him between the eyes.

The other one swung round and Mattei's fists grazed the man's forehead.

Renata darted forward and sat on the fallen soldier. The truck stopped abruptly and Mattei and the other soldier fell to the floor of the truck and then toppled over the tailboard with bewildering swiftness. Basil started forward instinctively and vaulted to the ground. He saw Mattei, hair ruffled and mouth wide open, breaking through the shouting crowd that opened before him like a door.

Basil whirled around and saw the sergeant appear from the front of the truck brandishing his revolver. For a split second their eyes met, then the sergeant's gaze switched to Mattei and he raised his gun. The crowd squealed and scrambled back and Basil, without thinking, hit the sergeant on the side of his head. He staggered and fired as he fell. Panic seized the crowd and they scattered in all directions and Basil darted off after Mattei.

Mattei ran with his teeth clenched and his body taut, catching brief glimpses of astonished faces as he passed—a child laughing, a black-veiled woman, a bearded old man waving some raffia, and a sheep's carcass dripping blood.

A bullet whistled past him. He darted into a side street, bumped into an Italian civilian, and ran on. His hip caught the edge of a sweet-stall and a stab of pain went through him. Though his breath seemed inadequate and his throat burned, he kept running. He slipped on some slimy rubbish, and a dog barked and jumped up at him.

He plunged into an alley. He felt sick and his head throbbed. Then he suddenly came to a wall—he was in a blind alley.

He heard shouts in the distance. He looked up at the wall, retreated a few yards and took a running jump. The handcuffs hampered him and he hung precariously to the top of the wall.

'Hurry up, old chap,' came a voice from below. 'They're on your heels.'

He felt a firm grasp on his ankles and then his feet felt the solidity of a pair of shoulders.

'Hurry up,' gasped the voice.

The Englishman straightened up. Mattei got an arm over the wall, hoisted himself up and rolled over, hitting the dust below.

And now, thought Basil, morally speaking, I ought to be shot on the spot.

But no one was in the blind alley, and Basil stepped back, ran and jumped for the top of the wall. His hands gripping the concrete, he heaved himself up, banging his chin against the stone, and dropped to the other side, landing near Mattei's prostrate body. They were in a small yard of beaten earth surrounded by walls on three sides and a one-storey house opposite them. In the middle of the yard lay a rusty bicycle, a green umbrella stuck in the ground, and a hen with one leg raised and its neck rippling with indignation.

Mattei turned over on his back. His breathing came more easily and regularly now.

Peace surrounded him and the entire town seemed to have ceased living. Only the clucking of the hen came to his ears.

'We're not out of the wood yet,' he said.

His voice surprised him.

'Pardon?' said the Englishman.

'We're not out of trouble yet,' Mattei said slowly. Then added, 'What on earth made you follow me?'

Basil wiped his face and the trace of a smile appeared on his white-ringed lips. 'I wish I knew. Rather stupid, wasn't it?'

Mattei shrugged his shoulders. 'One doesn't always do the clever thing.'

They both took long, slow breaths.

'Your girl-friend is still back there,' Basil said at last.

'I know.'

'I expect they've surrounded the district.'

'Very likely.' Mattei nodded towards the house. 'And if the people in there join in ...'

'And up there?' said Basil, pointing at the terraced roofs overlooking the yard.

Mattei looked up but the glare from the sun made the rooftops indistinct.

'Get on your feet,' said Basil, slowly standing up.

The hen stalked off towards the house, its head waggling in time with its step, and disappeared under the grey cotton curtain hanging over the doorway.

Mattei heaved himself up with effort, resting his back against the wall.

'We make an odd-looking couple,' he commented. 'Me with my handcuffs and a face like a hardened convict and you in that uniform. It's enough to set all the Italian watchdogs barking their heads off.'

Basil strode deliberately across the yard, lifted the grey curtain hanging over the doorway, glanced inside, then vanished.

'How odd,' Mattei said to himself, 'here's this guy who suddenly comes into your life again. He's the one who got you into this mess, and now he seems to be getting you out of it. For the present anyway.'

The Englishman appeared again and beckoned to him.

PART TWO

'Every setback is a hidden victory.'

J.-L. Borges

9

Lorena listened to the rasp of tyres from her husband's car on the gravel below. She lay naked on her bed, fair hair rumpled above slightly sunken cheeks. Her long slender fingers stroked her flat belly and hesitated at a scar that ran from navel to groin. In another two years it will be gone, she thought.

Her short, wide nose, green eyes and almost white eyelashes gave her the look of a lioness.

She was twenty-eight.

Amedée-Jean, she thought, was now on his way to Tripoli where he went every Tuesday. He'd make the rounds at army H.Q. and leave his claims in various offices, have lunch with the Swiss *chargé d'affaires,* and then at about five o'clock he'd go into the leather-goods shop in the Via Cavour to see that woman. Lorena had been there once, out of curiosity. The woman was in her thirties and her light gaberdine dress accentuated her large hips. Her dark hair was drawn back tightly and she held her head high as if in defiance. Lorena had looked around, fingered a few articles and then left. The woman had recognised her, but had remained silent and immobile behind the counter. Perhaps she had expected a scene?

After leaving the shop, Lorena had wondered why this woman attracted her husband. The ample figure, perhaps? A reminder of his beloved Switzerland? Or the aphrodisiac smell of leather. She was unable to imagine Amedée-Jean in the role of lover. She could only remember his awkward insensitive hands and his heavy breathing.

'He made love like a defrocked priest,' she mused.

Yet he did possess that Swiss appearance of vigorous health

combined with a certain Latin casualness which she had once found attractive. The appearance of a chamois hunter.

'But that's all. You made a mistake.'

She got out of bed and slipped on her pants, a pair of stained slacks and an old soiled sweater. Brushing back her hair she looked outside. Sunshine. What I wouldn't give for a little rain, she sighed. Even Swiss rain.

She remembered Zurich with its fairytale appearance and orderly sophisticated shoppers. But here the street below was teeming with people and noise. Tuesday was market-day, and everywhere Arabs were dragging heavy barrows piled with water-melons, oranges and bananas, dates and apricots. The noise and dirt pushed her back into the bedroom where polychrome wood carvings, which she had done in her first year in Tripolitania, hung on the white walls. She had made considerable progress since then but she liked the way the paint had faded with time on these carvings.

My Cheyenne period, she thought, running her finger over the carved surface of one.

She stepped out on to the wide landing and leaned over the balustrade, looking down at the red-and-white tiled floor of the entrance-hall. She heard the shrill voices of Tiken, the Senoussi man-servant, and Radah coming from the kitchen.

'Radah!' she called.

The girl came out and looked up. She did not wear her veil in the house, but never ventured outside without it.

'Yes, madam?'

'Will you bring me my coffee?'

'To the studio?'

'Yes, to the studio.'

Lorena went along the landing to the large room which she used as her studio. Opening directly onto a wide terrace, it was filled with light. A long work-bench stretched through the middle of the room and was littered with dark-coloured chippings, blocks of wood partly carved, trying-planes and chisels and stylets, tubes of paint and also cups and glasses full of cigarette butts. An empty bottle of Gordon's Gin sat on a stool, and an old-fashioned gramophone and some records were piled on the floor.

The air in the room was warm and pungent with the smells of wood, oil and tobacco. Lorena kicked a heavy block of wood sending it rumbling across the floor. She opened the slatted shutters and let in the street sounds.

Stepping out on the terrace bordered with large tropical plants, she looked across at the overlapping flat white roofs interrupted by the lines of washing hanging limply in the still air.

Below her dangled the Swiss flag strangled by smoke from the kitchen. The white cross is going to stink of rancid butter, she thought.

Radah shuffled in and Lorena made a place for the tray among the jumble of tools on the work-bench.

'Put it here . . .' she said in Italian with little trace of an accent.

Radah put the tray down and poured some coffee.

'Will you have lunch here, madam?'

'Yes. At about one. Bring me a large carafe of orange-juice without sugar, some apricots and a water-melon. Have you got a melon?'

'Yes, madam.'

'Tell Tiken to make me a little semolina.'

'Will that be all?'

'Yes. Have you been out? Is there any news?'

'It's being said that the Nazranis are coming to help the Italians, and that the other Nazranis are quite near.'

'I know,' said Lorena. 'They're not that close, however.'

'Everyone is saying they'll kill everybody and stick our heads on the ramparts,' Radah added.

'You frightened?' Lorena said with a smile.

'Yes.'

'Well, don't be. It isn't true.'

'Everybody says so,' said Radah stubbornly.

It's a thrill to be afraid, thought Lorena. I envy her.

'And they say that the soldiers are looking for some Nazranis who've escaped.'

'What, here? At Tarhouna?'

'Yes.'

Probably British prisoners, thought Lorena. The Arabs used the word 'Nazrani' (Nazarene) impartially for any kind of Christian. It was impossible to make much sense of any talk about British or Italian troop movements.

'What do you want for dinner tonight?' asked Radah.

Good heavens, thought Lorena, I'd forgotten about Maggiore

Sarfati and his little friends. And poor Amedée-Jean. He'll have to make love quickly.

'Water-melons, leg of lamb, *lasagna*,' she told Radah, 'with tomatoes, goat's cheese and fruit. I'll see about the wine myself . . .'

Radah looked at her, the glimmer of a smirk touched her lips. You little bitch, thought Lorena. So I drink, but I know it's you who tells Amedée-Jean where I hide my booze.

'Off with you, now!'

Radah sauntered out, and Lorena smiled to herself. The constant battle her husband waged about her drinking was the last semblance of marital authority. But then again he was only concerned with respectability. A consul's wife should never be an embarrassment. Lorena sipped her coffee. I wonder what she calls him in bed? Monsieur le Consul? Amedée-Jean? Or perhaps a pet name. A gentleness probably came into her husband's eyes as he bent over to kiss her and . . . oh, the hell with all that, she thought, and gulped the rest of her coffee. She lit a cigarette and took up her chisel and mallet.

Her features softened as she started work on the block of wood before her. Carving brought oblivion; a liberty of thought which came freely with no restraint or pain.

She worked slowly, chiselling sideways at the wood and pushing the round splinters away with her thumb. Gradually the bridge of the nose and the eye-sockets became distinguishable.

My African period, she thought.

She was interrupted by Radah: 'May I have the tray, madam?'

'Yes, take it away.'

Radah whisked past with a furtive and almost frightened glance around the room.

She probably thinks you're a bit mad, Lorena told herself. I wonder if Amedée-Jean has told her to check up on me during the day. Now don't be so positive of plots against you. Amedée-Jean is quite capable of being unfaithful to you yet priding himself on trying to save you. His Swiss woman must admire his strict virtue, she thought disgustedly.

She bolted the door after Radah and went across to the wooden masks hanging on the wall. Lifting one that bulged like a shield, she took down a bottle hidden in its hollow and drank.

'Ah, that's better,' she said to herself.

The liquid made her lips sting but she felt good. That early-morning listlessness seemed to be wearing off.

She passed her thumb over the dark wood and thought back to Switzerland and those days after she had returned from the hospital. She had been weak and despondent; shattered by the knowledge that she could never bear children. She had withdrawn into herself, never confessing her anguish to Amedée-Jean. Perhaps it was then that their ability to communicate had stopped abruptly. A sense of release had come at the initial stages of sculpting, the soft clay made her hands work with a kind of sensual eagerness. Then Amedée-Jean had told her he had been posted to Tripolitania.

'As well as the consulate I shall be responsible for the Mission school. It might remind you of New Mexico. There's lots of sand...'

Perhaps he too had been deeply disappointed when she lost the child he had expected. She'd never know.

Probably the best thing for you to do is return to New Mexico and leave him to his Consulate and Anita Payot. But then their secret meetings might lose their attractiveness.

Amedée-Jean must have reached Tripoli by now. She took another swig of whisky. 'Take it easy, girl, you're thinking too much. Maybe you have made a mess of everything—your marriage, your carvings, your whole life. But it can't go on like this forever. One of these days you'll leave. What's stopping you, anyway? The fear of being back in New Mexico, with the round of parties, the Community Centre on Friday evenings, and your mother and those everlasting cretonne curtains? Yes, she didn't want that. Amedée-Jean had rescued her from that boredom and she had set out in marriage as an adventure—fulfilling her fantasies of being the wife of a European.

Suddenly her eyes caught a flickering of light on the terrace. She watched it as it danced over the furniture.

She put down her file and went outside.

The bright light now shone straight on her and she shaded her eyes. Then it stopped. Was it some children playing with a piece of glass on one of the terraces?

The flashing started again, not directly on her but quite near, and in a deliberate manner; three short and then three long. It stopped again. But she had seen where it was coming from—a terrace about four streets away, probably somewhere near the

Via Savoia and not far from the ramparts whose white battlements could be seen between the rooftops.

She thought she saw a figure move, a man or a child raising his head and then ducking down again, as if playing a game.

Then she saw a raised arm and Lorena raised a hand in reply.

10

They had been lying on the terrace for more than an hour. At first it was a welcome reprieve, but the sun was relentless and they were thirsty. The bare white terrace provided no shelter from the glare above and they did not dare risk taking cover on the spiral staircase leading up to the trap-door.

In all probability they would have to remain until nightfall, which would be another eight hours. That is if they weren't discovered before then. The neighbourhood had most likely been surrounded and soldiers were probably searching the houses one by one.

'You've the knack of making life uncomfortable lately,' Basil was musing. 'Right now, if you hadn't pulled strings to get posted to Cairo, you'd be having lunch at Julia's apartment. Instead, you've almost been killed two or three times in forty-eight hours, you're exhausted on this ridiculous roof and if you're recaptured, you can expect to be treated with much less consideration. If you're recaptured alive, that is. The Italians have likely been ordered to shoot on sight.'

He was stretched out on his back with his cap over his eyes but he could feel the sun burning his chin and cheeks, and scorching his body through the thick battledress.

Mattei was asleep with his knees drawn up and his handcuffed wrists over his eyes, snoring evenly and peacefully.

'In any case, this is a stupid situation,' Basil said to himself. 'It's impossible to remain here for ever, and if we leave we'll be caught at once. You helped him; don't regret it, but the best thing you can do now is to part company.'

He pictured himself crawling to the trap-door, lifting it quietly

79

and slipping downstairs into the house. Then going to give him-self up. And if he was asked about Mattei he'd say he knew nothing, that they'd separated almost at once after escaping.

He heard the cries of fruit-sellers and also shouts in Italian, a patrol ordering the Arabs out of its way.

He fanned himself with his cap, but moving his arm was too exhausting.

Mattei took his hands from his face. He was sweating pro-fusely and his eyes were red and his face puffy from sleep.

'What time is it?' he asked.

'Look up at the sky,' said Basil.

Mattei squinted at the sun. 'Hell, I've been asleep.'

'You've even been snoring.'

Mattei stretched himself, holding his handcuffed wrists out in front of him. He felt rested but his mouth was dry. Getting awk-wardly to his knees, he looked carefully over the ledge.

'We're in luck,' he said.

'You think so?'

'Nobody goes out on their terrace at this time of day. Too hot.'

Basil began to get to his knees.

'Stay where you are,' said Mattei. 'With that army cap and your fair hair you're like a British flag.'

'And you with your handcuffs, what do you think you're like?'

Mattei made no reply; he was more interested in an escape route. The streets were narrow but not enough to jump from one roof to another. There remained only the trap-door. If they hadn't been discovered by nightfall, they could try to get away through the house.

'Curfew starts at eight,' he said.

'What do you mean?'

'People still in the streets after eight o'clock are stopped and checked.'

'You mean you're thinking of leaving this place?'

'Aren't you?' Mattei was not surprised at Basil's response. But he went on: 'You can stay here if you want, or you can make a bolt for it right now. In any case, I think we'd have a better chance if we split up.'

'I quite agree.'

Mattei continued to gaze at the surrounding buildings. His

eyes rested on a two-storey house about a hundred yards away with a red flag drooping from a pole over the doorway. There was a large room on the top floor that opened onto a terrace and he thought he could make out a figure in the room, a man in a white shirt. He dropped down again near Basil.

'Which country has a red flag?' Mattei asked him.

'There's the ensign of our Merchant Navy—the red duster, they call it.'

'You think the British merchant navy is at Tarhouna?'

'It's not impossible. Our merchant ships go everywhere.' Basil smiled with some difficulty. 'I don't know who'd have a red flag here. Unless it's a club for Communist prisoners.'

'I think it's red. Take a look, straight across there. A house with two floors. The flag's on the left-hand side.'

Basil knelt against the ledge and looked across.   .

'There's something white on it,' he said. 'It's the Swiss flag.'

'You're sure?'

'Yes,' said Basil.

Mattei looked at him in surprise and bit his lower lip.

'Suppose it's a consulate?' he said. 'It'd be neutral territory. See what I mean?'

'Christ, yes! D'you think they'd take us in?'

'I don't know,' said Mattei.

He looked across at the house. Screwing up his eyes, he saw that the figure was a woman bent over a table.

'There's someone over there,' he said.

Basil took a look. 'It's a woman. But not an Arab,' he added.

'No, not with light hair.'

'It's a Swiss woman.'

'You've got good eyesight.'

'Just simple deduction.'

A thoughtful silence fell between them.

'We can't get across the roofs,' Basil said at last.

'I wonder if we can draw her attention.'

'That shouldn't be too difficult,' said Mattei. 'But then how are we going to explain who we are? At this distance . . .'

'Yes, but in order to signal to her . . . What kind of signals do escaped prisoners make, in your opinion?'

The street sounds had died with the hot midday air and only an occasional sharp note, a raised voice, a dog's bark, the clatter of sandals could be heard across a courtyard.

Mattei was looking towards the terrace. 'Do you have a pocket-mirror?' he asked.

'No.' Basil felt annoyed that he hadn't thought of that first. Mattei glanced at his wrist. 'Your watch would do. Or better still, that bracelet.'

Basil slipped off the silver identity bracelet. It was a handsome, highly polished chain, slightly concave, and Julia had had his name engraved on the disc by the jeweller.

'You think this will do the trick?'

Mattei took it and rubbed the disc on his trousers, then turned it towards the sun. A bright reflection burst between his fingers.

'Yes, that'll do,' he said with a smile.

I I

It took a few minutes for her to understand what the man was trying to convey. She could not see his uniform very clearly but his pantomime consisted of pointing to his cap, then to his chest, making a wide gesture of refusal and pointing to something below him and then putting a finger to his lips. He ended by stretching his arms towards her.

She had thought at first that he was some drunken Italian soldier and then that he was crazy. Only a mad person would perform such comedy on a roof-terrace at midday.

The man disappeared and then began the same gestures with greater precision. Suddenly she remembered Radah's tale of escaped British prisoners. His uniform was indeed British. It made sense. He was appealing for help.

She nodded her head deliberately several times, then stretched out her arm and moved her hand up and down in a soothing manner.

Basil dropped down and wiped the sweat from his forehead.

'I think she's got the message. She went like that,' he said, imitating the woman's gestures. A smile came to Mattei's cracked lips. 'She's quicker than you,' he said.

Basil got to his knees again. The young woman was still look- ing at him with her hands resting on the terrace balustrade. Again she repeated her gestures.

'Yes, she's understood,' said Basil.

Mattei thought for a moment. 'Try and tell her that we'd like to take refuge in her house.'

Basil raised himself and placed his hand on his chest and then flung his arm out towards her. The woman remained still for a moment, then pointed towards Basil and turned sideways with an inviting gesture, indicating her terrace. She cocked her head in a questioning manner, as if awaiting assurance that she had understood correctly.

'Splendid,' said Basil. 'She's very astute.'

He nodded his head slowly and deliberately. Then the young woman went through the same action several times, making a soothing gesture with outstretched hand and then putting her forefinger to her brow.

'She's going to have a think,' said Basil.

'Come and lie down. There's no point in being spotted by the Italians just when we might be getting out of this mess.'

Basil waved a hand round him with a frightened air, then made as if to duck out of sight. The young woman nodded vigorously.

Basil dropped down next to Mattei.

'I'm dead tired.'

'Well, we've nothing to do but wait now.'

Basil looked at him. 'You're a great man,' he said.

'I'm a man who values his life, that's all. I only hope she won't tell the Wops.'

'She looks a decent sort,' Basil said.

'You're mad,' she said to herself. 'You didn't even think. You can't do anything for him except welcome him when he succeeds in reaching the consulate. If he succeeds . . .'

She tried to locate the exact position of the terrace on which the man was hiding. After a few minutes, one hand shading her eyes, she picked out two helpful guiding marks: one, a house with an ornamental pediment which belonged to Sheik Abou Brider whom she had met on two or three occasions; the other, a small minaret with a white dome. So she decided that the Englishman's house must be at the intersection of two narrow streets which she knew quite well, having sometimes gone there to shop or to look at the craftsmen's displays.

'And if . . .' she told herself, but her mind began to whirl from excitement and liquor.

Basil looked carefully over the ledge. 'She's still there,' he said. 'Perhaps she's waiting for us to go over there,' he suggested.

'There's no chance of moving from here until nightfall,'

muttered Mattei. 'And even then . . . The best thing would be for her to come and fetch us in an automobile. The street's wide enough.' He opened his eyes and looked up. 'Stop moving about. If you'd use your head you'd try and tell her what I've just said.'

Basil sighed. 'Where's the front door to the house?' he asked.
'On our left.'

Basil took off his cap, pointed at the woman, and then began turning an imaginary steering-wheel.

'You're going too fast,' Mattei said quietly. 'Looking at you, I'd think you wanted to escape in a racing-car.'

'Shut up, you,' Basil hissed. He then held up a finger and traced a curved line in the air from the consulate to just below him on the left.

'I think she's understood,' he said.

'That's very clever of her,' commented Mattei, impassively watching Basil's efforts.

He pointed to the sun, then curved his arm to the west. He waited for the woman to reply . . . She nodded her head, then repeated his pantomime.

'Great!' said Basil excitedly. 'I'm sure she's understood.'

'Good. Now all we have to do is to wait for eight hours.'

'How depressing you can be at times,' sighed Basil.

In front of her stretched the terraces and lines of washing. But somehow these familiar images took on new colour and life. The streets were no longer simply a place where the Arabs hawked their wares, but a means to a definite end.

'Something's happening to you,' she told herself. She had made a decision. She was embarking on a new adventure and one which involved danger.

The word fascinated her.

She went back to her studio and gazed at the tools and the chippings on the work-bench. Later for that—I've got something better to do. She picked up the liquor bottle, looked at it for a moment, then placed it behind the mask.

She went to her bedroom and got the keys to her car.

The first thing was to make a reconnaissance of the street. She was again surprised at making a decision but everything seemed to take on a new sense of order. The events of the morning followed one after another and left little room for doubt.

She met Radah on the stairs carrying a tray. 'Your lunch, madam.'

'Put it in the studio,' said Lorena. 'I'll be back shortly.'

'About the meal this evening . . .' Radah began.

'When I come back,' Lorena cut her short.

She continued down the stairs trying not to hurry and went out to the garden, the name given for a patch of ground in which a few palm-trees fought to survive. As she walked towards her Oldsmobile—bought secondhand soon after coming to Tripoli—she noticed that Amedée-Jean had once again scratched the back fender. His driving had been one of the early causes of clashes between them; he found it difficult to admit that his bold American wife was the better driver.

She backed the faded yellow Oldsmobile out of the garage and into the street. She felt calm and collected and knew exactly what she had to do. For the moment at least.

A quality of urgency seemed to be in the streets which matched her own. Many of the shops were already closed, and, in those still open, the customers were being served quickly without the usual interminable conversations. The few pedestrians walked along hurriedly.

Lorena drove slowly and suddenly thought that the safest way to get the Englishman to the Consulate would be to hide him in the back of the car, covered with a blanket or a rug.

An Italian patrol appeared ahead of her, and she sensed a new attitude in them also. They were not smiling. Two of the patrol stood guard outside the door of a house while the others followed a corporal inside.

Lorena spotted Second-Lieutenant Margheriti come out of a house, and she stopped. He was a short, dark young man and Lorena had met him several times at various dinners given by members of the European colony.

Margheriti was fond of jazz and had talked to Lorena about Duke Ellington and Louis Armstrong, whose records he had to listen to secretly since the Fascist government disapproved of these 'decadent musicians'.

'*Buon giorno, Signora.*'

'*Buon giorno, Tenente,*' said Lorena. 'You seem very busy.'

'I am. I'm playing at cops and robbers.'

'And which side is winning?'

Margheriti put on a look of disgust. 'The robbers always win,

Signora. Being a cop is the rotten role. Are you going out of town?'

'No. Just a call to make.'

'There are check-points at all the exits,' said Margheriti, mopping his face. 'Beginning tonight,' he added, 'you'll need a permit to drive anywhere.'

'Good Lord!' exclaimed Lorena. 'It's like war! Are these robbers so important?' she asked.

'A British officer and another man.'

So, thought Lorena, that explains it. That Englishman did at times seem to be speaking to someone below him and out of sight.

'And do you think you'll find them here?'

Margheriti shrugged his shoulders. 'In my opinion, they've already gotten away to the desert. But I must do my job.'

'You're a very conscientious cop.'

'I'm a cop who's feeling very hot,' said Margheriti.

A soldier approached and asked glumly if they should search the next house.

'Yes, of course. We're very conscientious,' he added, turning back to Lorena. 'We let prisoners escape, but then we really do try to recapture them. *Devvero.*'

This must be the place. She was almost certain. But the two buildings she had picked out to guide her—the small minaret and the Sheik's house—seemed less evident from this angle.

She drove a little farther down the street and stopped outside the Sheik's house. The gothic doorway was ornamented with yellow and blue tiles. A door-porter sat on the steps, wrapped in a dark cloak, and gazed impassively at Lorena as she stepped from her car.

She saw the minaret to her left and estimated the distance from it to what might be the right terrace. Then she started up the other side of the house in an alley ending at a tall fence with broken slates. A veiled woman came out behind her and threw a bucket of slops on the ground. Lorena peered through the fence and saw a small, white-walled courtyard with a green umbrella stuck in the ground and a rusty old bicycle.

She went back to the street and got into her car.

'Another five or six hours before it's dark,' she said to herself. 'If the Italians haven't found them before then.'

She moved off in low gear.

'She's back again,' said Basil.

He had opened his shirt but this brought no relief. The sun was ruthless and his bare arms were already covered with red patches.

'We've just got to wait,' muttered Mattei.

His swollen lips and eyes were painful and he wondered if the truck had taken Renata to Tripoli, or whether she was being held in some prison cell at Tarhouna until he and Ferguson were recaptured.

'I could do with a drink,' said Basil.

'So could I. But at best, we won't get one until this evening. It's surprising that they haven't come this way yet.'

'What'll we do if they do find us?'

'You do whatever you please,' said Mattei. 'But I'm not keen on being recaptured.'

'You think they'll be trigger-happy?'

'Don't know. You never know. But I'm not worth keeping alive. In your case, it's different. I'd hate to be shot or left hanging from a meat-hook to die slowly.'

'They do things like that?' exclaimed Basil.

'Yes,' Mattei quietly replied.

'It's difficult to believe.'

'No one ever believes that sort of thing.'

'I like Italians very much,' said Basil.

Mattei gave a shrug. 'You've never been in jail.'

'Have you?'

'Yes, for five years . . . I was twenty-eight when sentenced, nearly thirty-three when I came out . . .' Mattei was silent for a moment, then added, 'Jailers are hardly ever decent, what do you expect?'

'I've gathered that,' said Basil.

'No, you can't have any idea unless you've been inside. Perhaps everyone should be a jailer. It's impossible to know what you would do in certain circumstances—whether you would do the decent thing or not.' He glanced at the sun. 'The swine, it's hardly moving,' he said.

At about six o'clock the painful glare seemed to merge into the white walls.

'It'll be dark in an hour,' said Mattei.

Basil got up with difficulty. He felt dizzy and the skin on his face was raw and tender. I must be a fine sight, he thought. He saw the woman at once and waved. His head throbbed and his damp clothes clung tightly to his burning skin.

'I hope she's got some aspirins,' he said to himself.

The woman pointed at the sun, then held up one finger. In an hour, Basil interpreted. Next, she made the gestures of driving through streets and pointed to the right of Basil. Then she went back into the room and came out with a large yellow scarf; she waved this while repeating the driving gestures. He did not understand and gave a voluble shrug. After a moment of hesitation, she drew a shape in the air, made a steering motion, then held up the scarf.

'A yellow automobile!' Basil exclaimed.

'In an hour,' he said as he lay down again next to Mattei, 'she's coming to pick us up in a yellow automobile.'

A little before six-thirty, Lorena went down to the kitchen. Tiken was standing over the stove and Radah was muttering to herself while she prepared the vegetables.

'I'm going out,' said Lorena. 'I want you to prepare two carafes of orange-juice and some fruit and take them to the studio.'

Radah looked surprised. 'What, you're going to receive the Italian officers up there?'

'No.' Lorena hesitated, then added, 'And I don't want the Italian officers to know that I've some other Nazranis up there.'

Radah looked at Lorena with dusky eyes but said nothing. Tiken slowly turned and Lorena said to him, 'You know there's a search on for some Nazranis who've escaped. They are English officers.'

'I was the one who told you about that,' said Radah.

'They are coming here.'

There was no reaction from either of the servants.

'I'm going to fetch them now,' Lorena went on.

Still no reaction.

'They will be safe here until the other English arrive. You know that their army is not far away.'

Tiken nodded.

'It's being said,' spoke up Radah, 'that when they get here

the ramparts will be lined with the heads that they cut off.'

'I told you this morning that the English don't cut people's heads off,' said Lorena, determined not to lose her patience. 'But they punish people who have not been kind to their brothers. And they reward people who help them.'

Tiken nodded again. Encouraged, Lorena added: 'With rich presents.'

Radah gave her a sullen look.

'The English,' Lorena continued, 'will be happy to know that we have protected their brothers, and we shall all be well rewarded.'

In the silence that followed, Lorena realised that she was using the same unctuous condescending tone of Amedée-Jean when he spoke to the servants.

'And supposing the Italian Nazranis hear about it?' Radah asked with an almost triumphant air.

'They won't, if no one says anything,' Lorena replied.

'This house is protected by the laws of your master,' she told them. 'This house is part of the country of your master. That's why his flag is flying outside. No one has the right to come in here without his permission.'

Tiken seemed only half convinced. As for Radah, she went on staring sullenly at the peelings on the table.

'Does the master know?' Tiken said at last.

'Not yet,' Lorena replied. 'But I'll tell him and I know he'll agree.'

She could sense that the two Arabs did not go along with her there. They knew Amedée-Jean only too well.

'You know that I am English in a way,' she continued in a commanding tone. 'I speak their language, and the master would not want my brothers to be put in prison or hunted down like animals and shot.'

'No,' said Tiken limply.

'Especially,' Lorena added, 'as the master knows that the English army will soon be here.'

Tiken seemed a little more convinced. Even Radah approved. Lorena continued.

'If the Italian soldiers were after your brother,' she said to Tiken, 'he could take refuge here. He could sleep and eat here, and the soldiers couldn't arrest him.'

Tiken nodded, looking impressed.

'All your family could take refuge here,' said Lorena, indicating the kitchen with a sweep of her arm. 'Your brothers and sisters and your mother, they could all come here.'

If they're not convinced now, she thought, I can't do any more.

Radah was saying something in Arabic, and Tiken answered in a pompous manner. Lorena did not understand what they were saying. Then Tiken said, 'We won't say anything about it to anyone.'

'Good,' said Lorena, relieved. 'The master will know about it. And you and Radah. And myself. Four of us will know, that's all.'

'*Inch' Allah,*' said Tiken.

'*Inch' Allah,*' echoed Radah.

Thank God, thought Lorena.

As Lorena drove away from the Consulate she could hear martial music blaring from a loudspeaker. There were still fewer people out than usual, and most of the native shops were closed. Only a few foodshops were open where Arab women waited clutching their baskets.

The martial music stopped and an announcement in Arabic rose above the street noises. It was coming from a small khaki-coloured Fiat in which sat two Italian officers and an Arab in European dress reading from a sheet of paper into a microphone.

His voice surrounded her, but Lorena could not understand what he was saying.

She took the next right and saw a patrol coming in her direction. The soldiers were in single file, rifles slung, and their sergeant lagging behind, mopping his brow. As Lorena drove past she saw him looking at the Swiss pennant on the hood of the Oldsmobile.

As Lorena drew near the Sheik's house dusk filled the narrow street. She stopped by the entrance to the alley and revved the engine several times.

If they don't hear that . . ., she thought.

Reaching backwards, she opened the rear door and then kept her eyes on the rear view mirror and the street ahead.

To calm her nerves, she lit a cigarette. There was nothing to do but wait. Her heart beat violently. Then she heard whistling and spotted an Italian civilian coming up the street with his hands shoved deeply into his pockets. When he reached the parked car he stopped and peered in at Lorena. He had bulging eyes and his white suit was crumpled and shabby.

'*Signorina?*' he said, smiling with a gold toothed grin.

Lorena looked away. 'If only those two don't dart out just now,' she said to herself.

'*Signorina,*' the man ventured again.

'Clear off,' Lorena said in Italian and as calmly as possible. 'I'm waiting for someone.'

She looked up the alley but saw only a black dog lapping up a puddle of water.

'*Signorina,*' he said again. 'You're alone and I'm alone, why don't we ... ?'

'I'm not alone,' retorted Lorena. 'I'm waiting for someone.'

'I'm a leather merchant,' the man said.

Another of them, she thought, it's incredible. I ought to put him in touch with Anita Payot ...

She put her foot down hard on the accelerator and the engine roared, but the man did not budge.

'I'm not afraid,' he said. 'I was on the Isonzo in 'seventeen, and I'm not afraid. My name is Perfetini. Mario Perfetini, and since I was twenty ...'

'Clear off,' snapped Lorena as she caught sight of two figures coming cautiously down the alley. Despite the dusk, she easily made out the British uniform.

'Go on, clear off,' she said. 'Here are my friends.'

She switched on the headlights, and the man stood back. She felt the Oldsmobile sway to one side and heard the rear door bang shut.

'Here we are,' a voice breathed behind her.

Lorena immediately let the clutch out.

12

Amedée-Jean Dalloz was frustrated and furious at having to return to Tarhouna so early. He had completely forgotten about the dinner party for the Italian officers, and Lorena's phone call earlier in the day had spoiled his visit with Anita. He had planned to spend the night with her, telling Lorena that the confusion in the army offices due to the hurried retreat of the Italian troops would keep him in Tripoli another day.

Anita had been terribly disappointed and they had not been able to make love properly. In fact, they had not had time to make love at all.

As he approached the north gate to Tarhouna he was surprised to see Italian soldiers methodically searching all the vehicles leaving the town and shining torches on the faces of pedestrians.

'Something wrong?' Amedée-Jean said in Italian to Lieutenant Caleghani who was in command.

'There's been an escape, sir.'

'English prisoners?'

'One Englishman and a French gun-runner, sir. We're still looking for them.'

'Tarhouna isn't a very big place,' said Amedée-Jean.

'They've probably made it to the desert by now, unless someone in Tarhouna is sheltering them. I've spent the day searching houses.'

Amedée-Jean reached the Consulate and seeing Lorena's Oldsmobile parked by the front entrance he thought she must have been on another of her fast drives in the desert. Radah was crossing the hall with a pile of plates and greeted him with a loud, cheerful, and unusual, 'Hallo, sir!' What's gotten into her? he wondered as he went upstairs.

He went straight to the bathroom, undressed quickly and turned on the shower. The cold water felt marvellous. Then he heard Lorena call.

'Are you there?'

'Yes,' he replied. 'Just a moment.'

Wrapping a towel around his waist, he went into the bedroom where Lorena in an emerald dress stood looking out of the window.

'Sorry to have brought you back so soon,' she said, not turning to face him.

'You were quite right to phone. I'd completely forgotten.'

'That's what I thought. But I must have upset your plans.'

'Yes,' he said. 'You did.'

She gave that short mirthless laugh which always made him feel uncomfortable.

He said quickly, 'I have to return to Tripoli tomorrow afternoon and will be spending the night.'

'Oh?' she said.

'You don't mind?'

'Not at all.'

'. . . Still a number of things to settle,' he continued. 'Ever since the retreat began, half the officers at army H.Q. seem to have disappeared.' She made no comment and he went on, 'Panic seems to be setting in . . .'

She turned just as he took off the bath-towel. It was months since she had seen him naked.

'You're in good shape,' she said.

'Think so?'

'Yes. You're thinner.'

'I believe I am, yes.'

He slipped on his under-pants and sat on the bed to put on his cotton socks.

'What have you arranged about dinner?'

She walked slowly across the room and leaned against the bureau facing him.

'There's something I want to tell you.'

'Oh?'

'Something serious.'

94

'All right, what is it?' he said. Anita! he thought. My God, it had to happen.

'We have guests,' she said eventually.

He looked up, surprised. 'But . . . I know.'

'I'm not talking about the Italian officers.'

He got up and put on the white trousers Radah had left carefully folded on the chair.

'I've'—she smiled to herself—'I'm hiding escaped English prisoners.'

'What, here?'

'In my studio.'

It's not about Anita then, he thought with relief.

'Well, that is a surprise,' he said. 'What about the servants?'

'I've told them.'

'Ah, I see,' he said. 'How did you . . . ?'

'Oh, it would take too long to explain. They're here, and there's no question of anyone suspecting us.'

'I heard there was a gun-runner . . .'

'The Frenchman,' answered Lorena as if it went without saying. 'There's an Englishman and a Frenchman. They escaped together.'

'I see.'

He buttoned his shirt and began fumbling with his cufflinks.

'Oh, let me help you,' Lorena said, walking towards him.

'It's not a very easy situation, obviously,' she continued, 'but we couldn't very well do anything else. After all, this is neutral territory . . .'

'Provided the servants don't talk.'

'I don't see the connection,' Lorena remarked with sure logic, 'between the extra-territorial status of a Swiss consulate and servants' gossip.' She straightened up. 'There you are.'

'What sort of men are they?' he asked, selecting a blue tie with yellow stripes from his closet.

'The Englishman is all right—very English. The other one . . .' Lorena made a vague gesture, then added, 'I believe the Englishman's plane was shot down.'

Well, thought Amedée-Jean, it's probably only a matter of days before the British troops will be in Tarhouna.

'I'll speak to Radah and Tiken,' he said.

'Yes, I wish you would.'

He put on his white double-breasted jacket.

'Let's go and see your . . . guests,' he said.

The two men sat on either side of the work-bench. Amedée-Jean was struck by their drawn, exhausted faces and especially the red and scorched skin of the Englishman.

They got up as he entered; the Frenchman following his friend's show of etiquette. Amedée-Jean noticed the open hand-cuffs on the bench and eyed this well-built rugged Frenchman with suspicion.

'This is Lieutenant Basil Ferguson,' said Lorena. 'And Monsieur . . . ?'

'Mattei,' said the other. 'François Mattei.'

Amedée-Jean shook hands with them.

'Make yourselves at home,' he said in French, then added, 'at least for a few days. Then we'll see what's to be done.' He turned to the Englishman. 'Do you understand?'

'Oh yes,' said Basil. 'And we'd like to thank you.'

'It's a natural thing to do,' said Amedée-Jean. 'The extra-territorial principle is a good one. But in your case, I must make a clear distinction. If the Italians were to learn of your being here . . .'

'Yes?' said Basil.

'I should be able to use a certain amount of discretion in giving you asylum. Even though it might create some difficulty for me.' Then Amedée-Jean turned to the Frenchman. 'But your case is rather different.'

'I know,' said Mattei, taking his hands out of his pockets and looking sullen.

'If the Italians insisted on my giving you up, I should have to do so,' explained Amedée-Jean.

'I see.'

Amedée-Jean was not at all sure how to handle this fellow.

'But if I have to do that, I'll let you know first.'

'Thank you,' said Mattei with no semblance of gratitude in his voice.

'You're French?' asked Amedée-Jean.

'Yes.'

'What were you doing in Tripolitania?'

'Gun-running,' said the Frenchman as though it was the most natural thing in the world.

Amedée-Jean thought that the less he knew about this individual's dubious activities the better it would be.

'In any case,' he said curtly, 'being here only provides a temporary solution to your problem.'

The Frenchman cleared his throat and said: 'If I could get to the coast . . . I've a boat that's waiting for me near Zwara.'

Basil spoke to the Consul in English. 'It's thanks to him that I'm still alive. The plane I was in was shot down and crashed near his boat, and he picked me up.'

Amedée-Jean nodded approvingly. After a moment or two he told them: 'Some Italian friends are coming to dinner tonight and we're expecting them at any moment. You'd better not move from here for the time being.'

The two nodded in agreement.

'They'll sleep in here, I suppose?' Amedée-Jean said to Lorena.

'Yes, I've told Tiken to bring up two mattresses.' Two loud knocks on the front door echoed through the house.

'That's our friends,' said Amedée-Jean. 'Have a good rest. That's the best thing you can do tonight.'

He opened the door for Lorena and as they went along the landing they could see Major Sarfati and Doctor De Santi down in the hall giving their caps to Radah.

'Ah, my dear Consul,' exclaimed the major. 'Dear lady . . .'

13

The evening had gone smoothly. The table had been resplendent with ornate china and crystal sparkling in the light of the two seven-tiered candelabras. The lasagna, lamb and wine had been superb. The discussion of the war and the approach of the British had been the first topic of conversation but during dinner it had centred around the two escaped prisoners. Lorena felt that she and Amedée-Jean had asked good questions and shown the proper concern over the prisoners. She was also satisfied that the three Italian officers had been charmed by her. At the door they had kissed her hand with exaggerated gestures and clicked their heels.

Now upstairs in her bedroom, Lorena slipped into her dressing-gown and knocked on Amedée-Jean's bedroom door.

'Can I come in?'

'Yes,' he called from the bathroom.

She crossed the room and sat on the edge of the bed. 'What are we going to do about our escaped prisoners?' she asked.

'I can't do anything else but keep the Englishman here for a few days at least. As for the Frenchman...'

'You're not going to throw him out into the street, are you?' She envisioned Mattei's big body writhing at the impact of bullets.

'Throw him into the street? No. But he must leave soon on his own. If he doesn't...'

'If he doesn't?'

Amedée-Jean appeared framed in the bathroom door.

'Then I must inform the Italian authorities.'

He went back into the bathroom and Lorena heard him brushing his teeth.

'I take it that you'll be staying in Tripoli tomorrow night?'

'Yes,' he mumbled, then said in a clearer voice, 'I'm going to find out about the military situation and see what is the best thing to do. That's the main reason for going.'

'Main reason?' Lorena felt like laughing.

'One of the reasons,' he conceded. He wants to ask Anita Payot's advice, thought Lorena.

Amedée-Jean came into the bedroom.

'Who did you phone during dinner?' she asked.

He stopped in front of the mirror and began combing his hair.

'Stein,' he replied, then quickly added, 'I congratulate you. You drank practically nothing this evening.'

Thrust and parry, she thought; now it's my turn to lunge.

'Will you mention the matter to Stein?'

'Yes, of course,' he said. 'I've an appointment with him at four o'clock.'

'That early?'

'Yes.'

Lorena felt indifferent but continued the conversation out of amusement. But not entirely; she wanted to make her husband uneasy. He must not feel too confident during the next few days.

He continued to comb his hair with suspicious concentration.

'I thought Stein was always away at Homs on Wednesdays,' she said casually, examining her blunt nails and scarred fingers.

Amedée-Jean's hand remained suspended above his head. 'Yes, but due to the circumstances ...'

'Of course, due to the circumstances ...'

'Good Lord, it's late,' he exclaimed, glancing at the clock on his bedside-table.

'Half past twelve,' said Lorena.

'I'm ready for bed. Aren't you?'

'No, but I'll leave you.'

'Good-night then, sleep well,' he said with relief.

She stood up and stubbed out her cigarette.

'The odd thing,' she said to herself when back in her own bedroom, 'is that he hasn't reproached me at all. No mention of my rashness or lack of consideration in harbouring an escaped prisoner-of-war and a criminal under his roof.'

She drew back the sheets, then went out to the landing and started towards the studio. He's right, she thought. I only had one glass of wine tonight. But everything has gone so smoothly. This adventure has just begun but it already seems to be over. Then more days of loneliness, of my studio and liquor.

14

Mattei slept on the mattress with his cheek resting on his bent arm and a blanket pulled halfway up his naked back. His relaxed, almost boyish face seemed in direct contrast to the thick muscles of his shoulders and arms.

Basil sat against the wall smoking a cigarette and looked at the wooden masks and carvings illuminated by a single candle. The play of light gave the masks a hallowed-eyed look of death.

His headache was gone but he was thirsty. He wanted a drink —a sizeable shot of whisky with ice and soda. He remembered the two Arab servants looking out of the kitchen when they had arrived here and the ice-cubes in the carafes of fruit-juice.

He glanced at his watch from habit; it still remained at ten past five.

Immediately the vision of seething water and the gesticulating figure of the Australian pilot returned to him. Don't look at your watch, he thought. Ten past five triggers too many memories. Since you first climbed casually into the Beaufighter, you've lived a different life. You've seen four or five men die. No, six. The first dead bodies in your life, if you discount those bloody shapes, mockeries of men, being carried on stretchers in the streets of London. Who had once told him that the grief caused by loss of a loved one fades away in less than a year?

Supposing Julia was killed?

'You'd feel immense nostalgia for a long time,' he said to himself. 'You're a romantic and very fond of decorative sentiments. Nostalgia is terribly decorative.'

And Geoffrey? He was his brother, after all. Geoffrey, with

his bony build and long nose, thick spectacles and greying hair, digging about in Yucatan far from the convulsions shaking the rest of the world. His short letters home used to bewilder their father, who thought of little but Stock Exchange prices and golf.

'Dear Father,' Geoffrey would write, 'we've just excavated this delightful Quetzalcoatl, photo enclosed.'

'Heavens above!' their father would exclaim. 'Does Geoffrey really find this thing delightful?'

'Yes,' Basil said to himself, 'you'd grieve over Geoffrey too, though you haven't seen him in four years, not since 1937.' He remembered when Geoffrey had left for Yucatan as if he were merely going away for the weekend. They'd had a drink together at the Dorchester bar and he remembered Geoffrey's gentle smile as he ordered a pulque with a little lemon-juice.

This made Basil even more thirsty and he knew he couldn't wait another moment.

If there was anything to drink it would be in the kitchen.

Is it proper to burgle your host? he thought. Never mind.

He threw aside the blanket and silently got to his feet. His whole body smarted. He crossed the studio and gently opened the door and slipped out onto the landing. He felt for the rail and followed it to the top of the stairs. The marble stairs were deliciously cool to his bare feet.

He was halfway down when a door opened and a rectangle of light swept towards him. He looked around and saw the woman in a white dressing-gown outlined in the doorway. The light from behind set her flaxen hair afire.

She took a few hesitant steps then caught sight of him on the stairs.

Basil watched Lorena coming serenely down towards him and for a moment he thought she had not seen him. But when two or three steps away, she stopped with one hand on the banister.

'Can't you sleep?' she asked in a low voice.

'No. It's the sunburn.'

'I see.'

From the intonation, he guessed that she was smiling.

'I'm terribly thirsty. I was going down to the kitchen.'

'So silly of me,' she said. 'I should have thought of that. I'll go down with you.'

He followed slowly, testing each step with his feet.

'To the right,' she said and switched on the light in the kitchen. Some black beetles scurried along the tiled floor into dark corners.

'We're plagued with those things!' exclaimed Lorena. 'Just can't get rid of them.'

She put a hand to the neck of her gown. 'What are you looking at?'

'You,' he said. 'Forgive me.'

'No need,' she replied with a shrug.

'I was just thinking that I haven't had time to look at you. Everything's happened so fast.' He wasn't sure whether she was beautiful or merely desirable.

Opening the door to the refrigerator she asked, 'Thirsty or hungry?'

'Thirsty.'

'Are you against whisky?'

'Absolutely,' he said, smiling.

'I've a bottle of Bourbon—Early Times.' He watched as she opened the cupboard under the sink.

'That seems very good to me.'

She took the bottle out and held it up. 'The last of my reserve. My parents send it to me.'

'Nice parents.'

'Very understanding. With ice?'

'And some water.'

She put some ice-cubes into two glasses, uncorked the bottle and began to pour. 'Say when.'

He watched the ice turn a silky tan. 'Enough.'

She gave herself a liberal amount. 'I've the whisky habit too.'

'An excellent habit.'

'That depends,' she said. 'I drink a lot.' She added a little water. 'Never quite sober.'

'A big splash for me,' he said, holding out his glass.

'Never quite sober,' she repeated.

He felt uneasy by her insistent confession. Peering into his glass and swirling the ice, he finally said, 'If you say so, then it must be important.'

'Which? To drink or to tell you about it?'

'Both, very likely.'

'What did you do before the war?'

He raised his glass to his lips without taking his eyes from her face. 'I did cartoons for *Punch*.'

She started to laugh, a good-humoured, gay laugh, and he joined in.

'I know, I'm not very serious-minded.'

'And what are you doing here?'

'Drinking,' he said.

He took a long drink and sighed with pleasure.

Lorena began to smile. 'Thank your lucky stars I drink,' she said. 'If I hadn't been a little . . . high, I might not have rescued you. I wake up bored, I drink, I do carvings and I entertain my husband's friends. I carve most of the day.'

'So I've seen.'

'They're similar to cartoons,' she said gravely. 'Wood is very difficult to get here. What I use comes from Switzerland in the diplomatic bag.'

She was sitting on the edge of the table with her arms tightly folded across her chest, one hand holding her glass level with her mouth.

'What do you think of my husband?'

'He's been very fair.'

'Yes,' she said.

'We've put him in an awkward situation, I expect.'

'Yes,' she said again, still staring into her glass. 'What are you thinking of doing?'

'That's for you to say. I don't want to cause any trouble.'

'That's not the point. You must know what you want to do?'

'I've no idea.'

And it's true, you've no idea, he thought. You keep finding yourself involved in unplanned situations. You go looking for a cool drink, meet your hostess in her dressing-gown, hear her confess that she drinks too much as if she'd been waiting specifically for you to confide in.

'I don't know at all,' he repeated.

She looked at him, her face expressionless.

'And your friend?'

'Mattei?'

'The Frenchman, yes.'

'I'm sure he's got some definite ideas about what he wants to do. He's a very determined chap. He's sleeping now. He spends his time jumping from action into sleep and from sleep into action. A very odd character. Quite tireless.'

Lorena finished her drink and poured herself another, much weaker.

'I'd hate to see him handed over to the Italians,' she said.

'So would I.'

'You ought to have said so to my husband. He might listen to you. You know the Italians will shoot him.'

'I'm afraid so.'

There again, he thought, you're outside it all. She's probably annoyed at your passiveness.

'Only a week ago,' he said, 'I was working in the map section at the War Office. The biggest event of the day was at four o'clock—army tea. In the evenings I changed into civvies at an apartment in Mayfair and spent most of the night at the Dolphin Club, where a modern shelter had been converted into an Elizabethan cellar.'

'You've got very queer tastes,' she remarked.

'Decadent,' he said, looking up at her.

There was only five or six feet between them, no more than a couple of strides, he thought. Lorena's gaze wavered. 'Take advantage of the situation,' he said to himself, 'you've done it a hundred times. Well, perhaps not a hundred but often enough to know what her eyes are saying.'

She continued to look at him in an odd, attentive way, slightly ironical, as though challenging him. Suddenly he felt less certain that she wanted him. Maybe he misunderstood her gaze.

But there sat a woman within his reach wearing a fluffy white dressing-gown that revealed the shape of her breasts. Through the gap of the skirt, he could see her slightly parted knees and the soft flesh of her thigh.

The whiteness of the walls and the table, geometric shapes overlapping one another, seemed to press in on him.

He took a step forward and put his glass down—a sharp rap on the table. One more step and he would brush his hand against her ear and feel the warmth of the flesh on her neck. He would push aside the top of her gown and feel the smooth succulent breasts tighten under his touch. Her mouth would be close to his, and her legs would enclose the top of his thigh and her attentive look would remain emotionless.

'Hullo there,' came a voice.

Basil spun round and saw Mattei standing in the doorway, leaning casually against the side.

'I'm thirsty,' he said, and nodded towards the bottle. 'Can I?'

'Go right ahead.'

Mattei poured some bourbon into a glass.

Basil picked up his glass. 'Cheers,' he said.

Mattei looked at him with crafty smiling eyes. 'Cheers.'

15

Amedée-Jean had his breakfast served in the library, the only room bathed by the morning sun but not yet too hot. It opened onto the garden and he could see the lawn and palm-trees from his desk.

This room, moreover, came nearest to the Swiss idea of comfort. Bookshelves covered the walls and an antique French desk commanded attention in the middle of the room. On the desk were a large blue alabaster egg which served as a paperweight, a steel ruler, and a seventeenth-century hour-glass that Lorena had bought for him in London a few months after their wedding.

While eating his breakfast, Amedée-Jean read the *Tribune de Geneve* and the *Gazette de Lausanne,* which arrived in the diplomatic bag. Lorena usually sat opposite him with her back to the window. Amedée-Jean derived a certain pleasure in maintaining this ritual. 'After all,' he often said to himself, 'everything is basically the same. I still have a decorative wife even though I've taken on a mistress. And Anita's discreet so there's really no reason why anything should change.'

But this morning he had very little appetite. The two escaped prisoners made him tense.

Nevertheless, he finished most of his scrambled eggs (it was very difficult to get fresh eggs at Tarhouna, although the town was swarming with hens) and he pressed the bell on the floor. Radah shuffled in carrying a tray of toast, salt butter, apricot jam, and a pot of tea.

She put the tray on the desk.

'Isn't your mistress coming down?' he asked.

'She's gone out,' Radah breathed in a tone heavy with conspiracy. 'She said she was going to do some shopping.'

'So early?' asked Amedée-Jean cautiously.

Radah made a vague gesture and started to leave the room.

'And—er—the gentlemen upstairs?'

'I've taken breakfast up to them.'

Amedée-Jean wondered if he should breakfast with the two men. If the Englishman had been alone, he would definitely have invited him down to the library. But the Frenchman prevented this. A Consul of Switzerland surely could not eat with an escaped criminal. It was probably better like this anyhow. He needed time to make some decisions.

He intended telling the *chargé d'affaires* about the two men at the first opportunity. It was, after all, the responsibility of the Swiss Legation and there was no reason why he should continue to shoulder the burden alone. In a few hours he would be in Tripoli and shift the responsibility to someone else. He felt relieved.

Radah poured him a cup of tea.

'You—er—took them up some eggs?' he asked.

'Of course.'

Amedée-Jean was annoyed. If she had given them two eggs apiece, there would be none left for the end of the week.

'Your mistress told you to do that?'

'Yes, madam said so.'

'I see.'

'My brother,' Radah suddenly volunteered, 'says that if the Italians find out that the Nazranis are being hidden here, we shall all be sent to prison.'

Amedée-Jean dropped his knife. 'Your brother?'

'I have a brother,' Radah said impatiently.

'Yes, I know. Mohamed, isn't that his name?'

'Yes.'

Amedée-Jean had seen Mohamed in the kitchen after many parties. The excuse given was that Radah needed help. But he knew that this sickly and not too clean young man came only to eat the leftovers and stuff himself with Nestlé's chocolate.

Amedée-Jean tried to control himself. 'Your brother was here last night?'

'He gave me a hand. There was a lot of washing-up to do. Tiken was glad.'

'You told your brother about those . . . those Nazranis upstairs?'

Radah looked offended. 'My brother knows that the Italians are looking for the Nazranis.'

'Of course he knows.' He was now desperately rolling his napkin into a ball. 'But did you talk to him about it?'

'All three of us talked about it. My brother, me, and Tiken.'

'You talked about what?'

'The Nazranis,' said Radah as though it was obvious.

'Which ones? Those upstairs?'

'Of course,' she said with surprise.

'Now just a minute . . . You told your brother that the Nazranis whom the Italians are looking for are here in this house?'

Radah draped herself in dignity. 'The Italians are looking for them, yes. My brother Mohamed knows that.'

Amedée-Jean nervously wiped his forehead with the crumpled napkin. 'So do I,' he exclaimed. 'But what I want to know is whether you told your brother . . . you follow me? You understand what I'm saying? . . . that the Nazranis are *here*?'

A great weariness appeared on Radah's face. 'They're upstairs, aren't they?'

God in Heaven, thought Amedée-Jean, how fortunate for Switzerland that she hasn't any colonies.

'Did you,' he emphasised each word, 'tell your brother that the Nazranis are here in this house?'

'No,' Radah said sullenly.

'You're sure?'

'Yes.'

Amedée-Jean wanted to believe her.

Then Radah added, 'And besides, my brother and I are like one.'

Amedée-Jean's teacup rattled as he tried to lift it from the saucer.

'It was the mistress who said so,' continued Radah. 'She said that if my brother was being hunted by the Italian soldiers, he could take refuge here. I swear that's what she said.'

Amedée-Jean looked kindly at Radah.

'Look, if you told him, I won't scold you. But if you did tell him (Oh God, he thought), you must tell me.'

'Tell what?' asked Radah, who now seemed annoyed at this senseless conversation.

Amedée-Jean felt a pain begin above his left eye and slowly spread across his forehead.

'Now, let's go over it once more. All three of you talked about the Nazranis last night?'

'Yes.'

'But that's all. You talked about the Nazranis in general?'

Radah looked perplexed.

'You talked about the Nazranis, that the Italians are searching for them, but that's all?'

'Yes,' said Radah.

'You didn't say anything about the Consulate?'

'Why should we say anything about the Consulate?'

Amedée-Jean felt weary. 'All right,' he sighed.

'Can I go now?'

'Yes.'

Radah went silently from the room. Amedée-Jean picked up a piece of toast; it was cold. He had lost his appetite anyhow. One thing was clear, as soon as he arrived in Tripoli he would inform the Legation.

He looked at his watch. It was almost nine-thirty. He must be on his way to the Mission school which was a few miles south of Tarhouna. He was the administrator of the school and had an appointment there with Reverend Hirschbaum and the Italian army chaplain. Christ, he thought, I wish I could go directly to Tripoli.

16

Mattei cleared a space on the work-bench and spread out a map given to him by the American woman. The mid-morning sunlight forced its way through the slate of the closed shutters and cast bright wide stripes across the map.

It was forty miles to Tripoli and about the same from Tripoli to the inlet. A two-hour drive altogether, or at the most, three. That is if he had a car. Achmed would not sail until tomorrow evening and was probably far from anxious since Mattei had once or twice stayed ashore for several days.

He scratched his head with his pencil and turned to Basil. 'What are you thinking of doing?'

Basil finished his cup of tea.

'What would you do if you were me?'

'Stay, of course,' Mattei replied. Then he added, 'There are less pleasant ways of fighting the war.'

'Well look, Mattei,' said Basil, 'the front is two hundred miles away. The British army is mobile, I'm not.'

'I know.'

'And there isn't any point in trying to get to Djerba. You told me that you didn't want me on board, if I remember correctly.'

'Things have changed,' Mattei said evasively.

'Indeed they've changed.' Basil lit a cigarette. 'That was excellent tea. What's on your mind, old chap? We've nothing to hide from each other now.'

'If you decided to go to Djerba,' said Mattei, 'your good lady might drive us to my boat.'

'*Your!* What do you mean your good lady?'

Basil strolled across the room and peered through the shutters. 'Anyway,' he said, 'I'm not going to Djerba. Sorry to disappoint you.'

Mattei got slowly to his feet. He listened to the noise below them, the cries of the traders, the squeaking of barrows and that sound so characteristic of Arab countries—the tap-tapping of slippers on stone.

'You know,' said Mattei, 'I expected you to say that.'

'You're impossible,' smiled Basil. 'If I hadn't followed you, I'd be a peaceful prisoner respected by his jailers, a personality who would be consulted like an oracle, a unique phenomenon.'

'You're better off as you are,' said Mattei. 'There aren't any women in prison.'

Nothing but the memory of them, Mattei thought. Night after night, minute after minute, until you want to die. But you've never had to cope with unfulfilled desire, he mused, looking at Basil's thin nose and chiselled mouth. But you'd have to protect yourself against other temptations with that pretty face...

'If the British get here soon,' said Basil, 'all our problems will be solved. Yours as well as mine.'

Mattei shook his head. 'We French are always sceptical about the British. When they're our enemies, they're always where they shouldn't be. And when they're our allies, it's just the same.'

'You really are amazing. You're another Chamfort, with those maxims of yours.'

'Oh, go to hell.'

The door opened and Lorena came in wearing the same blue slacks and stained sweater as the day before. She was pale but her expression seemed less strained, almost calm.

You're a pretty bitch, thought Mattei.

'Well?' he said.

'There's a double guard at all the gates.'

'Road-blocks?'

'Road-blocks as well. But not everywhere.'

That's bad, thought Mattei, very bad. 'What kind of road-blocks?'

'Sandbags and barbed-wire.'

'Are they searching vehicles?'

'Not army vehicles. And not all civilian cars. But they're stopping everyone. But I think it'll slacken off soon.'

She went across to the work-bench and looked at the map.

'Why should it slacken off?' asked Mattei.

'I don't know.'

'Nor do I. But there must be some way out of this town.'

'It's possible. There are five gateways. No road-block has been set up at the north gate because it's used by the army supply convoys.'

She traced the line that Mattei had drawn on the map with her finger. It ended at a tiny indentation on the coast.

'Is this where you want to go?'

'Yes,' said Mattei, stepping closer to her.

He could smell her perfume and the memory of Claire came surging to the surface. Claire in evening dress with a small lamé handbag tucked under her arm, saying, 'Oh, wait a minute,' and snatching up the bottle on the dressing-table, shaking it gently, then dabbing the stopper on her ear-lobes, her neck, between her breasts and in her shaved armpits. She would smile at Mattei who looked on with irritation, his fists thrust into the pockets of his jacket. It was a week after his winning bout with Keller. He felt elated and carefree. He had plenty of money and above all this haughty woman who at night became a naked moaning girl. It was perhaps that contrast which attracted him most—the distant aristocratic-looking girl and the one who cried out with guttural desire in bed, the body adorned by costly garments and the other body stripped naked awaiting him. And it was François Mattei the heavyweight champion and the son of a quarryman who lay naked in bed beside this girl whose father owned the Lime and Cement Ferrieres Company, along with four factories in Provence, twenty apartment blocks in Marseilles and twenty-five thousand acres of vineyards in Algeria.

'Anyway,' said Lorena, 'it's out of the question for you to leave town today.'

17

Through the window of his office, Amedée-Jean watched Major Sarfati and Reverend Hirschbaum in the courtyard of the school. At last Lorena answered the phone. 'Lorena, it's me. The Italians are coming,' he shouted into the phone.

'The what . . . ?'

'I don't have much time. Sarfati caught up with me here at the school to tell me he has reason to believe the prisoners are in our house.' Amedée-Jean gasped and he again looked nervously at the two figures in the courtyard. 'He mentioned something about an informer . . . a youngster who works on the road. He must have seen you picking them up yesterday. Anyway, I asked Sarfati to come to the Consulate for a drink . . . You must get rid of those prisoners.'

Amedée-Jean was trembling and sweat poured from his forehead. 'Do you understand?'

'Yes,' said Lorena slowly. 'But how?'

Her indifference irritated him.

'Dump them anywhere in town. You've less than fifteen minutes. You realise,' he said slowly, 'my future is at stake.'

'Yes.'

'And be careful. The house may be watched.'

'All right,' said Lorena.

'I'll arrive . . .'

He heard the click of the receiver.

Mattei and Basil were playing poker when Lorena burst into the studio. 'We've been denounced. My husband just called. You must get out of here at once . . . Both of you,' she added, turning to Basil.

'How?' said Mattei.

'My husband . . .' she began, then said with a change of voice: 'I'll take you out of town in my car.'

Mattei looked at her. She seemed so frail and vulnerable now; though there was no trace of anxiety or distress on her face.

Mattei swept up the half-full bottle of gin that was standing on a stool. 'You'll need some of this.'

She looked straight at him and shook her head with her mouth set in defiance. 'No. I'll go and get the car out of the garage.'

'Wait a moment,' Mattei said, putting a hand on her shoulder. He could feel the delicate shoulder muscles and the knob of her collar-bone. She was not wearing a bra.

'I must have a gun,' he said.

Her eyes widened.

'I must,' he repeated calmly.

'Come with me.'

He followed her along the landing and into the last room on the left. She opened a drawer and took out a revolver from beneath a heap of files, photo-albums and old letters. Mattei took it and weighed it in his hand. It was a big Webley and already loaded.

'Have you any more ammunition?' he asked.

'Look in the drawer,' she told him. 'I think there's some there. I must go down to the garage.'

She ran out of the room. Mattei slipped the revolver into his trouser-pocket and started rummaging in the drawer. He found a small red cardboard box full of cartridges. Basil came into the room.

'I think I'll disguise myself as a civilian,' he said, opening Amedée-Jean's large closet. 'There's sure plenty to choose from.'

'Don't waste time,' Mattei said irritably. 'We've got to be off in five minutes. Meet us down below.'

Left alone, Basil selected a pair of cotton trousers and a blazer. This is ridiculous, he thought. What the hell am I doing?

He heard the roaring of the Oldsmobile and quickly dressed. The clothes fitted him very well.

He looked at himself in the mirror. His face was thinner and sunburned.

'It would be much easier to stay here and wait for the

Italians to come,' he said to himself. 'It would be rather amusing too.'

He imagined an armed platoon bursting into the house as he descended the stairs slowly to meet them.

'Hey, you coming?' Mattei shouted up from the hall.

Basil hurriedly snatched up his army uniform but could not find his cap.

18

Lorena's hands gripped the steering-wheel tightly as she edged the car along the narrow streets. The heat was oppressive. She had done her best to hide the two men under a tarpaulin in the back seat. She had put a wicker basket between the two in an effort to make the heap look more even but it could just as easily attract someone's attention as disarm a keen gaze. Although she knew that Mattei and Basil shared her anxiety, she felt completely alone at the wheel. The lives of these two men and her husband's future lay completely with her.

She slowed down to a crawl as she drew near the north gate. A group of Arabs squatted around the public scribe in front of one of the two crenellated white towers and some Italian soldiers and civilians played *boule*.

Three armed soldiers were on duty but no road-block had been set up to bar the wide exit. Under a wooden shelter a sergeant with his sun-helmet pushed to the back of his head sat reading the *Corriere della Sera*.

'Here we are,' she said as the car bounced heavily forward over the uneven ground. The *boule* players were forming an attentive line around the pitch; one of them was about to roll his metal ball, his feet together, knees bent, lower lip drawn in and his right arm stretched out behind him. The three soldiers were chatting amiably and it was only the sergeant who lifted his head above his newspaper at the approach of the Oldsmobile, his gaze concentrating on the Swiss pennant.

'Ah!' cried the player as he sent his ball up the pitch.

With the clash of one metal ball on another, shouts and applause rose from the onlookers.

The three soldiers turned as Lorena drew closer and one of them glanced inquiringly at the sergeant, who grasped the back of his chair and hoisted himself to his feet.

No movement escaped Lorena. As the sergeant strolled towards her giving a vague salute, Lorena braked gently and opened the glove-compartment to get out her papers.

'*Signora ...*'

She had never seen this particular sergeant before. Too bad, she thought, it would have made things easier.

'Swiss Consulate,' Lorena said in Italian, holding out the papers—the registration card, her driving licence and diplomatic passport. The sergeant hesitated, smiled at her then took them. Damn it! thought Lorena. If it had been Amedée-Jean, he would have let him through. But the fool likes my fair hair and blasted green eyes.

The sergeant's gaping shirt revealed thick black hair crawling up his chest to his neck. He smelled of garlic, sweat, and polished leather.

'Signora Lorena Dalloz,' he read aloud. 'You are Signora Dalloz?'

'Yes,' said Lorena, forcing a smile.

The sergeant opened the passport and flipped through the pages. 'All seems in order,' he said.

Okay—then just let me go—please, thought Lorena. Suddenly the roar of an engine resounded in the surrounding narrow streets. Some swallows took flight and Lorena, terrified, looked into the rear view mirror. An army motor-cyclist with his goggles pushed up on his wide-brimmed canvas helmet and a white cartridge-belt across his chest rode towards them.

The motor-cyclist swung to a stop as the sergeant was handing the documents back to Lorena.

'I can go on?' she asked.

'Just a minute,' he said, taking a sealed message from the motor-cyclist.

Lorena slipped into bottom gear. The Oldsmobile slid forward a few inches and the three soldiers stepped aside.

'Hold it,' the sergeant said gently.

He read the message and then looked towards Lorena.

'Wait a ...' he began.

Lorena stepped on the accelerator and the car lurched forward with screeching tyres.

'Halt!' yelled the sergeant, dashing forward, the message whirling in the air.

Lorena's hands stiffened around the wheel. She leaned back in her seat and swerved to avoid the soldiers. One of the tyres knocked against some projecting stonework but she put more pressure on the gas pedal and hurtled through the gateway, leaving the soldiers in a cloud of dust. The road opened straight and empty ahead of her.

19

The arid and threatening desert engulfed the car as it sped along the road that wavered in the distance under the sun's rays.

'I did what I could,' shouted Lorena.

'You did well,' said Mattei, throwing aside the tarpaulin, followed by Basil.

Mattei looked back and glimpsed the motor-cyclist through the cloud of yellow swirling dust.

'Faster,' he yelled.

The surface of the road was cracked and uneven, and the steering-wheel was shaking violently.

'I'm wobbling,' said Lorena in a strained voice.

'So's he,' said Basil.

Lorena called out something in English.

'What's she saying?' asked Mattei.

'That her shock-absorbers won't stand up to this lousy road,' said Basil. He pointed to the cyclist. 'What d'you think he's going to do?'

'I know what I'd do if I were him,' said Mattei.

'What?'

'I'd keep at that distance. He can make us do whatever he wants. All I can do is wait.'

Basil looked at him quizzically and Mattei continued. 'He's got a Beretta, I've only got this Webley, with a range of no more than fifty yards. All he has to do is keep us in sight.'

'He's drawing nearer,' said Basil.

They could now see the goggles over his eyes, the badge on his helmet, and his white cartridge-belt.

'We're doing eighty,' said Lorena.

'Don't push it, there's no point in blowing up the engine,' said Mattei. 'On that Guzzi, that guy can do eighty with his fingers up his nose.'

He gave the rear window a sharp hit with the butt of his revolver and then widened the jagged hole of splintered glass. The cyclist was now about one hundred and fifty yards away and the noise of his exhaust grew progressively louder.

'The bloody fool,' said Mattei.

'Are you going to shoot at him?'

'Not yet. He's still too far off.'

The Oldsmobile rose over a hump and came down with a thud that shook all the bodywork and the speedometer dropped to sixty.

'Stay at sixty,' Mattei ordered.

'D'you want him to catch up?' shouted Lorena.

'I don't know. I don't know a bloody thing. He's the one who's going to decide for me.'

The cyclist was nearing the hump, Mattei watched the machine leave the ground and come down again with only a slight wobbling of the front wheel.

'The bastard knows how to ride,' said Mattei.

'Look out!' cried Lorena.

Mattei and Basil swung around and saw an army truck careening towards them. By its speed, there was no doubt that the driver believed he was indestructible and was completely oblivious to any kind of wickedness in the world.

The Oldsmobile scraped past the truck, and the motor-cyclist signalled wildly but the truck maintained its speed and disappeared from view. The cyclist was now less than a hundred yards behind the Oldsmobile.

'He's set on winning a medal,' said Mattei, lifting his revolver to the top of the back seat. Just then the cyclist slowed down and drew to a stop.

'What's he up to?' said Basil.

'I don't know,' muttered Mattei.

The cyclist remained by the side of the road but it was impossible to make out what he was doing. Then he set off again, and Mattei understood.

'He stopped to load his Beretta.'

The motor-cyclist was gaining on them with disturbing ease. Mattei's calmness irritated Basil as he felt himself becoming increasingly tense. The Frenchman had a gun, Lorena was at the wheel; while he, as usual, was the onlooker.

'I mustn't miss him,' said Mattei.

'It's him or us.'

Mattei gave a shrug. 'There's a third possibility. When he hears bullets whistling past him, he might realise that the best thing to do is just keep his distance. In that case, we're done for. We'd arrive in Tripoli with him on our tail. That'd make a fine ceremonial entry!'

When the cyclist fired his first shot he was about seventy or eighty yards behind the Oldsmobile, and the bullet went wide.

Mattei leaned against the back of the seat and gripping the revolver in both hands, seemed to take no notice.

When the second shot rang out, Basil was sure the bullet had come much closer.

'He's not rattled,' said Mattei. 'He knows he can take his time.' Then he said to Lorena: 'I'm going to fire. Slow down when I tell you. Slow down to twenty as quickly as you can. Understand?'

'Okay.'

She must be condemning herself for getting involved in this fiasco, Basil thought. But maybe she hasn't even thought of that yet. She hasn't had much time for reflection.

'Slow now!' ordered Mattei.

The sudden deceleration threw him to the side of the car. The cyclist drew near quickly and Basil could see the man's little moustache, his collar flapping in the wind and his large hands gripping the handlebars.

Mattei squeezed the trigger and the gun jumped. Basil caught a whiff of gunpowder and saw the motor-cycle sway. The man stuck out one leg and scraped the ground with his foot.

'Slow down more,' ordered Mattei.

He lowered the Webley and again the butt bounced in his hand. The cycle swerved suddenly to the right in a cloud of dust; its rider hopped off but still clung to the handlebars.

Mattei fired twice in quick succession. The man crossed his legs drunkenly, then fell flat on his face. The motor-cycle moved beside him like a wounded animal.

'You haven't killed him,' said Basil.

The man was slowly rising on hands and knees, his head bowed. Then a rise in the road hid him from sight.

20

As he drove into the Consulate grounds, Amedée-Jean saw that the Oldsmobile was gone. He tried not to show his relief. Major Sarfati, sitting beside him with his legs crossed and his hands on his knee, maintained a significant silence.

'I really should be on my way to Tripoli,' said Amedée-Jean as he drew up to the front door.

'I'm sorry to make you late and I hope we don't inconvenience your wife,' said Sarfati, uncoiling his long body and pushing open the car door.

'Oh, I don't think so,' replied Amedée-Jean a little too quickly. 'She'll be delighted to see you.'

He opened the front door and followed the major into the entrance hall.

He felt relaxed knowing that Lorena had succeeded in getting the prisoners out of the house. Everything seemed quite simple. It was just a game.

'Lorena!' he called, then turned to the major. 'If you'd like to go into the library . . .'

The major glanced around the hall, taking in every detail.

'Lorena !' Amedée-Jean called again.

Radah appeared at the kitchen door, twisting a cloth in her hands. 'The mistress isn't here,' she said.

'She's gone out ?'

'She went out a few minutes ago.'

'Oh, well, never mind,' he said quickly. 'Bring us some drinks, will you ?'

'Yes,' said Radah gloomily.

Amedée-Jean stopped at the door of the library. 'Did she say when she'd be back?'

'No,' Radah replied.

Amedée-Jean deliberately left the library door open. 'You see, there's no inconvenience at all.'

'I do see,' said Sarfati dryly.

He probably knows exactly what is going on, Amedée-Jean thought. He must have guessed it was Lorena I was phoning from the school. But what proof does he have? And is he so set on having proof? In a sense, I've just saved the Italians from a difficult situation with a neutral country. Then he suddenly thought, 'Why, I've no need now to go and tell Stein or the Legation anything. As far as I'm concerned, it's as if these escaped prisoners never existed. They've never been here, I've never seen them, and when I get to Tripoli I can go straight to Anita.'

His joy lightened his movements. Radah came in with a tray of glasses, ice and whisky. Amedée-Jean poured the major a drink.

Sarfati gazed at his whisky, his mouth set tight and turned down in a disgruntled manner.

'If you'll excuse me,' said Amedée-Jean, 'I'm going to change my shirt.'

'Of course,' said the major.

Amedée-Jean crossed the hall and went slowly upstairs to his room. He saw a drawer half open, pulled it out and, finding all his papers disarranged, felt at the back. The Webley's gone! he thought. Damn Lorena.

And when he opened his closet he realised that someone had been going through his clothes and that at least one pair of pants was missing. That's all I need, he thought, to have those fugitives found wearing my clothes.

He angrily tore off his jacket and shirt, which was wet with perspiration. When he had put on a clean shirt, he went out into the hall and glanced towards the studio. The door was wide open. From where he was he could see a pack of cards and a British officer's cap.

'Bloody hell!' he muttered to himself.

He hurried into the studio and snatched up the cap. Opening a shutter, he sent the cap flying. It whirled beyond the terrace and came to rest on a roof on the other side of the street. Then he took a close look around the room. The mattresses and blankets had disappeared. He stuffed the pack of cards into his pocket and went back along the landing, greatly relieved. He saw Major Sarfati standing in the hall with the glass of whisky in his hand.

'I won't be a moment,' Amedée-Jean called down to him. 'But if you'd like to come up . . .'

'It doesn't matter,' the major said. He glanced at his watch. 'Besides, I must be off.'

Amedée-Jean went into his room for a jacket, then rejoined the major downstairs. 'You really don't want to stay?'

'No,' said Sarfati. 'You've got to go to Tripoli, haven't you?'

'Yes.'

The major put his glass on a small marble-topped console. 'Florentine, eighteenth-century,' he remarked.

'Yes, we bought it the year we were married.'

The major nodded slowly. 'I've one very similar, back home. Probably a little later than this one, but a very nice piece all the same.'

Silence fell between them. All is back to normal, thought Amedée-Jean. A little friendly conversation. Everything's as it should be.

Sarfati sighed. 'Well, I hate to go out into the heat again.'

He put on his cap and the two went out to the garden. The leaves of the palm-trees drooped motionlessly in the stifling air. The yellowish-grey sky looked like a leaded roof.

'I think I'm going to take a shower,' said the major as he got into his Fiat which had followed him to the Consulate.

'That's the best thing to do in this sort of weather,' Amedée-Jean agreed.

Just then, a soldier came cycling in from the street. He got off his bicycle, breathing heavily, and wiped the sweat from his face with his sleeve. '*Maggiore?*' he said.

'Yes?' said Sarfati impassively.

'I've come from the mission, *maggiore*. I was told I'd find you here.'

Amedée-Jean straightened up. The soldier handed the major a sheet of paper.

'I'm informed,' he said slowly, after reading the message, 'that the Oldsmobile belonging to Mrs. Dalloz broke through the check-point at the north gate a short time ago.'

Amedée-Jean remained quite still; his chest seemed gripped in a vice. 'I don't understand,' he said.

'Neither do I,' said Sarfati wearily. 'A motor-cyclist went after them, and he's been found wounded.' Amedée-Jean made no comment.

'Wounded by bullets.'

'But . . .' began Amedée-Jean, 'the . . . my wife was . . .'

'Mrs. Dalloz was at the wheel of the Oldsmobile.'

'I assure you . . .' This is impossible, Amedée-Jean thought. I must be dreaming. This can't be happening to me.

Sarfati was looking at him silently. 'Or . . . they must have forced her to . . .' went on Amedée-Jean.

Sarfati glanced at the piece of paper. 'There's no mention of that, consul.'

'I can assure you that . . . in any case, I was unaware that these men were in my house.'

'Perhaps you were,' said the major gently, 'but Mrs. Dalloz certainly wasn't.'

'What do you intend to do?' Amedée-Jean asked in a slightly hoarse voice.

'The matter's out of my hands now. I shall have to refer it to Tripoli.' Major Sarfati settled back in his seat. 'Carry on, Giuseppe,' he told the driver.

Amedée-Jean stood and watched the Fiat circle the lawn and disappear into the street. 'The matter's out of my hands,' the major had said; and Amedée-Jean thought, 'Everything's out of my hands.' He felt submerged in a matter quite beyond him. The British, he suddenly thought, if the British get here very soon, if there's a real disaster, a complete reversal, then this unfortunate affair will be forgotten.

21

The abandoned house sat about a hundred yards from the road. One wall had completely caved in and three dusty eucalyptus trees rose above the rubble in the courtyard. A rusty bucket still hung over the well and was pierced with round holes; probably used by some soldier for target practice.

The square, flat-roofed buildings of Castel Benito and the bright green splashes of palm-trees interrupted the otherwise barren horizon.

Lorena switched off the engine and sighed, her hands resting on the wheel.

'Tired?' said Basil.

'A little.'

'Let's get out,' said Mattei.

He opened the car door and walked into the courtyard. The sky had cleared, the clouds having been swept away by a north-west wind.

Basil got out and stretched his arms and legs. 'Aren't you coming?' he said to Lorena in English.

'Yes, I'm coming.'

But she did not move. Basil went towards Mattei who was sitting sideways on the edge of the well. He had opened the Webley and was dropping the empty cartridges into the well and reloading the chamber.

'How is she?' he asked, looking up at Basil.

'A bit on edge.'

'And you?'

'Everything happened so quickly. What do you have in mind, Mattei?'

'To avoid Castel Benito.'

'You think they've put up road-blocks?'

'It's very possible. And they'll shoot on sight now.'

'So?'

'So we could cut across the open desert, but we're likely to get stuck in the sand with this tank. I'd rather look for a track. There must be one.'

'Yes,' said Basil. He nodded towards Lorena. 'We've put her in a nasty situation.'

'Certainly have,' said Mattei, blinking in the sun.

'And that doesn't worry you?'

'No. But it does you?'

'Just a little.'

'Anyway,' said Mattei, 'she'll come out of it better than either of us.'

They heard the door slam and saw Lorena walking slowly towards them. In her faded slacks turned up above the ankles and her oversized sweater, she looked like a disgrunted teenager.

'How odd,' she said. 'I've often wondered what this old house was like. I always noticed it on my way to Tripoli.' She stretched herself, forcing her arms downwards. 'I feel a little better now. I wouldn't mind a cigarette.'

Basil took out a pack of Camels. 'These are yours anyway,' he said.

She took one and he gave her a light.

'We make a queer trio,' she said, putting her head a little to one side. 'I'm not a very presentable consul's wife, you're an unlikely Swiss consul, and as for Mattei'—she laughed—'anyone would wonder why the Swiss consul has a bodyguard.'

Mattei shrugged his shoulders. 'We could leave you here. You could always say that we forced you to drive us out here.'

'That's not a very convincing story,' Lorena said gently.

'No,' Mattei admitted, swinging his foot. 'But after all, you're doubly neutral. You're a kind of official person and you're a woman.' He smiled. 'There's another solution. You could take the car and leave us here.' Lorena said nothing and Mattei continued, 'If Ferguson is caught, nothing much is likely to happen to him . . .'

'And how about you?' interrupted Lorena.

Mattei evaded the question. 'Or we can head for my boat. Then split up or sail away together.'

'To go . . . where to?' Lorena asked.

'Djerba.'

'What would I do there?' she said, scraping the ground with the toe of her shoe.

'You'd have a choice,' Mattei replied. 'You could either return home or wait there for things to settle down again. You too,' he said to Basil.

'If the British get here . . .'

'Among other things,' said Mattei. 'Anyway, we've got to come to some decision immediately. My boat leaves tomorrow night.'

The old bastard, thought Basil. 'It's up to Mrs. Dalloz,' he said.

Lorena gazed at her cigarette, then dropped it on the ground and crushed it with her heel. 'I'll take you to the coast, to your boat,' she said. 'Then we'll decide from there.'

'Good,' said the Frenchman with forced casualness. 'Have you got the map?'

Mattei spread the map on the ground and squatted down to study the sparse road routes of the region. The other two followed.

'You're on holiday,' Basil said to himself. 'You just can't seem to take this situation seriously. You've always been on holiday, whatever you were doing. Even the incident with the motor-cyclist was dreamlike. Perhaps that's the tragedy of it all—you are unable to cope with the tragic side of life so you avoid it. Remember Malta and the Beaufighter? It was like a nightmare. Or, more precisely, like a film sequence which concerns you as little as . . . as this map and this present situation you've found yourself in!'

'We'll have to make our way around,' said Mattei. 'And there's only one way—by this track which crosses the road from Castel Benito to Tripoli. After that . . .'

'After that?' said Basil.

'I think we'll be all right then.'

Basil looked at the dotted line where Mattei had placed his finger. It left the main road a few hundred yards from where they were, going first in a northerly direction and then curving to the west.

'What surprises me,' said Basil, 'is that we haven't been followed.'

'We were too far ahead,' Mattei replied. 'The simplest thing for them to do is wait for us at a place we're bound to pass through.'

'So it appears, then, that I'm going to Djerba with you?'

'If you want to. Do you?'

'And finish up in an internment camp . . .'

'I can get you across to Malta,' said Mattei.

'That's a place to stay away from . . . full of officers playing bridge all the time. And I hate playing bridge.'

'Or send you off in a fishing-boat that'd sail around in waters patrolled by your navy.'

'Yes,' said Basil, without much enthusiasm. It all sounds so deadly boring, he thought. 'I could give myself up,' he went on. 'After all, I don't see much difference between being in an Italian camp or a French one.'

He was afraid to look at Lorena, though he could feel her eyes on him—a green, neutral stare.

'You could do that,' said Mattei. 'No objection.'

'If you get shot breaking through a road-block,' Basil said to himself, 'it'd be the kind of death you fear most—a stupid accident. And this fellow is going to run every risk to get where he wants. So it's quite possible that he'd dump you on that coast road and once again you'll walk towards Zwara, fall in with those charming cyclists who love sausage and beans, and make another entrance into town perched on the crossbar of a bicycle with your arms around the neck of an Italian smelling of garlic and red wine . . .'

'Oh, I'll go with you.'

Mattei folded up the map and then sat back against the side of the well.

'Aren't we going?' said Lorena.

'No,' Mattei replied. 'We're waiting here.'

His face was set in an ingenuous expression which Basil was beginning to respect.

'I thought you were in a hurry,' he said with some annoyance.

Mattei smiled. 'In theory, we ought to have reached Tripoli by now. If they're waiting for us there—which is very likely—they must be wondering what's happened to us. They probably won't consider that we're calm enough to sit and let the time go by. They're more likely to think that we've turned off to the south . . . or headed for the coast east of Tripoli.'

'Yes,' said Basil, not very convinced.

'We're very comfortable here,' said Mattei.

'Very,' Lorena agreed.

'Then let's wait. What time is it?'

'Twenty past two,' said Lorena.

'Until four o'clock, then. That'll be fine.'

My God, thought Basil, the French are supposed to be impatient. This chap mustn't have blood in his veins; it's ice.

As if echoing Basil's thoughts, Mattei said: 'You'd better relax. You'll be driving when we set off. Are you a good driver?'

'Not bad. I started driving when I was fourteen.'

'Oh, so did I,' said Lorena.

'Rich kids,' grunted Mattei. 'I didn't have a car of my own until I was twenty-eight. And then it was a secondhand one. I drove like a clot, what's more.'

His hands were folded over his stomach and he could feel the curved butt of the Webley in his side. He thought of Claire whom he had met the evening he had first driven his car. She had got in with that guy Patrice something-or-other and Mattei had driven wildly through the streets of Marseilles. They had gone to have dinner at the Rascasse, down by the old harbour, and he had felt dreadfully uneasy because he did not know which fork to use. She was not Claire that evening but Mademoiselle Ferrieres, the daughter of one of the ten wealthiest men in the city and whose loose behaviour was well known, as was her love for boxing matches and her affair with this Patrice. And it was all due to that blasted fish-fork that things had begun between her and Mattei. He remembered the wink she had given him and her finger pointing secretly at the right piece of cutlery. Mattei had smiled in thanks. Later, when Patrice had gone to say hello to some friends, he had thanked her and she replied, 'What for?'

'For everything,' he said solemnly, his lips and cheeks throbbing from the punches he had received in the fight that evening and his head swimming with too much wine. Then he had added, 'I'd like to see you again.'

'Oh really?'

'Yes,' he had said, suddenly conscious of his flashy suit and its poor quality, although he had been so proud of it a few days before. Then Patrice had returned. Mattei had left them at about two in the morning and he still remembered shaking hands with her, the feel of her slim hand in his and of a crisp piece of paper left in his palm. He had read the telephone number over and over as he left the restaurant.

'Really like a clot,' he said, bringing himself back into the cluttered courtyard and the flies and the merciless sun.

'Were you living in France?' Lorena asked. She was leaning sideways on one hand with her legs curled up under her watching a column of ants winding their way towards the well.

'Yes, at that time,' said Mattei. 'I was living in the south. Afterwards, I went to Belgium and Holland.'

'Afterwards?' Basil queried.

'Afterwards,' stated Mattei in his lethargic tone. 'I've always had my ups and downs. More downs than ups . . .'

'Like everyone else,' said Basil.

'No, not you. Not like me, in any case.'

'I can well believe it,' Basil said with a trace of hostility.

Mattei looked up at him. 'What I'm saying is that a situation like we're in now doesn't greatly surprise me.'

'We guessed as much,' said Basil laughingly, and Lorena joined in.

'Rich kids,' Mattei retorted.

'What do you mean by that?' exclaimed Lorena.

'It means that things happen to you as to everyone else, but they're not the same kinds of things that happen to people like me.'

'The same things happen to us sometimes,' said Basil. 'Right now, for instance.'

'No, it's not the same. You've nothing to lose. You're just playing with circumstances.'

'I had rather the opposite impression,' said Basil.

'You just drift along. But with you,' Mattei nodded at Lorena, 'it's different.'

'You think so?' she said.

'I don't know. But that's how it seems to me. What do you think?'

Lorena felt herself blushing. It was a long time since she had done that. Not since Boyd, she thought.

'It wasn't for us,' Mattei went on, 'well, not only for us, that you did this. Am I mistaken?'

'No,' she said.

Mattei spread his hands in an eloquent gesture. And there was silence.

He's gained a little time, Basil thought as he looked at the Frenchman. And he's got us in hand. Just like that. And he's right.

'In fact, I'm not very sure why I did it,' Lorena admitted.

'That's what I mean. One's never very sure.'

'You are, though,' Basil said to him.

'Me? I act on the spur of the moment. I can't do anything else. I've a margin of manœuvre as wide as that.'

Mattei stopped, raised his head and motioned the other two to be silent.

The air around them trembled and the ground vibrated. Mattei got up and went across the courtyard to the crumbling wall. The other two followed. Mattei was looking towards Castel Benito.

'An air-raid?' said Basil.

Mattei shook his head. 'I don't know.'

'If it's aircraft,' Basil said to himself, 'it means another offensive is under way, and you don't know whether to be glad or not. This inner emptiness you've got is becoming chronic. Nothing seems to matter but your own pleasure. Everything's divided into what pleases you and what doesn't.'

The houses of Castel Benito seemed to be quivering in the hot air. 'Look there,' said Mattei.

The first vehicle had just appeared a few hundred yards away and then was followed by others much larger. A few motor-cyclists led the convoy.

'All that for us?' said Basil.

The sight was so inordinate that it almost seemed reassuring. He imagined the three of them surrounded by these huge armoured vehicles and smashed to the ground by a barrage of bullets.

'No,' Mattei said calmly, a little smile on his lips. 'No, they're the Boche.'

'The what?'

'The Germans. Can't you see the Maltese cross?'

The vehicles were sandy in colour and Basil could see an emblem on their sides but could not make it out. I must really be getting short-sighted, he thought.

'You can see the crosses?' he asked Mattei.

'Can't you?'

'Yes, of course.'

The armoured column stretched out along the road, the cyclists in front, a few blunt-nosed armoured cars, a long line of heavy trucks carrying helmeted soldiers and then tanks bringing up the rear. In each turret sat the head and chest of the tank commander, looking like the figure-head of a ship. Then other squadrons surged forth from the walls of Castel Benito, armoured cars, trucks and tanks, one after another, like gigantic centipedes crawling easily over the ground, following the curves and the hollows, sometimes dividing into sections on undulating ground and then joining up again. The air resounded with the grunting and growling of engines.

'We'll have a good view of them from here,' said Lorena, as if watching some mammoth show.

'Yes,' said Mattei. The Germans did not concern him. They were not going to track him down or arrest him. He had nothing to do with them.

'Did you know they'd landed?' he asked Lorena.

She shook her head.

Germans, thought Basil as he looked at the approaching column. He had never seen German troops before.

Mattei gave Basil a teasing look. 'If the Germans are landing in strength, the British won't be here for some time.' Then he added, 'Let's get going.'

'Do we drive past the column?' Basil asked.

'No, we'll try to reach the track and turn off before they get that far.'

The Oldsmobile swayed and bumped over the rough desert track, its edges vaguely defined by the flocks of sheep taken along it.

'We just made it,' said Mattei, looking back at the armoured column rumbling slowly past the turn off to the track.

'You know,' said Lorena, 'I think I'm going to stay.'

'Why?' Basil asked her.

She smiled. 'It seems the natural thing to do. More honourable, if you like.'

'Then I wonder what's the honourable thing for me to do.'

'Not to let yourself be caught,' said Lorena. 'That's the most difficult.'

'And it's a difficult thing for you to stay?'

'Yes. In a way, yes.'

'You . . .' Basil began, keeping his eyes on the bumpy track. 'Never mind.'

'Yes, you were going to say something.'

'It was rather personal.'

'Well, carry on. We're past that stage.'

'Did you think of leaving before?'

'Before what?'

'All this.'

'Oh, vaguely,' said Lorena, running, her finger idly over the dashboard. 'You think vaguely about that sort of thing and then you find that time passes and you're still there.'

The Oldsmobile sank into a rut. Basil cursed, and started off again with a grinding of gears.

'But after all, I'm free to do as I like,' Lorena went on.

'Then you're free to come to Djerba,' said Basil.

Whatever am I going to do with these two, thought Mattei.

'No,' said Lorena. 'My freedom will begin when I've seen my husband again.'

There was silence. The Oldsmobile jolted over the track, which was climbing a sharp rise.

'What are you running from?' asked Mattei.

'From home. I spend my time running away from home. I ran away from Phoenix. Then from Zurich and now from here. I do a lot of running away.' She turned around to Mattei. 'You've taught me something.'

'Here we are,' said Basil, as if he had hauled the Oldsmobile up the rise by sheer force.

He braked gently at the top of the ridge. They had a good view of their surroundings.

On the horizon, the white band of Tripoli appeared with a deeper band behind, the sea. Nearer to them and to the left were the compact square houses and grey-green palm-trees of Castel Benito.

'No one in sight,' said Mattei.

'No, nothing at all.' Basil felt relieved.

'How far to your boat?' he asked.

'About forty miles. Two hours by this road.'

'Odd,' said Basil. 'I'm thirsty.'

'I've been thirsty for a long time,' said Lorena.

'We'll have a drink on the boat,' Mattei promised. 'I forgot to tell you—she's called the *Santa Clara.*'

'I knew that,' Basil exclaimed with a laugh. 'That's one of the ridiculous things I noticed when I came to the surface. *Santa Clara* in white letters on a blue background, isn't it?'

'Yes,' said Mattei.

'Why *Santa Clara*?' asked Lorena. She, too, seemed very relaxed now.

'Why not?' said Mattei.

It's the first time, thought Basil, that I've seen him looking happy.

'As a matter of fact,' Mattei went on, 'I named her that because I'd known a girl called Claire.' He smiled. 'But she was no saint.'

'Perhaps she became one after meeting you,' suggested Basil as he let in the clutch. Mattei laughed.

22

Lorena thought about Amedée-Jean and her abrupt departure from the Consulate. There had been no explanations or discussions about a separation. No farewells, no grievances. It was the perfect way of clearing out for good. Had she consciously left him? Did she know when she drove out of the garage that she would never return? Or at least never return for good? She wanted to leave behind that boredom and that confinement only dulled by liquor. But she had left Amedée-Jean in a difficult situation. And it was all her fault. She must return to take her share of the responsibility; it was impossible to do otherwise.

Lorena smiled to herself. And it was these two who set things off. This lumbering Frenchman, a bit vulgar and stubborn, and this Englishman with his head in the clouds. 'This Englishman,' she said to herself, 'who drives so well and whom you wanted very much last night. He aroused in you a longing you had not known since you left the hospital only half a woman or so you've always felt. His hands are loose on the wheel and he drives as if holding the reins on a horse. Good breeding. And this Frenchman, in his way, reminds you of Boyd, but without his kindness. But how can anyone be kind in such circumstances?'

She remembered the sound of Amedée-Jean's voice over the telephone—colourless yet with more than a hint of panic. She then recalled Mattei's deliberate tone in the studio when he had asked her if she had a gun. She glanced again at Basil, still with that look of reserve, or was it just complete unconcern. Basil with his air of being too well brought up to show excitement.

She told herself, 'You'll regret both of them. They're just the kind of men that tempt fate. This one because he lets himself drift and the other because of his activities. But even if you never see them again, they've begun to reveal a side of you that you didn't know about . . . or a side you never allowed yourself to acknowledge.'

It seemed impossible that in less than two hours' time they would vanish from her life.

The Oldsmobile rumbled over the uneven track strewn with goat droppings and marked by hooves.

'What's the chief of our expedition doing?' Basil asked.

'He's asleep,' replied Lorena, looking around at Mattei.

'He's amazing.'

'What an odd fellow,' she said.

'Very efficient. Too much so, at times. But very efficient all the same.'

Lorena murmured agreement.

'You know, on that terrace where we were all day, waiting for you, he slept almost without a break . . . as if we were in no danger.'

'And you?'

'I was scared stiff. But I must admit that the Italians I gave myself up to were really charming people.'

'They'd probably be much less so now.'

'Mattei's got a knack of putting one in an impossible situation.' Basil sighed, then continued, 'His boat is small but very comfortable. I spent about an hour aboard her, and when we went ashore I was as drunk as a lord.'

'Is your father a Lord?'

'No, merely a Sir,' Basil said with a smile. 'And he drinks only one glass of port a week. On Thursday evenings.'

'Why Thursday?'

'It's the day he goes to his club.' Basil waved a hand at the view. 'I like this country.'

'So do I.'

'I've never been in Africa before.'

'Neither had I. And now I'd like to go to Djerba.'

'What's stopping you?'

'Me, I suppose,' said Lorena. 'In any case, it's only a stage.'

'I know. For me too. But I'm beginning to get used to that. I go from one stage to another without having much idea where one ends and the next begins.'

Lorena looked at Mattei. His face was so innocent in sleep, a contrast to his strong, hairy forearms and his brown muscular neck. Like Boyd.

'Give me a cigarette,' she said to Basil.

The track began to run downhill and then followed the dried-up bed of a wadi that was studded with smooth round pebbles as white as old bones. There were cracks here and there in the baked, dry bed, forming what looked like irregular-shaped flag-stones. When the track crossed the wadi, Basil felt the car wheels sink in. He quickly changed gears and wrenched the Oldsmobile out of the mud.

'If it'd been me, I'd have gotten bogged down,' said Lorena.

'I almost did.'

The land was more broken now and the car sped along between two low hills. A dismantled watch-tower stood atop one, a herd of sheep browsing beneath it.

'You ought to come to Djerba,' Basil said suddenly.

'I don't know,' she replied.

If I go to Djerba, she thought. If . . .

'I can hardly believe that in less than two hours we will be saying good-bye.'

Basil drove in silence. Then, with some effort, he said : 'I don't understand you very well.'

'From what point of view?'

'You and your husband.'

'Oh, there's nothing to understand. It's all old history really. Poor Amedée-Jean.'

'I can't say I feel much pity for him.'

'The package is very good. I've always liked nice packages.'

She tried to speak lightly as she felt herself becoming much too serious.

'You see, I . . . I can't have any children.'

'Oh,' was all Basil could say.

'I expect that's the cause of much of the trouble. But I don't know. I think I'd have been a very good mother.'

'Yes, I agree.'

There was a short silence, then Lorena said, 'On second thought, maybe it was best. A child should respect his father.'

'Surely he would have?'

'Not if I'd had anything to say about it,' she said. 'And I would have.'

Basil laughed softly. 'You took the words out of my mouth.'

'Do you think America will come into the war?' she asked.

'I don't see the connection.'

'Neither do I. But there must be one.'

'I don't know,' said Basil. 'I haven't thought much about it. In fact, it's only been the last few days that I've realised that a war is going on, that it could alter the course of my life. Yes, I think America will come in . . .' He drove in silence for a minute, then added, 'later on. Much later, when things are going very badly. And then it'll take several years to restore the situation. Then a war against the Eskimos will start.'

'The what?'

'Or against the Zulus, I don't know. Another sort of war, different from this one. I'll probably be too old to take part in it. Anyway, I couldn't care less. What's that over there?'

'Some houses.'

'Should we wake Mattei?'

By the side of the track, about two hundred yards ahead, were half a dozen mud buildings.

'It's like a ghost town,' said Lorena.

For a moment she thought she was back in New Mexico, approaching some pueblo where under-nourished Indians would offer her basket-work and jugs of pulque.

Basil braked gently and Mattei sprang forward, the Webley clutched in his hand.

'You gave me a fright,' he said.

'Me too,' Basil laughed. 'Please, go easy on my nerves. I'm not used to it. This is just a hamlet and it looks deserted.'

Mattei smacked his lips. 'No, it isn't. There's a café, and I could use a drink.'

Six or seven square, squat buildings surrounded a well with a bucket and wheel. A scraggly dog was lapping up some water by the well and began to bark as the Oldsmobile drew near.

'*Basta,* Benito!' came a man's voice from the largest of the buildings. Above the door was a white-painted plank with the words *Stella d'Oro* printed in black. A curtain of thin metal strips hung stiffly over the doorway, glittering brightly in the sun.

Mattei stepped out of the Oldsmobile and looked at a swarm of flies buzzing around a heap of garbage. The dog bared its teeth and growled.

'Do you really think we'll get anything to drink there?' Basil said.

'Water, anyway.'

'Who's that?' a man called in Italian.

Mattei lifted the shimmering curtain and stepped inside. The room was dim and smelled of wine-dregs and burnt wood. A man sat behind the counter—a long plank placed on two barrels.

'Can we have a drink?' Mattei asked in Italian.

The man made no reply.

'Beer,' said Mattei. 'Have you got some beer?'

'Yes,' he replied. 'Yes, I've got some beer.'

Basil put his head in. 'Come on,' said Mattei. 'He's got some beer.'

Basil parted the curtain for Lorena.

'Two beers,' said Basil.

'And two for me,' added Lorena.

'Six beers,' Mattei said to the man.

The man remained seated. He had probably been sitting there for hours and would go on sitting there until evening, his big prominent eyes gazing into space and his hands resting on his fat thighs.

The dirty cotton door-hanging at the back of the room was drawn aside and a figure appeared. Mattei turned—Renata, he thought. Then the woman stepped into the light and Mattei saw her grey hair and dark, wrinkled face.

Idiot, he thought. Why would Renata be here?

'D'you want drinks?' said the woman.

'Six beers,' Mattei told her.

'There's only three of you.'

'Two for each of us,' said Mattei. 'We're thirsty.'

She was the same build as Renata, the same wide, sturdy shoulders; only the face was different.

'What's the matter?' Lorena asked in French.

'Nothing. This woman reminds me of someone.'

'Your girl-friend?'

'Yes,' Mattei said curtly. 'Renata.'

'Are you French?' the woman asked them in Italian.

'No, Swiss,' Lorena replied.

'Renata in thirty years' time,' said Mattei.

The woman stooped and opened an ice-box with no ice in it.

The man watched her without budging and Basil noted that they had said nothing to each other. She handed the bottles to the man who opened them one after another. The froth oozed out and he licked his fingers before putting the bottle on the counter.

'It's warmish,' he said.

'It'll do,' Mattei told him.

The woman looked at Mattei as she gave him a glass. 'I've seen you before,' she said.

'I don't think so.'

'I'm sure of it.'

'I've never been this way before,' said Mattei.

'No, but I've seen you at El Atsitia.'

'You may have. I've been there a few times.'

'At El Atsitia,' the woman repeated, still looking at him. 'You mentioned a Renata just now. I know a Renata at El Atsitia.'

How odd, thought Mattei.

'So do I,' he said. 'She keeps the *dopo-lavoro.*'

'Yes,' the woman said sullenly.

I don't like this woman, thought Mattei. I don't know why.

'We knew her father,' said the fat man. 'The father of this Renata. Did you know him too?'

'No.' Mattei drank his beer. It was warm and bitter, but it didn't really matter.

'Do many people drop in here?' Mattei asked.

'Before, yes,' said the woman. 'Before, there were soldiers all around here.'

'And now there aren't any?'

'No,' replied the woman. Then for no apparent reason she put a hand on the fat man's shoulder and said, 'He's my brother. We've been living here . . .'

'For ten years,' he said. 'We had a farm and goats and a Fiat for going into town. To Tripoli. Is the beer good?'

'Very good.' Mattei emptied his glass and refilled it. 'Any soldiers been by here in the past few days?'

'No,' said the woman. 'If there had been, they'd have stopped.'

The dog barked, and Mattei went to the door and pulled aside the metal curtain. The dog was playing with two naked children as flies swarmed around them.

Merde, said Mattei inwardly, what a life. He thought of the

Santa Clara and the sound of the waves splashing against her sides. He went back to the counter and emptied his glass.

'Let's go,' he said.

Lorena fumbled in her pockets. 'I haven't any money,' she said, quite calmly.

Basil smiled. This was the first time he had ever had a drink and was not able to pay for it.

The woman did not seem surprised.

'It's not important,' she said after a moment. 'Pay next time you come this way.'

Mattei thanked her. 'Yes, next time.' He was fully aware that they had aroused this woman's suspicions. But it did not matter. In an hour he would be a long way off.

The three of them went out into the sunshine.

'It's so stupid,' said Lorena. 'I should have brought some money.'

Mattei shrugged his shoulders.

'What a life,' said Basil as he slipped behind the wheel.

'Let's get out of here,' said Mattei.

'You're in a great hurry all of a sudden.'

'That woman makes me nervous.'

Basil started the car.

'You've nothing to blame yourself for,' said Basil, careful to avoid mentioning Renata by name.

'That's not the point. It's a nasty feeling, that's all.'

'You're getting superstitious,' Lorena said with a smile.

Mattei looked back at the diminishing hamlet. Its dried-up buildings looked as if they would crumble into dust at any moment. The woman had come outside and was standing by the door with her hands on her hips.

Then a rise in the ground hid the hamlet from sight.

'Another hour,' said Mattei.

23

The rocky ground gradually gave way to long stretches of fine sand with only tufts of alfalfa grass here and there on either side of the track.

'The air's cooler,' Lorena remarked.

'The sea isn't far off now,' said Mattei.

Basil was having difficulty in following the sand-covered track.

'I hope we're nearing the coast road,' he said.

He heard a rustling of paper behind him as Mattei opened the map.

'Another two or three miles.'

'You're sure your boat is still waiting for you?'

'Quite sure . . . This evening you'll be at sea.'

'And we'll drink your calvados,' said Basil.

'My crew will be surprised to see you again.'

Sand-dunes spread along the horizon about half a mile ahead. When Basil reached them, he sighed with relief at the wide expanse of deep blue that lay before them in the distance.

There was nothing more to fear, he thought. The boat would be waiting in the inlet and then he would be on his way to Djerba—yet another stage. He then recalled an incident that had happened while he was at Oxford. It was in 1934 and he was on his way to the Sorbonne to take a course. On the cross-Channel ship he had met this girl—Christa, an Austrian from Innsbruck, who was going to Klosters to ski. He had mentioned that he was going to Paris to study the works of St. Thomas Aquinas and she had jokingly said, 'You should come skiing with me instead.' So when they reached Boulogne he had taken the train to Strasbourg and from Strasbourg on to Zurich. He had spent two weeks with Christa, whose lover was away on business in Milan. An extraordinary two weeks free from all responsibility. He and Christa had lived out each day with no mention of any future obligations. Afterwards, of course, he had failed his paper on St. Thomas Aquinas but had made up for it with a study on John Collet. The ways of God, however pleasant, moved mysteriously. Klosters had been a stopover, a joyous escape. Djerba would be another.

'Do you think it'll be possible,' he said, 'to let my parents know from Djerba that I'm not missing?'

'Not from Djerba,' Mattei replied. 'But if I go to Sfax or Gabes I could ask the Red Cross to contact them.'

'They probably haven't been informed officially yet, but I'd like them to know I'm still alive ...'

He pictured his father opening the War Office telegram in his library. How would he react? His mother?

'It's odd, he mused; I've never seen them show any sign of sorrow or suffering. When Geoffrey's plane had crashed in Yucatan, he had cabled them three weeks later: 'Nothing broken but my glasses.'

A very sheltered life, thought Basil.

He caught sight of the coast road ahead and slipped almost voluptuously into top gear and sped towards freedom. The wheels no longer jarred and jolted on the compact surface. Splendid, he thought. He rounded a curve then stamped hard on the brake.

Barbed-wire barriers stretched across the road and two soldiers in desert uniform with long peaked caps stood guard. In the shade of an abandoned farmhouse an armoured car was parked with an officer sitting idly on the edge of the open turret. Three others were lying on the sand at the foot of the courtyard wall.

The two soldiers by the barriers, their hands resting on the Schmeissers hanging across their chests, calmly watched the Oldsmobile come to a stop.

'*Merde,*' said Mattei. 'The Boches again.'

The taller of the two smiled and raised his hand. '*Ein moment, bitte,*' he said in a clarion voice.

'What'd he say?' asked Basil.

'To wait a moment, I think,' said Lorena.

The soldier thrust his way between two barriers and walked

over to the car, clicked his heels and gave a salute that was smart yet casual. His eyes slid towards Lorena.

'*Schweizer?*' he asked, addressing Basil.

Basil nodded. 'Swiss consulate,' he said in French.

'*Ach so,*' said the soldier. '*Schweizer Konsulat.*'

Excellent, thought Basil, I can understand German.

The soldier put a hand through the window. '*Papier, bitte.*'

Lorena handed him the documents.

Behind her, Mattei's heart pounded as he looked towards the sea. On the beach sat a heavy Borgward truck and about a dozen men were bathing naked.

Gripped by anxiety Mattei turned his eyes back to the soldier who was looking through the documents.

'If we have to make a break for it,' Mattei muttered in Basil's ear, 'you'll have a job turning around.'

'I know,' said Basil. 'And I can't charge through the barbed-wire.'

The soldier gave the documents back to Basil. '*Gut,*' he said. '*Wohin fahren Sie?*'

There was silence; a silence that weighed heavily on the three in the Oldsmobile.

'Zwara,' Lorena said finally.

'Zoura?' queried the German, blinking in the sunshine.

'*Ja,*' said Basil. 'Zwara.'

The soldier nodded, then turned and shouted something to his comrade.

'The road-block isn't for us,' Mattei said quietly. 'It seems to be just a routine affair.'

The two soldiers began to move the heavy barbed-wire barriers.

'We're all right,' said Mattei.

The tight feeling in his stomach loosened. Then he spotted the officer climbing down from the armoured car and coming towards them. He was bareheaded and his field glasses dangled on his chest. His eyes surveyed the Oldsmobile, the Swiss pennant, and settled on Lorena. He was a young man, a little ungainly, with a long face, close-set eyes and a weak chin.

He gave a slight bow, clicked his heels, and said to Basil: '*Betrachten Sie die Möglichkeiten Vergnügungreisen in Afrika zu machen?*'

It's like an exam, Basil thought desperately. But there's only one passing grade. A Swiss consul has to speak German.

'*Ich entdecke das Land,*' the officer went on, looking attentively at Basil. '*Sind Sie schon lange hier?*'

Land, land, Basil thought urgently. What is he asking me about this country? If I think it's beautiful? If I've been living here long?

He could hear Mattei breathing heavily behind him. 'You've got to answer something,' he said to himself. 'Yes or no, something.'

'*Nein,*' he said in an apologetic sort of way.

The German gave a thin smile. A glimmer of doubt flickered in his eyes. He put a finger to the bridge of his nose and began rubbing it with a slow, thoughtful motion.

'*Verstehen Sie Deutsch?*' he finally said in a flat tone.

The hell with it, thought Basil. There must be at least one Swiss consul with no gift for languages, and it'll have to be me.

'What do you think?' he said in French.

The officer adopted an air of infinite patience. '*Papier, bitte,*' he said, holding out his hand.

'I've already shown them,' Basil said in French. He turned to Lorena. 'Give me the identity papers, will you, dear?'

The officer looked through them quickly.

'These are,' he said in laboured French, 'the papers of the vehicle, no?'

'Yes,' Basil replied.

'And of madame.'

'Yes,' said Lorena, flashing him a bewitching smile.

'Your papers, monsieur, I do want,' the officer said to Basil. Then he bent forward to peer in at Mattei. 'And also yours, monsieur.'

Mattei put his left hand on the top of Basil's seat and scratched his back two or three times, very quickly, while he felt for the Webley with his other hand. *Merde,* he thought, *merde, merde.*

He saw Basil looking in the rear view mirror at the road behind; the bend to the next straight stretch was fifty yards away. A ten-to-one chance, thought Mattei.

'*Bitte!*' said the officer impatiently, clutching the top of the lowered window.

The engine roared into life. The officer's blue eyes opened wide with surprise. Basil snapped into reverse.

'Lorena, duck down,' Mattei said urgently. At the same time

he brought the Webley forward, felt the barrel touch the officer's cheek, and squeezed the trigger.

The revolver jumped; the sound of the shot deafened him. The officer bounded backwards, arms flung wide, as if by some invisible force; there was a gap where his eye had been.

The two soldiers ran forward from the road-block unslinging their Schmeissers. The three who had been lying down sprang to their feet.

The Oldsmobile was zigzagging backwards. Mattei steadied the revolver on his forearm and fired. One of the soldier's helmets spun off as if his head had been twisted violently beneath it.

The Oldsmobile made a wide backward swerve.

'Look out!' shouted Basil.

A stream of bullets whined through the air and pinged against the side of the car.

Mattei knelt on the back seat and fired twice as the road-block quickly receded. Another burst of fire and bullets thudded into the padded roof above Mattei's head, making long jagged tears. All three occupants ducked instinctively.

In the distance, the naked bathers were swarming onto the road, which suddenly dipped and hid them from sight as though submerged by a large black wave.

A cloud of dust swirled across the whole scene.

PART THREE

'Every death is a suicide.'

J.-L. Borges

24

Amedée-Jean Dalloz gazed despondently at the brightly embroi-
dered cushions on the chairs in the waiting-room. They were the
work of Mrs. Stein herself and were also visible in every other
room of the Legation including the general office.

Amedée-Jean's hands were sticky and his headache had wor-
sened with the news of Lorena's mad escapade. Also, the atmosphere in Tripoli—reeking with the exhaust fumes of army
trucks and filled with the clamour of tanks and armoured
vehicles rumbling through the streets—did nothing to soothe his
mind.

He felt alone and floating in the midst of a chaos not of his
own making. He knew he could count on no one at this moment,
certainly not Stein. His relations with Stein, marked by outward
cordiality but mutual suspicion, gave him little hope. Not only
would Stein make no effort to cover up for him, he would be
happy to contribute to his downfall. He had always insisted that
his functions as *chargé d'affaires* were far more important than
those of a consul. Stein was making him wait now even though
he had told him to come to the Legation at once.

Amedée-Jean uncrossed his legs impatiently and heard Stein's
dry mirthless laugh come through the closed door to his office.

Stein gave a loud and lively *'Arrivederci!'* and then silence
followed.

He's doing it on purpose, thought Amedée-Jean. He's trying
to show me that the mess I'm in is not his responsibility. Five hours
ago everything was fine. Christ, how could Lorena have acted so
irresponsibly?

The door suddenly opened and Stein appeared—dressed in

white like a symbol of militant virtue, well shaved and holding himself upright to make the most of his height. He pretended to be surprised.

'Dalloz! What, here already?'

'You seemed in such a hurry to . . .'

'I am,' said Stein.

Amedée-Jean followed him into the office. Stein wiped his hands with his handkerchief as he walked around his desk. He's nervous too, thought Amedée-Jean.

'Sit down,' said Stein. He turned and looked through the window at the palm-trees.

Then he gave a deep sigh and said: 'I don't suppose I need tell you what it's all about . . .'

He swung around on his heels and gave a ghost of a smile, a cold smile. His thin lips expressed scorn easily.

'No,' said Amedée-Jean. 'No, not really.'

'When Italian headquarters telephoned me at midday I was shocked.' Amedée-Jean said nothing, and Stein repeated, 'Shocked.'

'My wife acted impulsively,' ventured Amedée-Jean.

'Impulsively? You realise she's the accomplice of a criminal and an escaped prisoner?'

'In the position . . .'

'I know what you're going to say . . . That you couldn't refuse to give asylum to an escaped British officer. True. But I should have been informed!'

'I was going to tell you this morning, but I was taken unawares by . . .'

'Taken unawares! You couldn't have put it better.'

Stein seemed almost satisfied. He enjoyed the position of accuser.

'And this . . . this'—Stein referred to a notepad on his desk—'gun-runner, Mattei?'

Amedée-Jean made a vague gesture. 'The British officer told me that they had escaped together, and I didn't . . .'

'I ought to have been informed!' Stein rapped out in a shrill voice. 'It's my job to have considered the matter. I alone! I represent the Swiss government here, and we shouldn't be in this situation if I had been able to take responsibility.'

There was silence. Amedée-Jean took a deep breath.

'And now,' Stein went on, 'I'm going to have to explain your wife's acts, which you've covered up and which have resulted in . . .'

Amedée-Jean interrupted. 'Aiding a British officer was not only my duty but the proper move since British forces are expected any day now.'

Stein again turned his back and gazed out of the window. 'My poor fellow! My poor fellow,' he repeated. Then he added, 'You don't know what they've done.'

'They broke through a road-block. Yes, I know.'

Stein spun around and leaned forward. 'Ah, you know? They broke through a road-block, and they fired on an Italian army motor-cyclist. You know it all, and yet that's all you've got to say?'

Amedée-Jean made no reply, and Stein went on in a voice that was almost gentle. 'But there's more to it. Barely an hour ago the automobile, flying the Consulate pennant, was stopped at a road-block manned by the Wehrmacht, west of Tripoli, and—and'— Stein banged on the table—'they shot and killed a German officer!'

My God, thought Amedée-Jean. This can't be happening to me.

'Killed him!' Stein repeated forcefully.

'But . . . Lorena . . .' Amedée-Jean began in a flat voice.

'Your wife was with them. It was she who broke through the Italian road-block—almost crushing two soldiers. She was driving when the motor-cyclist went after them.'

'It can't be. They must have . . . forced her,' Amedée-Jean said weakly.

'You don't really believe that.'

Amedée-Jean said no more.

'I'm very sorry,' Stein went on, 'but there's nothing more I can do for her. Except to pray . . . Meanwhile we still have a problem on our hands.'

'Yes,' said Amedée-Jean.

'The Italians are demanding sanctions. I don't know what the German reaction will be!'

'But I had nothing to do with it!' exclaimed Amedée-Jean.

'You may not be responsible for your wife's actions—though a diplomat is to some extent responsible for his wife. But you did permit an escaped criminal to stay in your house and now you can see the consequences of that act. Our situation here is now gravely compromised and I'm obliged to inform our government of all the facts—without omitting the slightest detail—before the Italians and the Germans do so.'

Amedée-Jean bowed his head. 'Yes,' he said.

'Unfortunately,' Stein went on, 'unfortunately that's not all . . .'

Amedée-Jean looked up at his torturer. What more could there be? Oh, God, what more?

'. . . And although I disapprove of such methods, I can't prevent the Italians from using what they've got against you . . .'

Major Sarfati, thought Amedée-Jean; he probably wants revenge for my duping him.

'I couldn't do anything else,' he told Stein. 'I don't have to account for my acts to Major Sarfati but to you.'

'To me?' said Stein, blinking at him.

'You've just been telling me . . .'

Stein waved his hand dismissively. 'This has nothing to do with the affair of the escaped prisoners.'

He picked up a pencil and began tapping his desk. 'Do you know a woman called Anita Payot?'

It came so suddenly that Amedée-Jean could not control his reaction.

'I see that you do,' said Stein.

'She's a compatriot,' Amedée-Jean hurried to explain. 'It's only natural that I should know her. All the Europeans go to her leather-goods shop.'

'Twice a week?'

Amedée-Jean jumped to his feet. 'I won't permit . . . !'

Stein tried to calm him. 'I don't approve of the methods of the Fascist police,' he began, 'but the facts have to be faced. We're all on file but as long as we behave ourselves a police-card is no more then a piece of cardboard with various items of information on it, of no interest to anyone. But from the moment—let me finish—from the moment we make a mistake, it can be used as a weapon against us. Your . . . visits to Mme. Payot haven't escaped the notice of the Fascist police. Personally, your private life is no concern of mine—it's purely your own affair . . . as long as it can't be used against us. But since this morning, that's no longer the case. In the protest that the Italians are sending to our government, they won't fail to draw attention to your misconduct. So there it is.'

Amedée-Jean was too stunned to reply.

'I wanted to warn you, in all fairness,' said Stein.

'It's outrageous,' murmured Amedée-Jean.

'Yes. But you're a public figure and should have realised that you lay yourself open to criticism.'

'What can I do about it?'

'Nothing, I'm afraid. Besides, this last matter is of minor importance.'

'I see. Do you think that my . . . my functions . . .'

Stein made an expansive gesture. 'At any event, you'll have plenty of time to defend yourself. And as communications with Switzerland have been out, you'll remain at your post until I'm able to get in touch again.'

'That means then . . .' began Amedée-Jean.

'I'm not presuming anything,' said Stein. 'You can count on me to make my report with complete objectivity.'

I hope so, thought Amedée-Jean, I do hope so, you son of a bitch. He felt himself reddening and wondered if Stein could read his thoughts. Apparently not, for the *chargé d'affaires* held out his hand.

'I'll keep you informed of what happens,' he said. 'You'll excuse me, but I've a hundred and one things to do today. I just wanted to let you know how matters stand.'

Amedée-Jean stood on the pavement outside the Legation. The air was filled with the noise of tanks rumbling along the Via Cavour; the tank-commanders were standing in their turrets and waving like victors to the people lining the avenue.

Amedée-Jean gazed at the passing masses of steel. Death would be so easy. He had only to step forward and be crushed into a bloody pulp. No more worries; no more Stein or Swiss government, no more Italian or German headquarters and no more probing into his private life. And Lorena . . . she would have to live with the fact that she killed her husband by her irresponsibility and selfishness.

His head swam with the shouts of the Italian civilians and the vision of little swastika flags. Each shout was like a drum reverberating in his head.

To die would be simple and dignified; he would be a victim of Stein's spitefulness and Lorena's thoughtlessness. Crushed to death in a matter of seconds by one of these jangling tanks . . .

With both hands he thrust apart the couple standing in front of him.

A tank thundered past, shaking the ground and sending its hot breath of gasoline and grease over Amedée-Jean. He felt dizzy and the huge moving treads of the tank mesmerised him.

Amedée-Jean jumped forward. He streaked across the roadway, heard a woman scream and then caught a glimpse of the startled eyes of the tank-commander turning around reprovingly. He cleaved a way through the crowd and headed towards a café. He stumbled to the counter, his legs quaking.

I might have been killed, he thought dully.

'Bring me a bottle of *grappa*,' he ordered.

'*Pronto!*'

25

The Oldsmobile was parked in a little street near the harbour. The smells of brine and fish permeated the air.

The street was deserted except for a big tabby cat.

'I wonder if it's such a good idea after all,' said Basil. 'We've put ourselves into a trap.'

'They'll never think we're hiding in Tripoli itself,' Mattei replied. 'And besides, there's that.' He pointed to the gasoline gauge with only three or four gallons left.

'Do you know Tripoli well?' Basil asked Lorena.

'Fairly well.'

'Have you any friends here?'

'A few. Italians.'

'Nothing doing,' said Mattei.

'I have a Swiss friend too, a woman,' Lorena added with a slight smile.

'Who'd lend you some money?'

'I hope so.'

There was a short silence, then Lorena said, 'Yes, I'm sure she'd lend me some.'

'I could always steal some gasoline . . .' said Mattei slyly.

Basil sniggered.

'. . . but, of course, I'd rather pay for it.'

'You need vouchers to buy gas,' Lorena reminded him.

'Okay, find me the money and I'll find you the gas,' said Mattei. 'I know someone here who'll fix that for me.'

The cat blinked at them.

'Let's break up,' said Mattei. 'You see about getting the cash, and I'll go and look for my friend.'

'And me?' Basil asked.

Mattei gazed at him despondently. 'Can't you look a little less English?'

'Can't do much about that. I'll just stay here in the car.'

'No, you find a way out of this town. I'm fed up with shooting my way out. We'll be going east. See if there are any road-blocks in that direction and whether civilians are being checked. What time is it?'

Lorena looked at her watch. 'Twenty after three.'

'We'll meet back here in two hours. You'll be able to find your way back?'

Basil and Lorena both nodded.

'All right,' said Mattei. 'I'll go first.'

He slid along the seat, opened the door and stepped out. As he hitched up his pants he leaned towards the others. 'Try and bring back something to drink too. I've a feeling we're not out of the wood yet.'

He hesitated for a moment then walked past the cat and disappeared around the corner.

'I wonder if he'll come back,' said Basil.

'Don't you trust him?'

'Not entirely.'

'And you?' said Lorena. 'If you had the chance to get out of this by yourself, what would you do?'

He smiled. 'I haven't much to lose one way or the other.'

They sat without speaking, looking at the empty street.

'I guess we'd better get going,' said Basil.

'You go first.'

'All right. But I'm afraid to go alone in the dark. No, I'm joking,' he added. 'That's a line I once heard.' He opened the door then looked at Lorena.

'Lorena,' he said, smiling.

Then he leaned towards her and brushed her lips with his. 'I've been wanting to do that for a long time,' he said. 'See you later.'

'Be careful.'

He got out and buttoned his blue blazer. 'You might very well be the one to let us down.'

'No,' said Lorena. 'Not now.'

'Out of pride?'

She looked at him with calm green eyes. 'Possibly.'

Basil went off in the same direction as Mattei. She watched him walk away in Amedée-Jean's pants. When he reached the corner he turned and waved.

The sounds of a brass band reached her and she imagined Basil sauntering among the Italians and looking abstractedly about him.

'If you were really sensible,' she said to herself, 'you'd go and see Stein at the Legation. But to hell with being sensible. For too many years now . . .'

I must get going, she thought. And for the first time in her life she felt like a vital part of a team.

She got out and set off in the direction taken by the other two.

She approached Anita Payot's shop with its pretentiously painted sign in English: 'Fancy Leather-Goods'. She turned the handle and walked in.

Anita sat at a small table.

'Good afternoon,' said Lorena.

Anita looked up but seemed too astonished to reply.

'I don't know if you remember me, but I'm Amedée-Jean's wife.'

'Yes,' said Anita faintly.

Lorena looked at the leather-goods displayed on small tables and in glass show-cases. Then she sat down. 'Forgive me, but I'm dead tired . . .'

'Look . . .' began Anita.

Lorena interrupted her. 'Have you any cigarettes?'

'Yes,' said Anita, and handed her a pack of Laurens.

'Thanks.' She drew on her cigarette. 'I haven't come to make a scene.'

Anita struggled for control. 'I hope not.' Her emotion made the curtness in her voice more pronounced.

'I could though,' said Lorena, smiling.

'Amedée-Jean has told you?'

I can do this much for him, Lorena thought, rather astonished at herself. 'Yes,' she said. 'He was very frank about it and very courageous.'

Anita flushed.

'But I haven't come to talk to you about that,' said Lorena. 'Has Amedée-Jean phoned you today?'

'No. Is something wrong?'

'Yes . . . We sheltered two escaped prisoners at the Consulate. And someone denounced us to the Italians.'

'My God!' exclaimed Anita, putting a hand to her red blouse.

Extraordinary, thought Lorena. She really loves him.

'We managed to get them away from the Consulate but everyone is looking for them. I want to get them across the frontier into Tunisia. But that takes money, and I . . . I went off without a cent.'

'Are you going to Tunisia with them?' Anita asked, a little too abruptly.

'Yes.'

'But how will you get back?'

There was a moment's silence. Lorena looked at Anita and could see that a man would probably take delight in arousing her rather set features and thick, sturdy body and in drawing cries of pleasure from her over-painted mouth, now pinched thin with curiosity and emotion.

'Won't you come back?' said Anita, her eyes opening wide with hope.

'It's unlikely.'

There, I've done it, thought Lorena. I can't go back now.

'And besides,' she went on, 'everything will be different when I do see my husband again.'

There was another silence and Lorena was touched by Anita's look. How easy it is to make someone happy!

'What I mean is,' she added, 'that I . . . that we'll get a divorce.'

'Is . . . is Amedée-Jean in any danger?'

'I don't think so. He might have some difficulties with the Swiss government but it is all my fault. I got him into this situation. But now I need money and you're the only person who can help me.'

Anita's lips began to tremble and tears came to her eyes. Oh no, not that, thought Lorena. Anita fumbled for a handkerchief and dabbed at her nose with delicate gestures.

'Come, come now,' said Lorena softly.

'You don't understand . . .'

'Yes, I think I do.'

'You can't . . .' Anita suddenly looked up anxiously at Lorena. 'You're not thinking of hiding them here, are you?'

Lorena smiled. 'No. No, I'm not. Can you let me have a thousand *lire*?'

'A thousand? Are you sure that will be enough?'

'Fifteen hundred then. I don't want to impose on you.'

'No, you're not at all.' Anita opened a drawer and took out a wad of lira-bills.

She's buying Amedée-Jean, thought Lorena. Or rather, I'm selling him to her. I should have asked for more. She'd give me all she's got.

'You came here once before, didn't you?' said Anita, handing Lorena the money.

'Yes.'

'And you didn't know at that time?'

'No.'

'I'm so sorry.'

Lorena smiled. 'There's no need to be. It was bound to end.' She stuffed the bills in her pocket. 'Well, I must be off. You've been very kind.'

'So have you,' said Anita, getting up.

'Good-bye.'

'Good-bye, and thank you.'

Lorena looked back. 'Whatever for?'

Anita shook her head and tears again appeared in her eyes. 'Good-bye,' she said again.

Lorena gazed at her thoughtfully. 'Do you know English?' she asked.

'A little.'

'You dirty little bitch,' she said sweetly, and went slowly out of the shop.

Basil sat on the terrace of a café beneath the shade of an arcade. The east gate of the town was on the other side of the square. It was flanked by two small buildings with colonnades and triangular capitals. There was a guard posted but the Italian soldiers weren't checking the vehicles that passed through.

Market-stalls lined the left side of the square and Basil listened to the cries of the traders as he slowly drank his chilled beer. He watched the crowds of people walking under the arcades, the men sitting at café-tables and army officers having their shoes polished. Ragged gaunt beggars squatted against the pillars with bony hands shaking copper bowls.

Basil took another sip of beer. He was in no hurry to leave especially since he would have to think up some excuse for not paying for his drink. Running away was out of the question. Too tiring.

He stretched out his legs and felt very relaxed. The waiter —an elderly, stooped Italian who wore a crumpled and stained white jacket—went slowly past and gave Basil a kind smile.

'Another beer,' said Basil.

I must prolong this and I'm doing something useful. Plus, I need the rest. There's nothing more tiring than being with other people.

He watched a Fiat driven by a civilian disappear through the gateway without anyone stopping it.

The waiter placed the glass of beer in front of him together with a check.

'*Grazie*,' Basil said.

The heat was making him sleepy. He wanted to close his eyes and take a short nap. No one seems to be taking any notice of me, he thought. It's almost as if I didn't exist. In fact, that's just what I am, someone without any real dimensions. He wondered what Tommy would have done in this situation; probably the same thing.

He began to hum a tune and thought back to the last time he had heard it. It had been about three weeks ago, in London, at that night-club where he and Julia had gone after hearing of his posting to Cairo. They had both got drunk in the midst of people dancing gaily around them. Then he remembered the calvados on board Mattei's boat. Then the prison; and the drive across the desert. Nothing made sense but it had all happened to him; he was the thread on which it all hung. And it had all begun that evening in London. Julia had even seemed distressed at his impending departure. Julia and her extravagances. Julia and her casual way, even when making love. Except on that particular evening. She had desperately run her slim hands over his body as if wanting to remember every contour and detail. Yes, Julia had been very distressed, he was quite sure of that. But the following day she had regained control. When she had seen him off at Waterloo Station a few days later she had merely said—as though he were going to Brighton for the weekend—'I hope you haven't forgotten your toothbrush.' And yet her eyes were clouded and he was almost certain that her smile had been forced. 'Oh darling,' she had suddenly said, 'I think I'm going to be ridiculous.' 'Go on then,' he had said, and grabbed her tightly and kissed her.

But it was absurd to be thinking of Julia.

Another Fiat crossed the square towards the gateway. This time a soldier held up his hand and stopped it. He said a few words to the driver and then motioned the Fiat to proceed.

Basil felt in his pockets for a cigarette but found the crumpled pack of Camels empty. Then he felt someone's eyes upon him. A swarthy-faced civilian sitting to his left was watching him attentively. Basil's heart beat faster.

'If you get up and go now,' he said to himself, 'the waiter who's only a few yards away is bound to notice.'

Basil pretended to be absorbed in the pageant of traders and pedestrians in the square. Then he stole a quick glance at the man. He was still looking at him. He wore white cotton pants and a short-sleeved shirt. A policeman in plain clothes perhaps, thought Basil, or more likely one of their informers. The man took a pack of cigarettes from his pocket and held it towards Basil with a broad grin. Basil took one and the man began speaking to him in German. The only word Basil understood was 'Tripolitania'.

'You can talk to me in Italian,' he said. 'I love that language.'

The man's eyes lit up. 'Will you allow me to buy you another beer?' he said.

'Oh, with pleasure,' Basil replied.

'Your arrival gives us confidence again,' the man said.

Basil made no reply. The other ordered two beers, then asked, 'Which part of Germany do you come from?'

'Hamburg,' said Basil, without thinking.

The man nodded, and Basil said again, 'Hamburg.'

The waiter came with two glasses of beer.

'My name is Carlo Taglia.'

Basil hesitated for a moment before replying. 'Basilius Schmidt.'

'Did you disembark last night?'

'No,' said Basil. 'I arrived two days ago by plane. Have you been here long?'

'Ten years,' Carlo told him. 'And you a professional soldier?'

Basil shook his head firmly.

'In any case,' Carlo said, still smiling, 'I guessed at once that you were a soldier in civilian clothes and that you hadn't been here very long.'

'I'm a journalist,' said Basil.

'Which newspaper?'

Basil felt himself plunging deeper into the mire. 'Actually, I work for a State agency. For propaganda,' he added as convincingly as he could.

Carlo seemed intrigued. 'Propaganda is a more powerful weapon than guns.'

There was a short silence, then Carlo asked, 'What's Hamburg like?'

What can Hamburg be like? Basil wondered.

'It's a big town,' he said. 'A port.'

Carlo nodded. 'How far does the port extend?'

'Fifty miles. It's a very big port, and'—Tommy had told him about this—'there are prostitutes sitting in shop-windows, just like playthings.'

'Like playthings!' the other exclaimed delightedly.

Basil finished his beer. After a moment the man asked, 'And being lonely here doesn't get you down?'

'Well, you see,' Basil said evasively, 'I've just arrived.'

'It's got everything, this town.'

'Really?'

'Are you interested?' asked Carlo, bending forward.

Basil made a vague gesture. Carlo looked at him for a moment. 'A girl of eighteen, perhaps? Very pretty, very expert . . . Would that do you?'

Good Lord, so that's what it's all about, thought Basil. What a fool I am . . . 'I'm afraid . . .' he began.

'Very clean,' the other put in hurriedly. 'And we could agree about the price. A hundred *lire* for an hour, one hundred and fifty for two hours. Is that too much?'

'From your description, no. But women, you know, just now . . .'

Carlo gave him a quick glance. 'Yes, I see,' he said thoughtfully. 'I've two young lads, cousins of mine,' he murmured. 'One's fourteen and the other's fifteen . . .'

Good God, Basil thought. This man is rather a disgusting beast but I'm still thirsty and want another cigarette.

'How about a mixture?' he suddenly asked. 'Would that be possible?'

'A mixture?'

'Yes, a mixed group.' Basil smiled. 'I've a couple of friends . . .'

'Ah, I see.'

'Let's discuss that, shall we? D'you happen to have another cigarette?'

The man hastened to hand him the pack.

'And,' said Basil, settling down on his chair, 'supposing we had another couple of beers . . .'

The café was full of people, noise and smoke. Mattei pushed his way to the bar and squeezed in between a *bersagliere* and a soldier eating a salami sandwich.

'*Prego?*' the bar-waiter asked Mattei.

'Is Federico here?'

The waiter was short and bald. He lowered one eyelid, and looked Mattei up and down. 'Who are you?'

'A friend of Colombani.'

'Which Colombani?'

'The right one,' said Mattei.

'Did he send you here?'

'Yes.'

The waiter nodded towards the end of the room. 'He's with someone.'

An old gramophone record was playing, and Mattei recognised the tune—*Sous les ponts de Paris,* Italian style.

'Tell him it's urgent,' he said.

'You having a drink?'

'Not right now.'

'I'll go and tell him.'

The waiter sauntered towards the back room and Mattei looked around the café filled with untidy Italian soldiers and a few civilians. It looked exactly like all those dives along the Mediterranean seaboard which endure every disaster and serve as a refuge for army deserters, a letter-box for secret service agents, a hideout for men on the run, and a market for smugglers and gun-runners. Mattei felt at home. And quite safe since the police shut their eyes to these dives. There must be four or five concealed exits, at least as many double partitions, and a dozen rooms where anyone could go with a woman for a few *lire*.

The waiter came back. 'I told him,' he said. 'What'll you have?'

'Nothing. I'm dead broke. But if you feel like offering me a drink on the house, I wouldn't say no.'

The waiter held Mattei's look and shrugged.

'Will he see me?' Mattei asked.

'Yes,' said the waiter.

Mattei was tired, thirsty, and wanted a cigarette. The music had stopped.

'It's you who's come from Colombani,' someone said.

Mattei turned and saw a tall man in soiled shorts and a string vest. He had the face of an ex-boxer, and his stomach bulged over the top of his shorts.

'Yes, me,' said Mattei.

'Come over there.' The other nodded towards the back room.

'*Ciaou*, Federico,' said a man at a table as they passed.

'*Ciaou*, Renaldo,' the other replied.

He pushed open a door and stepped into a dim room that opened onto a narrow courtyard. There were crates of bottles and boxes stashed in the corners and packs of English cigarettes lying all over the floor. Federico picked up a packet and split it open with his thumb.

'First class,' he said. 'D'you want one?'

Mattei took a Benson and Hedges. 'Remember to scrounge a pack,' he told himself. 'It would make Basil happy.' He was surprised at himself for thinking of this.

Federico gave him a light and then sat down heavily. Mattei looked around the room which smelled of cheap perfume. A leather couch stood along one wall with a pair of silk stockings draped on one corner. Federico smiled as he sucked at a hollow tooth.

'I was with someone,' he said.

'Sorry to have disturbed you.'

'I'd finished, anyway. If you feel like it, the girl's still around.'

'I'm dead broke,' said Mattei.

Federico looked at him closely. 'So Colombani sent you?'

'Yes.'

'Describe him to me.'

'On the plump side, going bald, and getting short-sighted too. He wears steel-rimmed spectacles to read with, but otherwise doesn't use them. He's got a daughter, Rosina, who went to a convent school in Tripoli. At the moment he's working a racket with a couple of guys who live on Djerba and come over here now and again.'

Federico nodded approvingly. 'You know a lot.'

'One of the guys is me.'

'Ah,' said Federico. 'I thought you'd been arrested.'

'You're well informed.'

Federico smiled. 'News travels fast. Especially when it's bad . . . those cigarettes in your last load came from here.'

'The army must be enjoying them now.'

'Not only the cigarettes. I've got news for you.'

Mattei's chest tightened.

'Your boat,' said Federico.

'Ah.'

'The coastguard boarded her this morning.'

Mattei nodded slowly and felt completely numb.

'It's a hard blow,' said Federico. 'Was any of the stuff on board?'

'No, we hadn't started loading.'

'Well, that's something. They've brought the boat here.'

'And Colombani?'

'So far he's not been questioned . . . Someone ratted on you, it seems.'

Renata, thought Mattei. She didn't hold out.

'Got someone in mind?' Federico asked.

'Yes. But I can't hold it against her.'

'The Vanucci girl?'

'Yes. They must have made her talk.'

Mattei's thoughts filled with the methods used by the Fascist police. They must have gone beyond the limit of what a person could endure to make Renata talk. 'And you're responsible for it,' he said to himself. 'If you hadn't escaped, they'd have probably left her alone.'

'Help yourself,' said Federico, pushing a glass and a bottle of White Horse whisky towards Mattei. 'You've been lucky.'

'You think so?'

'You're here,' Federico said matter of factly. Then, since Mattei said nothing, he asked, 'Was your boat worth a lot?'

'That's not the most serious thing at the moment.' Mattei poured himself some whisky. 'What's the port like here?'

Federico shook his head. 'Nothing doing in that line. The *Tedeschi* have landed here, you know? *Verboten* everywhere. Their Field police are guarding the docks. Yesterday evening they shot a couple of beggars who always slept in one of the warehouses.'

Mattei had not been impressed by Federico at first but he was beginning to feel that he could trust this rather stout, flabby fellow.

Federico stabbed his thumb towards the ceiling. 'You can hide up there until things settle down again.'

'I've told you, I'm dead broke.'

'Don't worry. I've a dozen deserters here, and the police never call. Except Colombani . . . and then he comes in plain clothes.'

'Thanks,' said Mattei. 'It's a possibility.'

'For you only,' added Federico, raising his glass with a hand that only had three fingers. 'You are by yourself, aren't you?'

'There's an English officer with me.'

Federico made a face. 'A week ago I'd have said bring your Englishman along too. But now . . .' He waved his mutilated hand.

'Sure,' said Mattei. 'Forget it. Got any other ideas?'

'The small fishing-ports to the east. I've got friends there.' Federico pointed at the cigarettes and the whisky. 'They got all that for me out of an English ship that went aground. They could take you to Djerba.'

The two were silent for a moment.

'The hideout up above,' Federico said. 'You can have it when you want. Right away, if necessary.' He smiled. 'I've been in jail too. Four years on the Lipari islands.'

'Political?'

'You're joking. Do I look like the sort of guy who'd get mixed up in politics?'

'No,' Mattei said laughingly. 'How did you know I'd been in prison?'

Federico scratched his stomach. 'It wasn't Colombani who told me. How many years?'

'Five. For assault and battery. Manslaughter in fact.'

'And you were a boxer, right? Me too.' Federico smiled. 'You can stay as long as you like in the hideout up there. If you get bored, I'll send you up a girl. Eat and screw, that's all you'll have to do.'

'You tempt me.'

'I've confidence in you. And besides . . . we could come to an arrangement later, the two of us.'

'I'm done for,' said Mattei.

'Not at Djerba. And I'm not done for here.' Federico shook

his head and smiled. 'I've heard much about you,' he added. 'It's a pleasure to know you.'

I could lay up here for a few days, Mattei was thinking. But he knew he would never do it. He thought of Lorena. He would never see her again if he stayed here. He had caused one woman, Renata, great pain. That was enough. He couldn't leave those two now, especially Lorena. She had helped him and he liked to repay his debts.

He drained his glass and put it on the table. 'I'll try to get back by sea,' he said.

'All right. What d'you need?'

'Gas, first of all.'

'There's no shortage of that. Can you come back at about six?'

'Yes,' said Mattei.

'The best place for you to head tonight is Misurata. Ask for Carlo Antonielli. He keeps a café down by the harbour. I'll give you the rest of the details later on.'

'Sounds fine,' said Mattei.

The other smiled. 'There's a man I've worked with in each of the fishing-ports east of here, and nearly all of them keep a café. You've only to say I sent you, or Colombani did. However,' he added, shaking his head, 'that's not taking you nearer to Djerba.'

'I know.' Mattei got up.

'If I see Colombani, what shall I say?' asked Federico.

'Nothing. You haven't seen me. One never knows which way the wind's going to turn.'

'You're right.'

'I trust him,' said Mattei. 'But things can happen.'

'True,' said Federico with a smile.

'Can you let me have two packs of cigarettes?'

'Take a carton.'

'Two packs will do.'

Mattei slipped the cigarettes into the pocket of his pants.

'See you later,' he said.

26

Amedée-Jean had been sitting in the café for a good hour and had just finished the bottle of *grappa*. He felt nothing now. The events of the morning seemed so far away and he was completely indifferent to the consequences.

He got up slowly and left the café. The air was close and the hot gusts of wind wrapped around him like wool.

His shirt was damp with perspiration yet Amedée-Jean walked briskly along the Via Cavour.

As he was about to cross the street, a soldier with his hands shoved deep in his pockets suddenly turned and bumped into him.

'Can't you look where you're going!' Amedée-Jean let fly in Italian.

'Pipe down, dad,' said the soldier. 'I didn't know you were right behind me.'

'Haven't you been taught to take your hands out of your pockets when you're speaking to someone!' he barked.

The soldier took his hands out, avoiding Amedée-Jean's gaze.

'. . . And to apologise!'

Amedée-Jean wanted to grab this man by the lapels of his jacket and shake the breath out of him.

'I'm sorry,' the soldier muttered.

'Sir,' Amedée-Jean prompted him.

Two or three passers-by stopped and Amedée-Jean felt their gaze.

'I'm sorry, sir,' the soldier said.

'All right, that'll do this time.'

Amedée-Jean crossed the road and pushed open the door of the leather-goods shop. It banged against the wall.

'I'm coming,' Anita called from upstairs.

'It's me!' shouted Amedée-Jean.

'Good heavens, Amedée-Jean!' she exclaimed.

He heard her footsteps hurriedly coming down the spiral staircase. His heart was pounding and the pulsing of his blood made it difficult to keep his balance.

'I'm late,' he said, then added, '. . . a spot of trouble.'

She came towards him and he noticed that her eyes were bloodshot, and that her face wore an excited rapturous look that he had never seen before.

'Your wife's just left!'

Amedée-Jean was too shocked to speak.

'She told me everything,' Anita added.

'What did she come here for?'

'I lent her some money for . . . for those escaped prisoners . . .'

Amedée-Jean's feeling of indifference was disappearing as he was engulfed by Anita's wild eyes.

'She told me about your decision,' began Anita, wringing her hands nervously. 'About your divorce . . . she told me that you had been very frank and brave—those were her own words— and that . . .'

'But,' said Amedée-Jean, trying desperately to understand this woman's words, 'were those men with her?'

'No, she was going back to join them.'

Anita suddenly cried out and threw herself into his arms. 'Oh Amedée-Jean, you're wonderful!'

He stared blindly at the leather handbags hanging above the counter. Her hair brushed his lips and he felt the warmth of her breasts beneath her thin red blouse.

'You're . . . you're . . .' she tried to say.

'Steady,' he said. 'Steady.'

'Forget it all,' he told himself. 'Stop thinking about the Italian and the German headquarters, the two escaped prisoners, Lorena, and Stein's report to Berne.'

Anita raised her head. 'You smell like you've been drinking.'

'I had some *grappa*. I needed a pick-me-up.'

His hands slid down to her hips and he drew her close. He kissed her and her lips parted slowly.

'I needed it,' he said. 'I went to see Stein about this affair . . .'

'Is it serious?'

'Serious enough. But I don't care.'

'Really?'

'I don't give a damn.'

A heavy truck rumbled past and shook the shop window.

'It doesn't matter anymore,' he said. 'Let's not stay here.'

'Just a moment . . .' She slipped away and locked the street door. 'Come upstairs,' she said.

He followed her and at the top of the stairs he suddenly put his arms around her waist and kissed her neck. He moved his hands up gently and cupped her uplifted breasts. Her head dropped back onto his shoulder and he felt her nipples stiffen, and she moaned softly.

'We mustn't . . .' Anita said.

'What mustn't we do?'

'Oh . . .' She was huddling against him now, responding to the pressure of his body. 'Oh, I don't know . . . How did you tell her?'

'What?'

'Well, all that . . . about me, us.'

'Do we have to talk about that just now?'

'I'm so happy,' she said.

'I couldn't go on lying any more. And things happened which made it . . . made it much easier.'

'That's not true,' she said. 'You were so brave. I'll never forget it.'

She put her hands over Amedée-Jean's and gently lowered them. 'Come along,' she said, and pushed open the bedroom door.

Lorena's gone, thought Amedée-Jean. She's left with those two renegades. And I had to hear it from Anita. I'm not sure I really wanted this to happen.

'But why did she tell you this?' he asked.

'Why shouldn't she have?' Anita replied with a smile.

He shrugged and then adjusted his voice: 'I wanted to tell you myself . . .'

'That's what she said. And she also . . .' Anita hesitated.

'Yes?'

'Oh, nothing. She was very pleasant about everything.'

Amedée-Jean was silent. Suddenly he thought, perhaps I'll never see my wife again.

'What are we going to do?' Anita asked.

'We'll have to wait and see . . . Did she say where she was going?'

'She spoke of Tunisia, I think.'

And supposing she's killed, he thought. He remembered Stein telling him that a German officer had been shot. But he must stop thinking about Stein, about Lorena, about this war.

'I can come here every night now,' he said.

'Yes, I know . . . My poor darling, how hot you are. Would you like to take a shower?'

Amedée-Jean made no reply. He was looking at Anita intensely.

'You know,' she said, 'I felt sure you'd have a talk with her. We had such an argument the other evening on the phone. You seemed so irritated . . .'

'I was. That dinner with those Italian officers was unbearable.' He laughed. 'I could hear those escaped prisoners walking above our heads and one of the Italians was saying, "In my opinion, these men can't be far away".'

'You're amazing,' said Anita.

'I could hardly keep a straight face.'

'You really are amazing. I can just imagine you. And your wife?'

'Oh, she took it all very calmly. One must grant her that . . .'

'What did you tell her about me?'

'Later,' said Amedée-Jean, pulling off his tie.

27

When Mattei returned to the Oldsmobile he found Lorena sitting in the back seat, one leg stretched out and the other coiled underneath her, sucking an orange.

He opened the door and heaved himself into the front seat.

'Help yourself,' said Lorena, remaining as she was. 'There's some oranges next to you.'

Mattei looked at the string-bag full of fruit and cooked-meats. 'Later on,' he said. 'Did you manage all right?'

'Yes.'

'What do I smell?' Mattei asked.

'The salami probably.'

'No, it's not that. A different sort of smell.'

'Soap, then. As soon as I got the money, I went to the public baths in the Via Savoia. I was beat. And how about you?'

'I've bad news.' He stared at the narrow street in front of him.

'What?'

'They've pinched my boat.'

'Oh no. How did it happen?'

'I've no idea. Renata must have talked. They succeeded in making her talk. I'd rather not think how.'

'And the gas?'

'We'll have what we want later this afternoon.'

'I'm terribly sorry about Renata,' she said.

He met her eyes in the rear view mirror. She looked rested and her hair was shiny and clean.

'To make her talk,' he said, 'they must have done some awful things.'

'I understand.'

'No, you can't possibly understand.' He turned around. 'Forty-eight hours ago, we were in bed together. It was just a light-hearted affair between us. We saw each other, we made love. But it didn't matter that much if we didn't see each other.'

'I understand,' she said.

A silence fell between them.

'I'm coming with you,' she said abruptly.

'You've made up your mind?'

'Yes.'

'This is a fine time to decide that. We've got to go at least as far as Misurata to find a boat.'

'But that's two hundred kilometers.'

'One hundred and ninety-eight,' said Mattei.

'And what is there at Misurata?'

'A guy who can take us to Djerba. What made you decide to come with us?'

She hesitated. 'Well, I can't go back now.'

'You can always go back in your kind of life.'

'Then let's say I've acted impulsively.'

He looked round at her again. 'It's damn stupid.'

'Maybe, but so what.'

She tossed the orange out of the window and watched it roll down the street. A cat sprang out of a doorway, stared at the orange and then tapped it with its paw. The orange moved slightly and the cat leapt at it with claws outstretched and shook it playfully.

Mattei thought of Renata, of her body and her throaty voice which grew deeper as their love-making became more passionate. It would be senseless to risk going to Misurata, he told himself. It would be far better to take advantage of Federico's offer.

'You've got to make up your mind. Maybe you can only get out of this by yourself. Anything can happen between here and Misurata, but Federico's place means safety at least for a while.'

The cat suddenly leapt back, arched its back and began to strut slowly round the orange.

'What time is it?' Mattei asked.

'About five-thirty.'

'What the hell is Ferguson doing?'

If he's been caught, thought Mattei, that makes everything

simple. I'd rather send this woman back home or take her to Federico's with me. There are worse ways of passing the time. She'd probably be good in bed.

He did not want to look around again but knew she was still sitting with her slacks stretched tightly over her parted thighs which emphasised her hips and the roundness of her belly.

'This is the worst situation you've ever been in,' he said to himself, 'yes, the worst, and why are you thinking of this woman as a woman. If the Englishman doesn't come back . . .'

'It's time he was here,' he said aloud.

'Perhaps he's been delayed.'

'Or caught.'

'You sound almost hopeful,' Lorena said gently.

'At the worst, he'd be a prisoner for a few years. So what?' Lorena remained silent, and Mattei went on : 'That'd give him a chance to put his blasted casualness to the test. And besides, in wartime being in prison is the common fate. It's in peacetime that it's tough. When everyone else is free.'

'How long were you in prison?'

'Five years.'

Mattei turned around. His eyes travelled slowly from her sturdy shoulders to her parted thighs.

'What for?' she said offhandedly.

'Manslaughter.'

'Oh? Through negligence?'

'That's what my counsel pleaded.'

A slight breeze carried the smell of seaweed and fuel-oil to them.

'I meant to kill him,' said Mattei. 'And I did.'

She held his gaze. 'There's no need to be apologetic. After all, you've killed a man in front of my eyes, and it's quite obvious that you're no saint. What was it like?'

'What?'

'In jail.'

'Rotten.' He suddenly felt very old and tired. 'Eighteen hundred days without a woman,' he added.

'Tell me about it.' She changed her position and crossed her legs.

He was silent for a moment or two. I've never spoken about it to anyone, he thought. Not because I didn't want to, but because I've never felt the need.

'It was in Marseilles,' he said. 'I was a heavyweight boxer at the time. Pretty good, I think. Probably with a future. Anyway, I'd had thirty fights and never been dropped for a count. I had money. Not much, but at the time it seemed enormous. And I had a girl too. Not just any girl. Her name was Claire . . .'

'Like your boat?'

'Yes, like my boat.'

He offered her a cigarette and noticed that his hands were shaking. Fool, he thought, sentimental fool.

'She wasn't just any girl,' he said. 'She was a bit of a bitch, but it's impossible for you to understand what it meant for a guy with my background to have a girl like that . . . the footman sleeping with the daughter of the house, if you see what I mean. But that's how it was. My old man worked in the quarries, and I started the same way. Hewing stone out of a quarry develops muscles but not fine feelings. But she . . .'

Lorena was listening with obvious interest, yet not unduly curious; with a wooden face, as he had expected. He drew on his cigarette, and continued.

'She belonged to one of the wealthy, influential families over there . . . We became lovers, that wasn't very difficult. She was that kind of girl. And after all, it would have ended sometime. We'd have got tired of each other. She more quickly than me. But as things turned out . . . What time is it now?'

'Twenty to six.'

'What the hell is he up to?'

'Go on,' she said.

'Well, I'd had a fight two days before. Against Colomani. A very hard fight. The bastard had given me a pasting. A vicious guy, and with a jaw like concrete. And then that evening, Claire and me went out together. To a concert. I didn't know a thing about music . . .'

He saw Lorena smiling, and smiled back.

'It was Brahms, I think . . . I had a cracked rib and swollen lips, and all I did during this concert was shift about in my seat to find a comfortable position. She was a well-educated girl and you can't believe what she knew about this Brahms. When we left the concert hall—full of women in evening dress and jewels and men in black like undertakers, me too—when we left, we met some of her friends and went to have a drink. They were all talking about the concert, and I didn't have a thing to say. I felt like a damn fool but knew in an hour I'd be screwing this girl and Brahms and his concerto wouldn't matter. I'd be the one in charge. There was a guy there, Patrice somebody'—it's a fact, he thought, I really have forgotten his name—'and he was the one I'd taken Claire from. And he was there with some friends, three or four of them. They were all the sort who talk in a high and mighty way, you know, because they've been used to giving orders since the cradle —first to their nurse, then to their governess, and then to poor fellows like me that they've had as orderlies, workmen or flunkies. They were drinking a lot, and so was I . . .'

Mattei stopped. He was sweating. Sweating out memories, he thought. He did not know why he had started talking like this, but it was far from disagreeable. He liked the way she listened in her cool distant manner. Like Claire, he thought.

'I've forgotten how it all started,' he went on. 'I was in a bad mood, I know that. And I don't know what the other guy was after—trying to get Claire back, perhaps, or to make me look like a fool in front of her. It wasn't very difficult, anyone like me would be very touchy. Anyway, they started in on me . . .'

'What do you mean?' said Lorena.

'Taking the piss out of me. It took me a little while to realise this but when I did . . . We ended up on the pavement outside. There were five of them, four or five anyway, and Claire was there too. Looking on. She liked that, I think, to have men fighting over her.'

And in his mind he was back again on the pavement which was wet from the rain and he could smell the dampness that hung everywhere. He was fighting with just one of them—that tall, casual, elegant young man, half a head taller than himself—and the others were looking on with amused smiles. He, Mattei, had simply ducked the punches at first, smiling and pretending that the whole thing was a joke—until the other's fist caught him above the eye where Colomani had opened a cut two days before. He felt the blood running down his face and dropped heavily to his knees.

'Go on, Charles!' someone shouted.

The other swung a left hook as Mattei rose to his feet and he stumbled backwards from the blow. Then he caught sight of Patrice's amused grin and of the torn sleeve of his tuxedo—his new tuxedo, the first he had ever had. He lost all control of himself, lunging forward and hitting where he knew a punch could kill. He felt a keen pleasure as his fist crashed into the man's windpipe, crushing the cartilages; then he pounded at the face as it went blue from suffocation. Impervious to the others who were trying to drag him away, he hit Patrice again and again. Suddenly he broke away and fled through the narrow streets as the others chased him and shouted murderer....

'And he died?' said Lorena.

'Yes,' said Mattei, astonished that he had been speaking aloud to this woman with the green acute stare. 'Then later, there was the trial.'

'And the woman?'

'She wasn't a witness. Her family sent her off to Morocco. I was sent up for eight years but the sentence was reduced. Afterwards, I had to leave Marseilles and just wandered all over the place. When the war broke out, I was in Holland under a false name.'

'What were you doing there?' Lorena asked.

'What d'you think?'

'A bit of everything.'

'Exactly. And even a little more. Well, there you are.'

Lorena smiled. 'And here's Basil.'

He had just appeared around the corner, strolling along like a tourist.

'I've spent,' he said, falling into the seat next to Mattei, 'a most delightful afternoon.'

'Good for you,' said Mattei. 'We thought you'd been caught.'

'Really? I've been with an Italian pimp who thought I was a German journalist from Hamburg. He bought me lots of drinks, gave me cigarettes, and offered me a Syrian dancing-girl of eighteen and two of his young cousins. Twenty-five years between them.'

'Oh really,' said Lorena.

Mattei said nothing. He was irritated that Basil and Lorena belonged to a world in which things were treated so lightly, a world where all was amusing and for amusement....

'Don't worry,' said Basil, 'I only had the cigarettes and the drinks, and I'm half drunk. Now don't look like that, Mattei. Does it annoy you so much to see me come back?'

'Only a little.'

'It's odd,' Basil said in a plaintive tone, 'but the beer has made me fearless. Would you like me to give myself up?'

'That's probably the best thing you can do,' replied Mattei and then told him of the latest developments.

'This new idea of going to Misurata,' said Basil, 'takes us right away from Djerba, doesn't it?'

'On the whole, yes.' Then Mattei added, 'Mrs. Dalloz has decided to come with us.'

Basil and Lorena said nothing. Mattei went on: 'You haven't told us about getting out of this town.'

'It's quite easy. There's no check. Neither on civilian or army vehicles. This Misurata business—are you serious about it?'

Mattei gave a shrug. 'I'll tell you when we get there. If we ever do. It's a risk, but we've taken plenty since yesterday, and bigger ones.'

You still don't know exactly what you want to do, Mattei thought. What's scaring you? What they'd say about you?

'Let's get going,' he said. 'We're late as it is.'

28

Mattei elbowed his way through the crowd that was being held back by a line of Italian police armed with truncheons.

The street was teeming with army trucks, helmeted *Feldgendarmen,* and Italian and German officers. Shouts and the sounds of breaking furniture were coming from the café.

Merde, thought Mattei, *merde et re-merde.*

'What's going on?' he asked the man next to him, a short perspiring Sicilian.

'It's the *Tedeschi.* Their police aren't so patient as ours ...'

'Get back! Get back there!' shouted a plump sergeant. The Italian policemen immediately linked arms and moved forward, forcing the crowd back. As the sergeant turned, Mattei recognised Colombani buttoned up tightly in his uniform.

The door of the café flew open and six men came out with their hands clasped behind their necks. The Germans followed, urging their prisoners on with the butts of their revolvers.

'Schnell!' they yelled. *'Alle heraus!'* The six men, made up of civilians and Italian soldiers in ragged uniforms, started to run towards a covered army truck with its tailboard down.

Colombani mopped his face with a large handkerchief and spotted Mattei.

One of the prisoners stopped and called to the Italian officers. *'Per favore, maggiore, per favore.'* A German hit him in the face with his revolver and the man fell to the ground, his hands over his head.

'Scum!' yelled the Sicilian.

'Traitors!' yelled another onlooker. 'Dirty Commies, the whole lot of them!' Then he stood on tiptoe and shouted, 'Death to the Reds!'

'*Basta, basta,*' snapped Colombani. His big face was shining as he approached Mattei and gave him a discreet wink.

'Death to all traitors!' shouted a man behind Mattei.

'I didn't know you were here,' said Colombani in a low voice. 'I thought you were somewhere else.'

'I was,' said Mattei.

'Then go back there. Did you have something to do here?'

'Yes. But not now. What's going on?'

Mattei had raised his voice with this question and the Sicilian answered. 'The Germans came to pick up Federico . . . He won't get away with it this time. He's not well in with the *Tedeschi* . . .'

'Precisely,' nodded Colombani.

The *Feldgendarmen* had closed the tailboard and the prisoners were leaning out of the back shouting and waving their arms, appealing to the small group of Italian officers. Now the screams of women came from the café.

Mattei and Colombani moved a few steps away from the Sicilian. 'Renata?' Mattei asked.

Colombani shook his head gently. Judging by his puffed eyes and ashen complexion, he had not had much sleep recently.

'Is she here?'

'In Tripoli, yes,' said Colombani, glancing towards his men. 'At the military police.' He spoke calmly as though giving news of a niece who was taking a vacation.

'I've heard that the *Santa Clara* is here too,' said Mattei.

'That's right.'

'Here come the girls!' shouted the Sicilian. 'Oh what lovely whores!'

Several young women, their hair tousled, barefoot and wearing bright dressing-gowns, were brought out. They were all screaming as the *Feldgendarmen* pushed them roughly forward. One of them slid to the ground; a German hauled her up by the arm and her dressing-gown fell open, revealing her large well-formed breasts.

'She's got nothing on!' yelled the Sicilian.

'And Renata?' Mattei asked Colombani. 'D'you know what they did to make her talk?'

'It's Carolina!' shouted another onlooker. 'Hey, fellers, get an eyeful of Carolina's buds!'

Colombani looked straight at Mattei. 'Don't think about Renata. Think about yourself and clear out of here.'

Two *Feldgendarmen* were dragging the screaming Carolina towards the truck.

'What a temper that Carolina has,' said the Sicilian. 'Now there's a woman for you!'

'Get out of here,' Colombani said again, in a low but direct tone. 'Don't stay in this town.' Mattei remained silent. 'I can't do anything for you,' added Colombani.

Not only won't you do anything, Mattei thought, but if you could bump me off so there'd be no fear of me talking, you'd do it at once.

Colombani looked old and worn and Mattei realised that he was terrified about his own future.

'So long,' said Mattei, moving away.

Colombani looked at him blankly. 'See you again sometime, perhaps.'

Mattei turned and made his way through the crowd.

Basil and Lorena were waiting for him in the Oldsmobile which was parked near the Banco Commerciale di Torino. Mattei got in behind the wheel without saying a word. The other two looked at him.

'Well?' said Basil.

'Nothing doing. We've got to get out of here.'

'How about gas?' Lorena asked.

'We'll get it somewhere else.'

He had no idea where. He thought of Federico with his sad, dark eyes and bulging stomach. Perhaps he'd had time to get away.

He switched on the engine.

'I've just seen Colombani,' he said.

'Who's Colombani?' Basil asked.

'The cop who was waiting for me on the beach.'

'A charming fellow,' said Basil, turning round to Lorena.

'I wouldn't say that,' said Mattei. 'If he met you now, he'd shoot first and ask questions later.'

He came to the Via Balbo and turned left.

'If I've got it right . . .' Basil suddenly began.

'Exactly. If you'd arrived back on time, we'd have probably been in Federico's when the police raided the place . . .'

'There, you see.' Basil was all smiles. 'And I didn't do it on purpose.'

'One of these days,' said Mattei, 'one of these days you'll turn up on time and . . .' He snapped his fingers. 'How do you manage it? I'd like to know how it's done.'

'It just happens. I drift on quite happily—or if you prefer, I take things as they come. The convoy I came out on was attacked three times by U-boats. And the ship I missed sailing on was blown up a hundred miles out from Gibraltar . . . It just occurred to me now.'

'Who made you late?' asked Lorena.

'No one. I missed the train. I could have caught it if I'd hurried. But I felt certain that the next train would still get me to the ship in time. At least, I thought so. And anyway, I didn't much care either way.'

Mattei stopped the Oldsmobile in the shade of some palm-trees near the end of the avenue. Ahead of them was the gateway and the guard post.

'Is this where you were?'

'Yes,' said Basil, and pointed to the café under the arcades. 'That's where I was sitting with the pimp.'

Mattei's head was aching and he felt exhausted. He folded his arms on the wheel and closed his eyes.

'Want me to drive?' asked Basil.

'Wait a bit.'

'Are you all right?' Lorena asked.

'Whacked,' said Mattei.

He needed peace and quiet far from all the noise of traffic and people that now surrounded him. But he felt sure that he'd find a way out of this too. It was not so much the check-point ahead that worried him but the fact that he was being imperceptibly drawn farther and farther away from Djerba . . . as if by a magnet, as if everything was at work to keep him from his destination.

He looked up. The daylight was beginning to fade and the yellowish clouds seemed thicker and heavier.

The other two said nothing but he could feel their uneasiness.

In slow motion, as if his actions were weighed down by the heavy sultry atmosphere, he switched on the engine again.

'Would you like me to . . .' Basil began.

'No,' snapped Mattei. He angrily shoved the car into

gear and they moved forward slowly. 'Here we go,' he said.

But no one paid any attention to them as they drove through the gate.

'There, what did I tell you,' said Basil.

'Oh, shut up, will you,' snapped Mattei.

And he started down the road to Homs, the road to the east.

29

Lorena had driven along this road two or three times during the summer of 1940. She remembered an army fuel dump somewhere south of Homs and about forty miles east of Tarhouna.

'You're sure about that?' said Mattei.

'Yes,' she replied. 'But you reach it by a branch road and I'm not sure which direction.'

On a good road, Mattei thought, there would be enough gas to get them as far as Homs. Since Lorena had no vouchers it would be impossible to obtain gas at any of the coastal road stations. In any case, all the stocks of gas had most likely been requisitioned for the German army convoys on their way to Sirte. Also, the gas stations would certainly have an army guard.

'The annoying thing is,' said Basil, 'that it's going to take us out of our way again.'

'What's another fifty miles,' Mattei retorted.

Night had fallen and they had turned off the road to have something to eat and drink. They were about a hundred yards from the coast road and watched as a single truck or a convoy rumbled along with their headlights illuminating only the roadway. Also, the singing of the convoy soldiers broke the silence of the desert night.

They ate the salami with thick, rather chalky biscuits, and then had some cheese and fruit with beer. Their dinner was shrouded in darkness and they ate eagerly in this nocturnal security.

The night air brought a welcome release from the sun's heat but the clouded sky warned of the coming *khâmsin*.

'Perhaps not before tomorrow,' said Mattei. 'What did you come around here for, you and your husband?'

'To see the Roman remains.'

'Are there any?' Basil asked.

'Quite a lot. Especially near the coast.'

'Temples?'

'Yes, and amphitheatres,' said Lorena. 'Also, ruined reservoirs are all over the desert, usually near a wadi to collect rainwater. We took some photos . . . Wait, we also found a Roman tomb, it was near the fuel dump.'

'Would it be on the map?' Mattei asked.

'It might be. But it certainly was no work of art.'

Mattei went to the car and fumbled around for the map. 'Come over here and make a screen for me,' he said.

'Who's got the matches?'

'I have,' Basil answered.

'Lorena,' said Mattei and hesitated for a moment since it was the first time he had called her that, 'keep an eye on the road. Basil, cover me.'

Basil took off his blazer and held it behind Mattei as he struck a match and followed the road with his finger.

'I think we've gone about thirty miles since leaving Tripoli,' Basil said, looking at the speedometer.

The match went out and Mattei struck another. 'I can see a little circle marked in this area, but there's nothing to indicate that it's a Roman tomb. A track leads to it, which is something . . .'

The second match went out. Lorena tapped on the windshield. 'Trucks coming,' she said, and joined them inside the car. They listened to the throb of heavy engines coming from the west, then dim lights appeared and a dozen trucks swept past.

'Italians,' said Mattei. 'Now, your Roman tomb, was it before or after the fuel dump?'

'After, I'm positive. Have you found something?'

'I think so. We'll have to go on for another six or seven miles, and then there's a track off to the right. But we better wait for dawn.'

'What exactly are you thinking of doing?' asked Basil.

'I don't know yet . . . If Lor . . . if Mrs. Dalloz goes and asks for some gas, they might fill the tank for her.'

The wind rose suddenly and the rumble of the disappearing convoy was carried back on the strong gusts.

'Do we stay here for now?' said Basil.

'No, we'll go on as far as the track. Then we'll see.'

It was after ten when they reached the track veering off to the right. Basil, who was driving, had difficulty in following the track which was covered with sand and pitted with holes.

'At this rate,' he said, 'we'll be out of gas in half an hour.'

'Stop then,' said Mattei.

Basil parked on solid ground and switched off the engine.

'Does this track look familiar?' Mattei asked Lorena.

'No. But since I've lived here, I must have driven thousands of miles along desert tracks, and they're all very similar. Perhaps I'll recognise it when daylight comes.'

Basil gave a long yawn. 'I'm sleepy.'

'Well, go to sleep,' Mattei told him. 'Are there any blankets?'

'Yes, in the trunk,' said Lorena.

'There's room for two to sleep in here,' Mattei said. 'You, and one of us. Which?'

'We could toss for it,' Basil suggested.

'I don't have any money.'

'I do,' said Lorena. She fumbled in her trouser pocket and brought out a few coins.

Basil took one and spun it, calling 'Tails.' He caught it and smacked it down on the back of his hand. Mattei bent forward. 'You've won.'

'It's in my nature,' smiled Basil.

Mattei got out and took a blanket and the tarpaulin from the trunk. He could see no more than five yards ahead and stepped forward gingerly, testing the ground with his foot.

The wind was blowing in gusts again, bringing a dry, warm feeling to his face. He could hear Basil and Lorena talking. Spreading out the tarpaulin at the foot of a small sand-dune, he sat down and folded the blanket around him. He was not sleepy but welcomed the chance to stretch out and relax. Staring up at the sky, he lit a cigarette and inhaled slowly. His thoughts drifted towards Djerba. 'I'm getting farther and farther away from there,' he said to himself. 'Will I ever see it again?'

He stubbed out his cigarette in the sand, turned on his side and closed his eyes.

A crunching sound awoke him. He could not have been asleep for long, half an hour at the most. Raising his head, he peered into the night and was soon able to make out a figure moving slowly towards him.

'I'm over here,' he said, propping himself up on his elbow.

The figure turned in his direction.

'Here,' he said again.

She came and sat down near him, clasping her arms around her raised knees. 'I couldn't sleep. I wanted a cigarette and you have the matches.'

He took out the pack of Bensons and handed them to her. The match made her features teutonic below the yellow glow of hair.

'What's that?' she asked.

'An air-raid probably.'

Lorena got up and clambered to the top of the dune and Mattei followed her. They saw pink gleams low in the dark sky to the north-east.

'That's Homs.' Then looking back towards the car he asked, 'Is our friend asleep?'

'Yes,' said Lorena. 'It's odd how safe one feels here.'

'So quiet, eh?'

'With just enough sound to keep us aware that a war is going on.'

In the distance the pink flashes suddenly quickened.

'You don't feel too disheartened?' Lorena said gently.

'A bit. But I'm still alive.'

She laughed. 'Now own up . . .'

'What?'

'Own up that this afternoon you were ready to drop everything.'

'True. And if the occasion arises, I'd drop you two for good. Understand?'

'Yes.'

'I still don't understand why you stayed with us.'

'You and Basil came along just when things were coming to a crisis in my life . . .' She stopped, then went on in a more cheerful voice. 'You know, I have the feeling that we've no control over what happens to us—that things occur without any conscious action on our part. At least, that's how it is with me.'

The distant noise had ceased and now the sky over Homs was tinged with red. 'A fuel dump hit,' said Mattei.

'In Tripoli, I got the money from my husband's mistress,' Lorena blurted out.

'You've got some nerve. Besides, I'd never have thought your husband had a mistress.'

'Oh, he keeps it very secret. And I really don't hold it against him. But when I was with her . . . words came faster than thoughts. It seemed the ideal moment to make the break . . . No, not quite that. It all happened in spite of myself.'

'I see,' said Mattei, looking at the red glow above Homs. 'That's a good guide over there—we'll see the smoke tomorrow. We couldn't ask for a better compass.'

Silence fell between them. Mattei felt that Lorena was waiting for something and he looked at her closely as she stood with her back towards him.

His hand rose as if impelled by some force outside himself and wavered above her shoulder.

It can't be helped, he thought.

She made no move as his hand gently touched the back of her neck. Then he drew her slowly around towards him. Their eyes met but he could not make out her expression. He could smell her breath as his hands slid down her arms and rested on her hips. Then he lifted her sweater and felt her skin come alive under his touch. He drew her closer as his hands explored her back and rose to her damp armpits and then pushed softly at the rise of her breasts.

He could see her eyes now.

'I don't understand why I want you,' she murmured.

'Just relax,' he breathed.

His hands tightened around her firm breasts and then he lowered his head to suck at her nipples.

'Just relax,' he repeated softly. 'Let's just enjoy each other.'

She was lying on her back now, legs together and arms by her sides with Mattei stretched out next to her.

He put his hand to her waist and slipped his fingers under the belt of her slacks, feeling her soft belly rise and fall with her breathing. Then he pulled down the zipper and gently edged her slacks over her hips and down past her thighs. He sought her lips as she kicked her slacks off. His hand travelled up her legs to her opening thighs, his fingers revelling in the softness of the flesh. Her lips quivered as his hand reached the fork of her legs and she moaned softly. With sudden impatience he pulled down her cotton pants and stroked the pubic fleece. She arched her back, and her lips parted under his mouth.

'Don't hurt me,' she murmured.

He stood up quickly and undressed. He lay down beside her again, drawing her close to him and with patience and tenderness fondled her breasts, his penis erect between her thighs. Then he turned on top of her.

'Don't hurt me,' she murmured again softly.

He had pulled the blanket over them and was holding Lorena tightly in his arms.

She was breathing evenly now but she felt as if Mattei was still in her. The sky was dark above and the hot wind swept across the dune, sprinkling sand on them.

'What's your first name?' she said. 'I've forgotten.'

He laughed softly. 'François.'

'François,' she repeated. 'François the Frenchman.'

'That's it,' he said gaily. 'May I call you Lorena?'

'Yes, of course.'

'Lorena,' he repeated.

'Very good. You can speak English now.'

'I can say "Good-bye, good-morning, Churchill and Lorena".'

She smiled: 'It's a long time since . . .'

'I know. Did you really want a cigarette when you came out looking for me?'

'Right now, I'm not at all sure. But I think I did.'

'I thought it was Basil you were interested in.'

'I thought so . . . I'll leave you so you can get some sleep.'

'Don't go yet. I'm not tired.'

They were silent and listened to the distant heavy thuds that rolled like thunder through the air.

'What will you do at Djerba?' she asked.

'I'll see how things are. I might move to Tunis. I don't know. Anyway, I'm not there yet. And you?'

'I think I'll go back home.'

'Where's that—back home?'

'Phoenix.' She paused and then said, 'You know, I'm glad of what's happened.'

'I hope you'll still feel the same tomorrow.'

'I'm sure I will,' she said eagerly. Then after a moment she said: 'I'd forgotten that I have a body.'

'I'm sure you were the only one who had forgotten that.'

'Did you long to make love to me?'

He hesitated before replying. 'I haven't had time to think about it until just now. But yes, I was longing to . . .'

'Did you . . . ?'

'Shush,' he said. 'You ask too many questions.'

30

Basil was dreaming of being jammed in the Beaufighter between the crates of beer and beneath a dangling body. It was not Skinny's body but Julia's. She was dressed in black leather and she was smiling despite the gaping wound in her throat. Basil said to her: 'I can't move an inch because I missed my ship.' And she replied curtly: 'You must try, Calloway has jumped.' Basil saw that the pilot's seat no longer held Calloway but a small Quetzalcoatl statue. He tried to reach it, struggling with the crates that held him captive. He continued to push the crates madly, knowing the importance of getting to the statue before the plane plunged into the sea.

He woke up with a start, and it took a moment for him to realise that he was curled up on the front seat of the Oldsmobile with the handbrake sticking into his ribs and his arms resting on the steering-wheel. He sat up and saw a bleak greyish light spreading across the desert. He looked at Lorena still asleep in the back seat.

Quietly he opened the door and slipped out. He took an orange from the string-bag and clambered up to the track and walked along it a little way, sucking eagerly at his orange. All around was silence and the grey dawn. The sky in the north was flecked with black. Over Homs, he thought. But everywhere else stretched only the still billows of pebbly sand.

He went down the slope, which gave way under his feet, and saw Mattei with a blanket over his shoulders sitting below a sand-dune and smoking a cigarette. His black hair was ruffled and his face was dark with stubble.

'Hullo!' Basil called cheerfully.

' 'Morning. Sleep well?'

'Very well. Just a bit stiff.'

Basil looked at the ground and easily recognised Mattei's large footprints in the sand. But there were other smaller marks converging on the tarpaulin.

'Something's burning over there,' he said with a nod towards the column of smoke.

Mattei looked up. 'Yes, there was an air-raid during the night. Didn't you hear it?'

'No. I was asleep.'

Mattei smiled. He cast off the blanket and got up. 'We must keep that smoke in sight,' he said. 'It'll show us which way is north. Did you notice how much gas we have left?'

'There's about two gallons.'

Mattei made a face. 'That's running close. I hope we're on the right track.'

Mattei sat down again and put the blanket over his shoulders and watched Basil finish his orange.

Then they heard Lorena calling. 'Where are you?'

'Over here!' shouted Mattei.

She appeared on top of a dune and stood there with her hands on her hips.

'I know where we are,' she said. 'I recognise that tower over there. The dump can't be far off. A few miles.'

'Are you sure?' asked Basil.

The silence of the desert made their voices strangely distinct.

'Absolutely. We're going in the right direction.'

She ran down the slope in long strides.

'Good morning. You look like a couple of castaways.'

'We are,' said Mattei.

'The castaways of the Oldsmobile,' Basil added.

'Mattei,' she said, and something in her voice made Basil look at her with surprise, 'Mattei, anyone would take you for an old squaw.'

'I am an old squaw,' Mattei said in a tone that Basil did not recognise. 'Didn't you know? Weary, ugly as sin, and past caring.'

Lorena laughed. She rubbed her arms and suddenly sneezed twice.

'You'll catch cold,' said Mattei. 'Come over here.' He opened one side of the blanket. 'It's warm in here.'

Lorena's eyes shot towards Basil and she seemed to hesitate. Then she gave a slight shrug and went and sat by Mattei, who folded the blanket round her.

'You see,' he said.

'Yes, you're right.' She snuggled up against him.

'Good old animal warmth,' he said.

Basil saw that she was blushing.

'Did you notice that the fire's still burning over towards Homs?' she asked.

'Yes I did,' replied Mattei softly.

So that's it, thought Basil, gazing at the footprints again.

'When you've warmed up a bit,' said Mattei, 'we'll be on our way.'

The three of them were lying on top of the rocky mound. Daylight had come but the sky was overcast. The sun looked like a large tarnished silver coin as it tried desperately to break through the heavy clouds. The army fuel dump was about a hundred yards square and surrounded by barbed wire; the drums of gasoline were stacked in pyramids. A mud hut stood to the left with a sand-coloured truck parked in front under a tented tarpaulin.

'Can't see anyone,' said Lorena. 'They must be sleeping.'

'If these were normal times,' said Basil, 'I'd go and ask them to fill up the tank. It's the sort of thing that's done between civilised people.'

Lorena glanced at the two dirty, unshaven men. 'Yes, but you two don't look at all like civilised men.' She began to recite:

> ' "Half a league, half a league,
> Half a league onward,
> Through the valley of death
> Rode the Six Hundred."

Shall we charge down like at Balaclava?'

'I don't know what your Balaclava is, and anyway . . .'

'They all got killed,' Basil put in quietly. 'It was one of the more idiotic episodes in our military history.'

'I've no intention of getting killed,' said Mattei. 'Especially not here.'

'In that case,' said Lorena, 'I can see only one solution. I'll drive down there alone.' She turned to Basil. 'Imagine five or six

British army storekeepers in the same situation as that group down there. What would they do?'

'Failing gas, they'd give you some tea.'

Mattei and Basil stood by the Oldsmobile as Lorena got in behind the wheel. The track made a wide curve around the rocky mound before running down to the fuel dump.

'Well, see you later,' said Mattei.

He and Basil were going to follow her on foot.

'I'd like a cigarette,' she said.

Mattei lit one and then passed it to Lorena.

Basil felt annoyed at this childish show of intimacy.

'That ought to last you ten minutes,' Mattei said. 'See you in a little while.'

Stepping back from the car he waved and asked, 'Okay?'

'Yes,' she nodded.

She watched as the two men vanished behind the mound and then looked at herself in the rear view mirror. Bluish rings circled the bottom of her eyes and her lips were slightly puffed.

It's obvious, she thought. She felt a twinge in the pit of her belly—not quite a pain exactly, something else—and she knew she wanted Mattei again.

'Come off it, bitch,' she said to herself. 'Now is not the time to plan when you can again have him in you.' She thought of his eyes bearing down on her with their look of violence yet fleeting tenderness. So fleeting, in fact, that she didn't know whether she had only imagined it. It—what had occurred—was very different from what she had experienced with Amedée-Jean. With Boyd, on the other hand . . .

'You must be depraved. You don't enjoy sex in the marriage bed and most of all not in Swiss consulates.'

She clenched her knees together and shut her eyes. After drawing deeply on her cigarette, she looked up at the yellow, pebbly track curving in front of her.

A strong gust of wind blew sand in through the window, stinging her face. She rolled up the window and again felt a gnawing ache deep in her belly. Mattei, François Mattei, she thought. She remembered the silence before he had put his hand on the back of her neck. It had seemed so natural for him to turn her around and slide his hands up her body to her breasts. And yet she had not really been expecting it. She had been merely a lonely woman who had left behind a sterile existence and found that she was still a woman who could want and be wanted.

And supposing it had been Basil?

You can't say, she told herself. She stubbed out the cigarette in the ashtray, switched on the engine and drove off slowly.

Lorena stopped near the entrance to the dump, got out and looked at the heap of gasoline drums shining dully in the leaden light. The smell of smouldering wood came from a camp fire. Walking towards the hut, she looked up and saw a man standing in the doorway. He was tall and slim, with deep-set eyes; quite handsome, in fact. His shirt was open on his smooth, suntanned chest.

'You frightened me,' he said. 'I thought it was the *maggiore* come to inspect us.'

'I'm no *maggiore*,' Lorena said impassively.

'So I see,' he remarked. 'It's a pleasant surprise.'

She laughed. 'I've lost my way. I'm going to Homs.'

'If you get to Homs this way, my name's Adolf Hitler.'

'You don't look like him.'

The soldier laughed loudly. 'You're not German, are you? You've got some sort of accent...'

'No, I'm American.'

'*Mamma mia!* An American woman! And to think I had to come out here to meet one. You're the first American woman I've ever seen.'

'I'm flattered.'

'I'll go so far as to say you're the first woman I've seen since'— he flapped his hand—'the last one ... well, let's leave it at that.'

He winked at her in such a comic manner that Lorena could not help laughing.

'So you're American? My name's Sergio Passi. Sergeant Passi,' he added, drawing himself up lazily. 'At your service, *signora* ... *signorina* ... ?'

'Parker,' Lorena replied at once. '*Signorina* Parker.' And she was astonished at having called herself by her maiden name.

The sergeant held out a big, solid hand and she shook it. He looked down at her, and his blue eyes sparkled gaily. Everything's going to be all right, she thought.

'And what are you doing here?' he asked.

'I told you—I've lost my way.'

'Yes, but apart from that?'

'I belong to the American Agricultural Mission,' said Lorena.

'Agri . . . what?'

'Agricultural. And to tell you the truth, I need your help—I'm out of gas! Not a drop left.'

The sergeant broke into a hearty laugh. 'That's the craziest thing I've heard in a long time!'

'I can believe it.'

'But it's a lot funnier than you think!'

He pointed to the drums. 'There's not enough fuel there to fill a cigarette-lighter! Not even a tiny one.'

Lorena's heart sank. 'What d'you mean?'

'Povera Signorina! There hasn't been any gas at this dump for the past three months by order of the top brass. There are a lot of other phoney dumps like this one. The purpose is to keep the enemy from bombing the real dumps.'

The sergeant looked amused. 'Does it really matter?'

'Yes.'

There was silence.

'But then . . . your truck?' Lorena said finally. 'You have to have gas for that.'

'Just enough to go and fetch supplies once a week. But no more!' He made a face. 'All of us here belong to the disciplinary company. So the officers keep a tight watch on us. But we manage as well as we can with what's available . . .'

Lorena looked around her.

'All the others went off on their bikes this morning to buy stuff from the nomads.' He smiled. 'And to have a girl or two, for all I know . . .'

The smile lingered on the sergeant's lips.

'So we're alone here,' he said. 'You and me.'

'Yes,' Lorena managed to say.

'Very much alone.'

'Well,' said Lorena, 'I think I'll be on my way.'

'Without any gas?'

'Can you give me some then?'

'Of course, I'll give you some. What did you think?' He jerked his thumb at the hut. 'I've a couple of jerricans in there. Will that do?'

'It's better than nothing,' said Lorena. 'I've some money, I can pay you for it.'

'We'll see about that. Come on in.' He hitched up his trousers, and drew back the curtain hanging over the doorway. '*Signorina* ... after you,' he said, giving a comic little bow.

Lorena hesitated for a moment. 'Don't be so silly,' she said to herself, there is nothing to fear, and stepped into the hut. Four camp-beds lined the sides of the hut and photos of film stars covered the walls. Flies buzzed around the dirty mess-tins on the paper-covered table.

'Sorry,' said the sergeant, behind her, 'it's not exactly the Farnese palace.'

He pointed to two jerricans in a corner. 'But there's your gas.'

'You're very kind,' she said.

'I am. And I can be even kinder.'

His smile had vanished and his lips were now trembling.

'I'll ... I'll pay you for ...' began Lorena.

The man shook his head as he stood by the door, legs apart and hands thrust into his pockets.

Lorena felt her heart pounding.

This is ridiculous, she thought, and walked towards the door. 'Let me pass,' she said.

He shook his head. 'No.'

'Let me pass,' she said again, her voice breaking.

'Come on now,' he said coaxingly, 'don't be nasty.'

They looked at each other and Lorena was frightened by this man's intense gaze.

'This is absurd,' she said to herself. 'Last night you made love with a man you hardly know but this man—his lust—he terrifies you.'

'You're making trouble for yourself,' she said in a voice that did not seem to be her own.

'Don't worry . . . I've had many others and they all wanted more . . .'

He took his hands out of his pockets.

She opened her mouth, felt the cry rising within her and heard herself scream. The man was immediately on her.

Seizing her wrists and forcing them behind her back, he pushed her onto the nearest camp-bed, turning her face down. Then gripping both her wrists with his left hand and pressing on the nape of her neck with the other, he thrust her face into the blanket.

This is how people are murdered, she thought. The soldier's

knee was digging into her back, holding her down on the bed. She felt her head splitting and was vaguely aware that he had hit her on the back of her head. She was completely limp and yet conscious that he was pulling her slacks over her hips and down her thighs. She tried to arch her back and free her face from the blanket. She screamed. The man hit her again and lights flashed before her eyes. She could smell his sweat and could hear his feverish breathing. She was trembling uncontrollably.

She managed to free her face and saw the room spinning slowly around her—a mess-tin, a steel helmet on a stool, a film star on the wall.

Suddenly she felt him turning her over and wrenching her knees apart. A succession of images passed swiftly before her eyes: the soldier kneeling on the edge of the bed, his chest glistening with sweat and the muscles standing out on his bare stomach; the soldier with lowered eyes and an enigmatical smile on his lips gazing at her open thighs; the soldier again bending over her, leaning nearer and grasping both her wrists. A nightmare. Coming nearer, his hard eyes intent on her and his trembling lips curled back above his teeth.

Suddenly he jumped off her and sprang round.

He stood listening and then grabbed a rifle from the rack. The curtain at the door parted and a figure sprang into the room.

'Look out, Mattei!' Lorena shouted.

The rifle-butt swept down and Basil heard a sharp crack above his head as the butt smashed the rotten wood.

Carried forward impulsively, Basil stumbled over a stool, fell, and whirled around on his back to meet the Italian who was rushing at him with the rifle-butt raised.

He means to kill me, thought Basil. The heavy, steel-plated butt battered the floor an inch from his head. He drew back both feet, then kicked forward and caught the man in the stomach. He heard a cry, jumped to his feet, and struck the man's ear with just enough force to unbalance him. The rifle fell to the floor, Basil kicked it aside, then turned to meet the other's attack.

He led with his left and crossed with his right. The voice of the boxing instructor at his public school, a short, broad-shouldered Welshman in long shorts and a red-and-black striped vest, came back to him. 'Left, left, right!' Basil dabbed at the soldier's eye twice with his left and then put all his force behind a right swing to the jaw. Pain shot up his arm as his knuckles hit the man's chin; but he brought up his left and his opponent grimaced and swayed.

'Nice uppercut!' came that Welsh voice as his fist sent the other flying backwards onto the table, scattering the mess-tins and the flies.

I've won! Basil thought with surprise. But then the Italian lashed out with his foot and caught Basil hard in the stomach. He doubled up, almost vomited.

Then his ears were deafened and a shower of glass broke around him.

From the floor he saw Mattei leaning casually against the door-post, a wisp of grey smoke curling from the Webley in his hand. The Italian was rising slowly to his feet.

'The next time,' said Mattei, yawning, 'don't fight like a gentleman. It's dangerous for all concerned.'

31

The strong wind of the *khâmsin* whipped the sand against the doors and windows of the Oldsmobile.

They had left the decoy dump and were travelling north between rocky ridges that the wind had beaten into odd shapes. Overhead, the sky was the colour of sulphur. The track was a good one and Basil was able to maintain an average speed of forty miles an hour.

Lorena was sleeping, or resting, on the back seat and Mattei sat silent and sullen in front.

Basil thought back to the fuel dump and admitted to himself that his reaction on first hearing Lorena scream had been very dramatic but not at all sensible. Her scream had started him running and he had ignored Mattei's shouts. 'You silly bastard! You'll get yourself killed . . .'

It was not until he had reached the entrance to the dump that he began to worry about how many Italians he would have to grapple with in order to save Lorena.

Then his mind skipped to the scene immediately following the revolver shot: the fear on the soldier's face as Mattei pushed him out of the hut and the soldier sobbing continually as Mattei forced him to empty the gas from the truck. When the Oldsmobile's tank had been filled, the soldier, half crazed with terror, fell on his knees before a callous-looking Mattei and then raised his tear-stained white face to implore Lorena to save him. It was all so pitiful and embarrassing.

Basil, thinking that Mattei was going to shoot the man, intervened, saying, 'Let him be.' Mattei had turned on him with a cold, disdainful look and snapped, 'D'you think I'm going to waste a bullet on this skunk . . . ?'

As Basil had driven away he watched the soldier in the mirror lying in the dust and banging his head on the ground. He wondered if those moments of unbearable anguish had really driven the soldier mad.

'Mattei,' he suddenly said, 'talk to me. I'm falling asleep.'

'D'you want me to drive?'

'No, just talk to me.'

'I've nothing much to say,' Mattei replied after a moment or two. 'It's very windy.'

'Yes,' said Basil solemnly. 'I haven't thanked you for stepping in and saving me.'

'I almost didn't budge. That would have taught you a lesson.'

'Perhaps once and for all.'

'Exactly. I thought of that.'

'All right,' said Basil, 'let's be beastly. What have you been thinking about?'

Mattei looked at him without a trace of a smile on his lips. 'The time when I first saw you struggling in the water.'

'I see.'

'Your death would have saved the lives of others, who were probably as good as you. Skoda, that German officer . . . Saved a lot of trouble too.'

Swirling sand tinkled like rain against the Oldsmobile, and Mattei twisted around to wind the window up next to Lorena.

'She seems to be sleeping,' he said softly.

'You hold it against her, don't you?'

'Yes.'

'Yet it was you who sent her on ahead,' Basil pointed out.

'She went on her own accord. And when a man gets the idea of screwing a woman it means she's encouraged him one way or another.'

'How aggravating you can be at times,' said Basil. 'There are moments when I feel like bashing your face in.'

'Who's stopping you?' Mattei said a little too calmly.

'Now look . . . !' exclaimed Basil.

'Careful,' Mattei said with a smile. 'Be careful what you say.'

'You're not embarrassed about something by any chance?'

'Oh, not at all. No, it's to save you from making a fool of yourself. I know quite well what you're going to refer to, and it doesn't bother me in the slightest. Want to continue?'

'No.'

'Wise fellow,' Mattei said in English.

'So you can speak English now?'

Mattei puckered up his eyes. 'I'm taking private lessons.'

'Now you're being vulgar.'

Another flurry of sand beat against the Oldsmobile which swung to the right from the force of the wind.

'Why did you frighten the life out of that wretched man?'

'Because he deserved it,' Mattei replied. 'When you're as handsome as that guy you get your women by fine words. Not by force.'

'I don't say I acted very intelligently,' admitted Basil, picturing Lorena spread across the camp-bed. Was sexuality that too, he wondered, those tears and shouts and that brutality? 'But I ran faster than you . . .'

'Because I had more to carry,' Mattei pointed out ironically. 'I had the Webley.'

'Even if I'd had it, I shouldn't have used it.'

'That's stupid.'

'A question of character.'

'No, circumstances.'

Basil straightened up. 'It seems to me that I did what was necessary in the circumstances.'

'I don't think you had the faintest idea of the danger.'

'I jolly well did! That chap seemed to want to kill me!'

Mattei shook his head slowly. 'When you really know danger, you'll fight for your life. And when you're fighting for your life, you don't give a boxing exhibition.'

'Sorry,' said Basil. 'I'm lacking the experience.'

'That's just what I'm saying.'

A short silence followed. 'Mattei,' said Basil at last, 'I think relations between us are going to deteriorate.'

'That doesn't worry me.'

The Oldsmobile swayed under the impact of another gust of wind. The engine began to knock and Basil changed gears. Lorena sat up and Basil caught sight of her bruised face.

From pleasure or pain, Basil wondered a little bitterly.

'The *khâmsin,*' she said. 'This is it. What a nuisance . . .'

The wall of wind caught the Oldsmobile sideways. Basil felt

the wheel stiffen and the automobile sway to the left. He drove on fighting this seemingly invisible and intelligent force.

Another heavy shower hit the windshield and the visibility was reduced to less than five yards. 'A tale told by an idiot, full of sound and fury,' Basil quoted to himself as he battled against the elements. He turned on the windshield wipers; they made a pathetic attempt to move but were forced back.

The sand was thick now and Basil could see nothing. Suddenly he felt the tyres sinking into a muddy, boggy patch but he pulled the wheel hard and the car was snatched from the grip of the quicksands. Basil was tense and sweating as he tried to keep the car on firm ground.

'I can't see a thing,' said Basil, wiping a hand across his eyes. Even with the windows tightly shut the sand forced its way into the car.

Mattei bent down and brought out two pairs of motor-cycle goggles.

'Where did you get these?' Basil asked.

'Pinched them from the hut back at the dump.'

Basil slipped the elastic band over his head. 'That's a lot better.'

'I thought they might come in useful,' said Mattei.

Basil looked at him from the corner of his eye. 'You couldn't be a little less perfect, I suppose?' he said with a smile.

'Don't talk so much, just drive.'

Mattei turned and said, 'Lorena, give us a drink.'

Lorena unscrewed one of the jerricans of water and drank. It was lukewarm and tasted a little rusty but it was refreshing nevertheless. She wiped her mouth with the back of her hand and passed the jerrican over to Mattei.

She looked at the back of his brown neck and thought of last night when her lips had pressed against that tanned skin. She remembered him penetrating her with a slow, regular movement until she blended into him. She was angry now. She had only been resting when she heard Mattei's voice saying '. . . it means she's encouraged him one way or another'. It had cut her like a knife.

'And the worst of it is,' she said to herself, 'he's right. In a way you did encourage that soldier. When you were on that bed you were terrified yet excited. Perhaps it was because of last night. Because Mattei had reawakened you to feelings you thought quite dead.'

A bit of masochism too, she thought. Or the sexual fantasy of the pathetic female and the brutal male. She had wondered if the soldier would tie her to the bed. This thought had revolted her yet for a fleeting moment had fascinated her.

It must be the experiences of the past few days which have revived a passion for life, she thought. Life in all its aspects. She remembered as a girl galloping along for hours across the red plains of Arizona or going off to see Boyd who was always saying, 'We'll do this . . . we'll go there . . .'

Mattei turned and handed her the jerrican. 'Screw the top on properly,' he said.

She glared at him, put the jerrican down by her feet, and pushed the pair of goggles at him. 'You take them,' she said. 'I don't need them.'

She stretched out on the seat and closed her eyes. She was back in the adobe hut with Boyd. She saw the flames of the fire and thought she could hear—it was the same sound as outside the car now—the whining of the wind and the spattering of sand in the chimney, and Boyd saying, 'Next week, we'll bring some meat and grill it over the fire . . .'

It shouldn't be too difficult to find out where he is, she thought. His parents must know. Somewhere in the Philippines, she was sure of that. In Manila, perhaps.

As soon as she got to Phoenix she'd phone his parents. He might be married, but she didn't think so. 'It's not in my nature,' he had told her many times. 'And remember this—its not in your nature either.' And he was right.

She had not listened to her body but only her intellect when she had married Amedée-Jean. She had never forgotten Boyd.

'No, we'll never be able to forget what's happened between us,' he had said to her one day. 'Whatever we do, I'll always remain a part of you as you will of me. You understand, darling? Wherever I may be, you'll be with me. In any event.'

You're crazy, she thought. He's ten thousand miles away . . .

Mattei had revived in her that folly, that inner tumult and passion.

She opened her eyes and looked at the two men in the front seat. What was the chemical term? My catalysts . . .

The howling wind and the swirling sand beat relentlessly against the car. Suddenly the rear of the Oldsmobile sank into the sand.

32

There was nothing to be done. All their efforts to push the car free were in vain as the rear wheels sank deeper and deeper into the sand.

'I'm terribly sorry,' Basil said, sweat pouring from his forehead.

Mattei made a weary gesture. 'It's not your fault.'

Lorena got out of the car. 'Where do you think we are?'

Mattei stood up and peered through the swirling sand.

'I don't know exactly. About on a level with Misurata. Perhaps a little farther on. In any case, we're not lost.'

'You don't think so?'

Mattei shook his head. 'If we go that way,' he said, pointing to the north, 'we're bound to come to the Via Balbo. Or perhaps a track that crosses it.'

'If only this wind would drop,' Basil sighed. His eyes were two dark holes in a face streaked with sweat and grey sand, and his shirt and trousers were stained with grease.

'It might go on like this for a week,' said Mattei, leaning against the car.

'I imagined the desert very different from this,' Basil said.

Mattei made no reply. 'You're trying to recover,' he said to himself. 'But what for? To have the strength to carry on. Carry on where? Three, no four, days have gone by and your situation is the same. Plus you're a couple of hundred miles out of your way. If things go on like this, you'll soon find yourself in Cairo.'

'If things go on like this,' exclaimed Basil, 'we'll find ourselves in Cairo.'

'Shut up!' growled Mattei.

'Oh, I'm sorry.'

A strong gust of wind blew around them and they hid their faces from the sand.

'You can do what you like,' Mattei said suddenly, 'but I'm getting the hell out of here.'

'Where to?' asked Basil.

'Cairo or Djerba or Paris—I don't care. But I'm not staying here.'

'Mrs. Dalloz is worn out.'

'No I'm not,' Lorena protested.

'She'll be worse off if she stays here,' said Mattei. He went and fetched the three jerricans of water from the Oldsmobile. 'Take the one you want,' he said to Basil.

'If I'm not mistaken, you've made your decision and don't care what we think about it?'

Mattei looked at him and then at Lorena.

'And suppose Mrs. Dalloz can't keep up with us?' Basil added.

'She will.'

'Yes, I'll be able to keep up,' said Lorena.

'You see.' Mattei held out one of the jerricans to Basil. 'Here, take this one.'

Basil just looked at it.

'There's nothing else to be done, Basil,' Lorena said in a calm tone, as if speaking to a discontented child.

Basil clasped his hands behind his back. 'If Mrs. Dalloz is unable to carry on, what will you do?'

'I won't be crazy enough to carry her,' said Mattei. 'And stop saying "if"—I'm fed up to here with "ifs". We've got to get out of here, and there's only one way to do it. Walk.'

'You'd leave us in the lurch'—Basil clicked his fingers—'like that.'

Mattei gave a shrug. 'Don't dramatise things. We've got four or five hours' walking ahead of us. We're also in the area of convoys. There's nowhere busier than the desert in wartime.'

'Mattei's right,' said Lorena, getting to her feet. She took one of the jerricans and slung the strap over her shoulder.

Mattei thrust the Webley into his pocket and set off. His progress was slow as his feet sank into the sand at each step.

Lorena put a hand on Basil's shoulder. 'Let's go,' she said.

Basil watched her as she followed Mattei's tracks, her head lowered against the irascible sand. Mattei did not once look back.

Where's all this leading us? thought Basil. Then he chuckled, maybe we will find ourselves in Cairo.

He imagined Shepheard's Bar and Tommy perched on a stool next to him. They were drinking double whiskies with plenty of ice in them and were surrounded by girls.

Basil got up to follow the other two. 'Will I ever get to Shepheard's Bar?' he asked himself. Then he answered his question immediately: 'Oh, you'll find a way.'

Mattei still led the small safari. The three had been trudging along about an hour, with the wind sweeping across the dunes, rushing into the hollows and sending the sand high.

Mattei went doggedly on, never looking back; and Basil, tagging far behind, was irritated by this indifference. But whenever the burly figure ahead disappeared behind a dune, Basil increased his pace until he had Mattei in view again. Then his irritation returned. He found it an effort to drag his feet out of the sand, and the continuous wind and the flying sand that stung his face sapped his patience and increased his nervous exhaustion.

'But you're not really exhausted,' he said to himself. 'You're just making a fuss because Mattei takes the lead in everything. And, he's not as sensitive as you are and whatever you do he lords it over you. It's anger and frustration that's exhausting you, the stupidity of this whole thing, and never knowing how it's going to end...'

He wanted to sit down and wait. But for what?

He caught up with Lorena—whose pace had slowed considerably—and together they trudged up and over a dune and then dropped down into the sand to rest.

Mattei was disappearing over a dune ahead, a gap in the ridge marking his passage.

'That man's like a tank,' said Basil. 'He's got the build of one and just about as much feeling. We'd better push on. Once he's started, he'll never stop.'

He got slowly to his feet, putting an arm before his face to keep the sand out of his eyes. He took a few steps then turned round. Lorena had not moved.

'Tired out?' he said.

She smiled, making cracks in the caked sand on her face. 'Give me a hand.'

He helped her up, and they looked at each other.

'I'm fed up, Lorena. I wonder if it's really worth going on.'

'It was only yesterday that everything started,' she said.

'For you.'

She made no reply and they started walking. When they reached the top of the next dune they saw Mattei trudging along stubbornly, his clothes billowing out in the wind.

'If someone had told you that you'd be only a few miles from Misurata today,' said Lorena. 'would you have believed him?'

'Good Lord, no! Back there, I was thinking we'd end up in Cairo, one way or another.'

Then he tried to slide down the side of the dune, but fell. She could not help laughing.

'You seem to find that funny!'

'No, but—oh, I don't know—so much is happening to me!'

'Yes, something's happened to you all right,' he said a little bitterly, getting to his feet.

'Well, and why not?'

'Don't be so aggressive about it. This is neither the time nor the place.'

They moved on again. 'Well,' began Lorena, 'unlike you, I believe that everything's possible. That everything has become possible. In the space of twenty-four hours, I've struck five years out of my life and I'm starting afresh.'

'You can say that again,' he said, looking around them dismally.

'I don't regret those five years,' she went on. 'They had to be lived, to bring me where I am . . .'

Basil staggered ahead. Another hour of this, he thought, and I'll be raving mad.

He caught sight of Mattei about a hundred yards ahead, waiting for them on flat ground. When they came up to him, he pointed to a track winding into the distance.

'It's going north-east,' he said. 'Just right for us.'

'You see?' Lorena smiled at Basil.

To hell with it all, Basil thought. I'll give myself up to the first Italian I meet. This time, I mean it.

33

Maggiore Flaiano and his driver bumped along the track in his staff-car with the windows rolled up tightly against the flying sand. I shall be almost disappointed to arrive at Fort Cadorna this evening and leave this moving, jolting home of steel and canvas, he thought.

'I wonder,' he said aloud, 'what Fort Cadorna will be like.'

He saw Bartolomeo's broad shoulders lift in a shrug. 'Nothing to write home about, *maggiore*. And the *Inglesi* are quite near.'

'Not all that near. I've seen the operational map at headquarters.'

Bartolomeo, in front and with both hands on the wheel, shrugged again. Then suddenly he shouted, 'Look, there's someone ahead.'

Flaiano looked up as Bartolomeo slowed the car. Three figures were staggering along the track with their backs to the approaching car.

'They look like civilians,' said Bartolomeo. 'Shall I stop?'

One of the men had turned around. He was a tall, slim young man and raised both his arms to stop the staff-car.

'Glad to see you!' he called with a wide smile that split the sandy mask on his face.

Well I never, thought Flaiano, and wondered what he ought to do. He was not prepared for such a situation.

'You are English, are you?' he asked most politely.

Meanwhile the second person had run forward, and said to him quickly: 'My name is Parker. And we are members of the American Agricultural Mission in Tripoli.'

'Oh, but you are a woman,' exclaimed Flaiano.

'Not very obvious, I'm afraid,' she said ironically, patting her hair with a natural gesture. 'I'm Lorena Parker, and this is my husband.'

Flaiano got out and shook hands with them.

'Maggiore Flaiano,' he introduced himself. 'I'm on my way to join my unit.'

'We had a breakdown a few miles from here,' said the woman. 'It's lucky that we met you.'

The third member of this group had stopped some distance away but now began walking slowly towards them.

'Here's our chauffeur,' said the woman.

What an odd trio, thought Flaiano.

'Where were you going?' he asked.

'To Misurata.'

'I'm not going that way, but I can take you to Fort Cadorna, which is farther east.'

'How much farther?' the chauffeur asked in Italian.

Flaiano stared at him. 'About sixty miles,' he said. 'But I don't think there'll be any difficulty in getting you to Misurata from there.'

A strong gust of wind whipped the sand up around them.

'Let's get in,' said Flaiano, indicating the back seat.

The chauffeur took the seat next to Bartolomeo. In the back, the American woman sat between her husband and Flaiano.

'Carry on,' Flaiano said, tapping Bartolomeo's shoulder.

Flaiano sat back and his glance fell on the American's silver chain and identity-disc on his left wrist. It was encrusted with sand and Flaiano was unable to make out the engraved lettering.

He unbuttoned a pocket of his jacket and brought out a pack of cigarettes. 'Do you smoke, *signora*?'

'Yes, thank you.'

Flaiano gave her a light. 'I'm sorry,' he said to the man, 'but I've forgotten your name?'

The American looked at the woman, then replied: 'Parker. Basil Parker.'

Mattei was listening to the conversation in the back with only half an ear. He was preoccupied with other matters. Again they were taking a course which would bring him further and further from his destination. Each improvement in their situation seemed to be penalised by an extra distance to cover—like the game of snakes and ladders that he had played as a child.

'Where are you making for?' he asked the driver.

'Fort Cadorna.'

Mattei liked the look of this man with his big face and full lips. His cap was too small and perched precariously on his balding head.

'Is it on the coast?' he asked.

'A few miles inland,' the driver said in a disgruntled tone. 'Just my luck. My hometown's Genoa, so I'm used to the sea . . . especially after a day like this. And you?'

Mattei thought quickly. 'I'm from Sardinia. But my mother was French.'

'I've a cousin who lives at Monaco.'

'Nice place, Monaco.'

'I've never been there.'

Bartolomeo was silent and Mattei heard the *maggiore* saying: 'And what do you think you're going to get to grow here?'

'Trees,' said Basil in that easy manner which annoyed yet made Mattei envious.

Chauffeur, he thought—that little bitch found just the right thing to say. To her, I'm just a chauffeur, and that's what made her fuck last night—being screwed by a guy with horny hands and as much sentiment as a fighting bull.

'You'll have plenty of work,' said Flaiano.

Lorena laughed softly, and Mattei remembered her breath against his ear.

'Fort Cadorna,' he said to the driver, 'where's that exactly?'

'It's on a level with a fishing-port—Boueirat.'

'That so? We could go and have a swim, eh?'

'If we arrive in time. Is he decent to you, your boss?'

'Not bad, as bosses go.'

'I was a truck-driver,' said Bartolomeo. 'In the vegetable trade. Sometimes we did the Genoa-Rome run in one night. It's at dawn that your eyes start to hurt. And you?'

'I worked in the quarries. Then I became a boxer.'

Bartolomeo shot an admiring glance at him. 'I was just thinking—with your shoulders and that nose . . . You know, I'd have liked to have been a boxer. I wasn't bad at it. You were a pro?'

'For four years.'

'My God.' Bartolomeo whistled between his teeth. 'What made you pack it in?'

'Mistakes,' said Mattei. 'Loss of breath.' He was talking easily now.

'Yes, I suppose you age quickly at that game,' said Bartolomeo. 'But there must have been compensations?'

'Oh, yes.' And Claire immediately flashed through Mattei's mind.

'Us truck-drivers, you know, we used to pick up a girl now and again. Once I had one on a load of lettuce while my mate was driving.' The memory of it made him laugh, and Mattei joined in. 'Among the lettuce, can you see it?' He nudged Mattei with his elbow. 'I knew a driver who once did it among a load of egg-plants. She didn't know where the hell she was . . .'

They both roared with laughter.

'Does you good to laugh,' said Bartolomeo, wiping his sleeve across his eyes. 'You know, it'd be great to have a swim in the sea.'

'It would. If Boueirat is as near as all that.'

'We'll see about it,' said Bartolomeo, winking. 'I say, what's this mission of yours, with your boss—is it to do with priests?'

'No. Agriculture.'

'Ah, that's better. I don't think much of priests. Not having a woman, that can't be good for them. Hey, I've heard there's a brothel at Boueirat. How about going there tonight?'

Mattei caught sight of Lorena's face in the rear view mirror.

'No,' he said. 'Not tonight.'

34

On their arrival at the fort—a shoddy building with a squat tower from which a torn flag flew—Maggiore Flaiano had put Basil and Lorena in the care of his junior officers. The lieutenant in charge of transportation had promised that the mail truck would take them to Misurata in the morning, or even to Tripoli if they wished.

Their room was on the south of the fort, but the thick walls and the narrowness of the window kept out much of the heat. A bed and a small table and chair were the only furnishings.

Basil could hear Lorena humming softly in the shower. He could hardly wait to feel the cool water running over him and rinsing away the sand that stuck to him everywhere.

He looked out of the window and watched some soldiers below struggling to put up large tents.

I might be in a cell, he thought. There are even iron bars on the window. I've often felt that if ever I were to do anything creative and worth while I'd have to commit some heinous crime so that I'd be shut away from all worldly temptations.

'I've never enjoyed anything so much!' came Lorena's voice from behind the curtain that separated the shower from the bedroom.

'What's happened to Mattei?' she called.

Basil eyed her clothes left in a small heap in front of the shower. 'He went off with the major's driver,' Basil said at last.

'They seemed to get on famously together.'

'Yes, but he's not very pleased,' said Basil.

'Well, would you be? Djerba is farther away than ever.' She

215

laughed. 'And we're less than a hundred miles from the nearest British. This is really becoming ridiculous.'

Basil made no reply.

He looked around at the almost medieval austerity of the room

'I don't know how to get out of here,' said Lorena.

Basil smiled. 'I can turn my back or go outside.'

'Go outside, will you? I think I'll lie down for a little while. What time is it?'

'Ten after six,' said Basil, surprised that his watch seemed to be running perfectly again.

'Oh, that gives me plenty of time. Dinner isn't until eight.

How funny, he thought, we're talking like a couple of tourists in their hotel room.

'I'm going out,' he said. He shut the door behind him and stood in the dim musty corridor which had a number of doors spaced along it, all exactly alike.

'You can come in again,' Lorena called after a few minutes.

He went back into the room. She was lying on the bed with the sheet lying softly on the contours of her body, pulled up to her chin.

'I feel marvellous,' she said. 'You ought to try it.'

'I'm going to.' He smiled at her. 'I can recognise you again.'

'Oh, it's still me all right,' she said lightly.

He took off his shirt then stepped behind the curtain to finish undressing. He turned the faucets and delighted in the cool feel of the water as it fell over his hot bruised body. He could not tell which bruises came from the fight with the Italian and which came from the plane crash. He picked up the soap and washed himself slowly and carefully. The lukewarm water soothed his sunburned arms and face.

'Marvellous!' he called.

'Isn't it?' she replied.

Mattei walked slowly out of the water. Higher up the beach and overlooking the harbour he saw sandbagged anti-aircraft emplacements and gunners naked to the waist strolling about in the sunshine or bathing in the sea. The grinding and grunting of army convoys on their way east to Sirte was continuous and frequently planes flew low over the town.

Mattei slipped on his shirt.

'Where are you off to?' shouted Bartolomeo from the water.

'To have a look around. I'll meet you in that café over there.'

Mattei went up a short flight of steps and followed the quay to the little harbour which was formed by a jetty and a landing-stage. He lit a cigarette and stood looking at the six or seven moored boats rocking gently and rubbing against one another. An old Arab sat in one, mending a net and seemingly oblivious to the army trucks rumbling along the quay. Two larger boats were anchored by themselves near the landing-stage and one of them, Mattei guessed, was equipped with a fairly powerful engine. Too powerful for just inshore fishing. The colour of the boat was light green and painted in black along the stern was the name, *San Benito.*

Mattei sat down on a rusty bollard and gazed out to sea. A squadron of bombers flew over and an anti-aircraft battery opened fire, then stopped after a few moments.

Then Mattei saw the hatch rise on the *San Btnito* and a short, thin man appeared on deck. He dipped his arms in a bucket of sand and began rubbing them vigorously. Noticing Mattei on the quayside, he looked at him while he continued to clean his hands and arms.

'Is that your boat?' Mattei eventually called.

The man raised his head. 'So what?' he said shortly.

'So nothing, if she doesn't belong to you.'

The other straightened up and wiped his hands on his trousers, then sprang onto the landing-stage and went towards Mattei. 'Who are you?' he said.

'Federico sent me,' Mattei replied, without getting up.

'From Tripoli?'

'Yes.'

'How's he getting on, Federico?'

'Badly, I'm afraid,' said Mattei. 'The *Tedeschi* raided his place yesterday afternoon.'

'Aie.' The other made a face. 'And you were there?'

'Yes.'

The man looked around him and passed his tongue quickly over his lips.

'What proof have you that Federico sent you here?' the man said at last.

'None. But I'll show you something that'll prove I'm in a spot.'

'We'd better not stay here then.'

'It's all right,' said Mattei. 'What I've got to show you is nothing at all.'

The other frowned, not understanding. Mattei spread his hands and smiled. 'I haven't any identity papers.'

The man gave a low whistle 'And you move around like that?'

'What else can I do?'

The man's thin, wrinkled face, deeply sunburned, gave the impression of health and vitality. He looked at Mattei with some sympathy.

'You've got a nerve,' he said. 'Here you need an identity-card, a pass from the army authorities, a resident's permit, a work card, a certificate from your employer, and last but not least, a Fascist Party ticket.' He cleared his throat. 'I've got the lot. I'm no fool.'

Mattei shrugged his shoulders. 'I'm French.'

He glanced at the *San Benito*. It reminded him of the *Santa Clara* and his heart tightened; it was the first time that he was so acutely aware of the loss of his boat.

The owner of the *San Benito* was frowning down at Mattei. 'And just what d'you want?' he said at last.

'To get to Djerba.'

'By sea?'

'I don't particularly like the roads,' said Mattei. 'I've my reasons.'

The man smiled for the first time. 'They're good reasons, I take it?'

'Very good.'

'We'd better not stay here,' said the man. 'We'll go and have a drink at the *Due Sorelle*. It'll be crowded at this hour.'

The two crossed to the other side of the quay, just as a long line of army trucks full of Italian soldiers were going past.

'The Ariete Division,' said the man. 'They're moving up to Sirte.'

'They can go to blazes for all I care. I'm not interested in this bloody war.'

The other clapped him on the shoulder. 'Come and have a drink, and we'll talk things over.'

As they reached the square, Mattei saw German tanks trundling into the town.

'After all, you're a man and she's a woman,' Basil was saying to himself. 'She's free and desirable. In her kitchen the other night, I'm sure she wanted me. If only Mattei had not interrupted us. And right now, she can only be having the same thoughts as

I am. The trouble is, you're not quite sure what attracted her to Mattei. But what's really bothering you is how to approach her without making an ass of yourself. Are you scared of that green, cold look of hers . . . ?'

To hell with it, he thought angrily, and said aloud, 'Lorena . . .'

Just then the walls and windows began to shake and the metal ashtray rattled on the table.

Lorena raised her eyebrows. 'Planes?' she said.

'No. It sounds like tanks.'

Basil got up and went to the window, just in time to see the leading tank swing to the right, followed by four others. Then the sixth tank swerved to the left and was followed by four tanks. This manœuvre was repeated as each section arrived. One behind the other, they disappeared from view under large tents and soldiers swept away the marks in the sand with brooms.

'Good show,' said Basil. Then as the silence returned, he became aware of Lorena standing next to him, wrapped in the sheet.

'That was very impressive,' she said in a low voice.

'Yes.'

'They're heavy tanks, aren't they?'

'Mark Threes. I'd never have thought they could have got here so quickly. They're the tanks we saw soon after leaving Tarhouna.'

Lorena stood looking down at the big tents.

'What do you think this means?'

Basil said nothing for a moment, as if the reply was distasteful to him. 'A big offensive is being mounted,' he finally said.

Lorena waited for him to continue.

'And with those tanks, it could be timed for the first glimmer of light tomorrow. They could overrun our forward positions by dawn and make a breakthrough.'

'Do you think the British know?'

Basil felt uneasy.

'They must know that the Germans have landed in strength,' he said as calmly as he could. 'But they very likely don't know that the German armour is only sixty or seventy miles from their forward positions.'

'I see,' said Lorena, still looking out of the window.

'And,' Basil went on, 'those positions are very likely unprepared to meet a powerful attack, as generally happens when pursuing a defeated enemy, in this case the Italians.'

'You mean that if the Germans attack, they'll crash through the British positions?'

'I don't know, but it's possible. On the other hand, the British may know about this build-up and may be preparing a strong air attack.'

'Or they may not.'

'Quite so,' admitted Basil.

'All the track marks have been obliterated, did you see that?' said Lorena.

'Yes.'

She turned away from the window and went and sat on the bed. Basil lit a cigarette and felt Lorena looking at him.

'My great-uncle Geoffrey would have been quite at ease in these circumstances,' he said.

'Why? Who was your great-uncle Geoffrey?'

'Leaving aside his distinguished bearing and his stupidity, he was much like Mattei. The sort of man who has only one aim and never loses sight of it.'

Lorena listened patiently, but was more interested in his behaviour than his words. She seemed to be waiting for him to reach a decision. Basil went on talking with a faint note of anger in his voice.

'Great-uncle Geoffrey was the hero of the family. I never knew him, fortunately. He was the colonel of some regiment or other and had only one idea in his head—to defend the far-flung outposts of the Empire. He was killed at Omdurman. There's a picture of him at home. He was unredeemably stupid but had a great style all his own.'

He stopped.

'You'll need an automobile,' Lorena finally said.

'Of course.'

Basil glanced at the young woman sitting on the bed draped in a sheet. What a knack she has of getting people into difficult situations, he thought. Anyone would think she took pleasure in it.

'You said that the British are only sixty miles away?' Lorena prompted him.

He nodded. 'I'll have to think about it.'

But he had a hunch that events were going to decide his future for him.

35

Lorena was seated next to Major Flaiano at dinner in the officers' mess.

'Have you been given comfortable quarters?' he asked her.

'Yes, very comfortable. This officer gave us his room,' she replied, turning to the young lieutenant on her right.

'Ah, Svevo,' said the major. 'That's very kind of you.'

'Oh, the least I could do, sir '

'I hope it hasn't inconvenienced you,' said Lorena.

'Not at all. The main thing is for you to be comfortable.'

'We are. Basil, my husband, thinks that your room is like a monk's cell.'

'But I am a monk,' said Svevo. 'By compulsion, but a monk all the same. One becomes an ascetic in the army.'

'I don't know about that,' said Lorena.

'There are long periods of meditation while preparing to go into action, as when preparing for some act of faith.'

'I'd have thought you to be a pacifist.'

'I am. Very much so,' Svevo said, smiling. 'But I can put on a good show.'

Lorena glanced across the table at Basil who was sitting next to a young German officer wearing the ribbon of the Iron Cross. She then noticed that Major Flaiano kept looking at Basil with quick furtive glances.

The mess waiters brought in dishes of *tagliatelli* and Lorena helped herself. She was hungry and thirsty, and was tired of Basil's passiveness.

If only it was Mattei instead of him, she thought.

Basil helped himself to some *tagliatelli* and Lorena realised what Major Flaiano had been staring at—Basil's identity-disc!

Lorena could not make out the name engraved on the disc but it was evident that it was not 'Parker'. She tried to attract his attention but he was too busy talking to the German officer.

'Basil, go easy with that *tagliatelli*,' she said, raising her voice. 'You know that tomato sauce doesn't agree with you.'

Basil looked quickly in her direction. She had put her elbows on the table and was absently tapping one wrist with her finger.

'You must miss American cooking,' said Major Flaiano.

'There's no such thing,' she replied. 'It's European cooking badly adapted.'

He laughed good-humouredly

Perhaps he's already noticed the name, she thought, and in that case he's a very good actor.

Basil had not understood her gesture but kept glancing at her inquiringly. She repeated it, and saw him (oh the idiot! she thought) look at his watch; but then he suddenly went red and, putting down his knife and fork, thrust both hands under the table.

'What part of Italy do you come from?' Lorena asked Svevo, aghast at Basil's abrupt reaction.

'My home town is Trieste,' said the lieutenant.

'You're not a professional soldier, are you?'

'Is that so very obvious? You know, it's civilians who fight wars in the end.'

'What is your profession then?'

Svevo looked at her. 'I haven't one.'

'I don't understand.'

'I've always refused to work.'

'If you were lucky enough to manage without . . '

'Oh, I never had that luck.'

Lorena smiled at him. 'Then how did you live?'

'By sponging,' he replied gravely. 'I was kept by rich friends in return for my sparkling conversation. Or by women in return for certain favours. And now I'm being kept by the army in return for risking my life. In short, I've always lived very well.'

Lorena looked perplexed.

'I could be telling you this to make the most of myself,' Svevo continued in a lower voice. 'Or to arouse your curiosity . . A little more wine?'

'Yes, please.'

Svevo filled her glass with deliberation. The icy look in his eyes and the determined set of his chin were offset by his rather feminine slim features.

'But in fact,' he went on, 'it's to reassure you.'

'Oh, really?'

A smile spread across his thin lips as he skilfully rolled some spaghetti on his fork.

'You feel a need to reassure me?' Lorena said in an amused tone.

'More than that. For you to trust me.'

A burst of laughter came from some German officers and Svevo glanced wearily towards them.

'There are two ways for a man to make sure that a woman will remember him,' he said softly, turning back to Lorena. 'Either to make love to her, which is much the more preferable, or if time is too short—as in your case—to make her curious.'

He stopped for a moment and then went on. 'If we had more time I'd suggest that we make love.'

Lorena felt uneasy as she felt herself being propelled into unfamiliar depths.

'And you would agree. Because you're intelligent, and because the man you're with is not your husband.'

Lorena felt herself go pale. Svevo smiled gently. 'Nor your lover. But something else.'

Lorena hung on his words, aware that only she could hear them.

'I'll tell you something else—your name may be Parker, but his is not. And although you're certainly an American, he is quite obviously English . . .'

Lorena hung on his words, aware that only she could hear tried to speak but he silenced her. After making sure that Major Flaiano's attention was directed towards the German captain on his left, Svevo continued.

'You may be wondering why I didn't denounce you. And this is the point, in theory, where you ought to be puzzled . . .'

'Oh, but I am,' said Lorena as lightheartedly as she could.

'That's fine, then. There could be two reasons. First, that I'm applying a little blackmail to have what you'd readily give, that's to say, your body. Right?'

'Right,' said Lorena.

She felt as if she were fencing with this man who was far more experienced than herself and who was merely biding his time to finish her off. And she realised by that thin smile on his lips that he enjoyed sending her into a panic.

'If I insisted, we could find some excuse for leaving here and going off together. Your . . . husband wouldn't make a move, and for a very good reason. And we'd go, of course, to my room.'

'Now look . . .' she began, truly alarmed.

'But I shan't do anything of the kind,' said Svevo, pouring some more wine into his glass.

'What then?' she asked, bracing herself for the finishing thrust.

'Nothing,' he said after a short silence. 'I simply won't say anything. It's one way of making sure that you'll remember me. Whatever you do' (his smile became almost tender), 'you'll never forget me. And that, for me, matters more than such outworn ideas as love of one's country or duty. Have a little more wine. I think you could use it.'

He filled her glass and she drank the wine nervously and quickly. However, her heart was beating more normally.

'And now,' he said with a smile, 'between ourselves, and really between ourselves'—he nodded towards Basil, who was still talking with the German officer—'he is English, isn't he?'

'Yes,' breathed Lorena.

'There, you see. It's not so terrible after all.'

Major Flaiano turned to Lorena. 'What have you two been talking about?' he asked. 'It appeared most interesting.'

'About having scruples,' Svevo replied with a cold smile.

He's quite right, thought Lorena. I'll never forget him. She looked at his strong, well-kept hands, and wanted to hear his steady, slightly harsh voice saying, 'To return to our subject' or 'Now as I was explaining'. She wanted him to continue his subtle game which made her feel alternately anxious and relieved.

But he appeared to be engrossed in conversation with Major Flaiano. Finally, she took the initiative.

'Has it occurred to you,' she said quietly, turning towards him, 'that our intention might be to reach the British lines?'

'I would hope so,' said Svevo.

'We might have to shoot an Italian soldier in order to escape.'

'Really?'

'You, perhaps?'

He smiled. 'I may be killed,' he said in an equable voice, 'and that's something I've faced up to, but it will certainly not be while doing my duty. Don't even consider that I'd raise a finger to stop you from getting away or from shooting anyone sitting at this table.'

'Supposing I asked you to go further than that . . .' She broke off, her heart pounding. 'Supposing I asked you to find us the means of getting away—an automobile, for instance?'

Svevo put down his fruit-knife and slowly produced a key from his pocket and placed it on the table near Lorena.

'My automobile is parked outside with the rest,' he said. 'It's number 17.707. A lucky number, don't you think? And it's got a full tank.'

Lorena was speechless.

'Be quick. Take the key,' he urged. 'No one has noticed. You've only to put out your hand.'

'I don't understand you,' Lorena said in a voice so low that Svevo did not hear her.

She took the key and put it in her pocket. 'I suppose I ought to thank you.'

'Don't be so ceremonious.'

He watched the mess waiters make their way around the table pouring port. He waited for everyone to be served and then rose suddenly to his feet and called for attention by tapping his glass with a knife.

'Gentlemen,' he said loudly. 'One moment, please.'

Lorena looked up at him, terrified. 'This is it,' she said to herself. 'He's bored with his games and is now going to denounce Basil and me. Innocent Basil who looks so happy and vulnerable.'

'Gentlemen, your attention, please,' said Svevo when the hum of conversation had died down. He lifted his glass and said slowly, 'I would like to welcome our two guests who are dining with us this evening.' His eyes fell on Lorena's hand which was gripping her glass hard enough to crack it. 'I drink,' said Svevo, 'to Mr. and Mrs. Basil . . . Parker, citizens of the United States of America.'

Lorena felt the tightness in her chest gradually slacken.

'To the United States of America,' said Flaiano, rising and giving a disapproving glance at the lieutenant (after all, it was up to him to propose a toast if he thought one was required), 'and to President Roosevelt, whose neutrality we all appreciate.'

Lorena closed her eyes in relief. When she opened them, she

saw Basil on his feet and raising his glass to Major Flaiano.

'Gentlemen, I raise my glass,' Basil began (he smiled at Lorena, and she knew he was enjoying himself), 'to the Italian Imperial Army to whom we owe this magnificent hospitality and to its German allies. I drink to the health of His Majesty, King Victor-Emmanuel, and Chancellor Adolf Hitler.'

'Well done,' murmured Svevo. 'Your friend has a nice sense of humour.'

Everyone raised their glasses to their lips.

'I thought for a moment that you'd decided to denounce us in proper style,' Lorena said softly to Svevo.

'*Prosit!*' shouted the German officers. '*Prosit!*'

Svevo drank a little of his port and then leaned towards Lorena. 'I had thought of doing that,' he said with his most charming smile.

And she knew that he meant it.

The next thing was to tell Basil that she had the keys to a car. After that, it was up to him.

Then she suddenly thought about Mattei.

36

Mattei, sitting in the shadow of the ramparts, watched the lights in the officers' mess glimmering through the thick curtains.

'*Ich brauche keine Millionen*,' someone sang in an unsteady voice. '*Ich brauche keine Pfennig . . .*'

The sky was spangled with misty stars and the wind which swept across the courtyard made Mattei shiver in his light clothing.

They'll come out soon, he thought, and they're bound to pass this way.

Above his head he heard the sentry coming around again. The man cleared his throat and coughed and Mattei saw the outline of his face as he stopped to light a cigarette.

What the hell are they up to? Mattei wondered, looking again at the windows of the mess. He would have to talk to Basil and Lorena first and then he'd ask Bartolomeo to drive them to the harbour at daybreak. Bartolomeo wouldn't be surprised at that. Or else Lorena could ask the Italian major to arrange transportation for them.

'My driver,' she would probably say, 'has succeeded in finding a boat to take us from Boueirat to Misurata . . . My driver is a very resourceful man . . .'

'Bloody fool,' he sighed. Why did he come back to the fort when he could have forgotten about these two and left without them.

The owner of the *San Benito* had 'worked' more than once with Federico, and with Colombani too. He knew exactly who Mattei was and what he could expect in return for helping him.

Federico had been right in saying, 'I've friends in all the small fishing-ports to the east.'

You bloody fool, he thought again, this woman doesn't give a damn about you, she's shown that. He tried to recall the brief moments during their love-making when tenderness had been stronger than sexual desire. He wanted to remember what he had said and how he had acted, as if hoping it would provide him with the reason for his present behaviour.

'You left Renata in the lurch,' he told himself, 'and she gave you what this woman did and was much better at it, but you've hardly thought of her, whether she's dead or mutilated. Here you are waiting for this American woman who's used you and then cast you aside, and thinks of you—quite naturally—as a chauffeur. And you don't even know how to tell her that you want her to go to Djerba with you.'

He put his head in his hands. '*Merde,*' he muttered, 'I'm going to turn in.' But he knew he would stay where he was. Just then the door of the mess opened and two figures appeared, clearly outlined against the lighted interior. He recognised Basil; the other man was a German officer.

Mattei pressed back into the shadows as the two men strolled into the courtyard. Then he heard Basil speaking in English.

After two glasses of port, Lieutenant Steiger had turned to Basil and suggested taking a stroll outside. Without waiting for Lorena (she and the Italian officer next to her seemed deeply preoccupied) Basil followed the German lieutenant into the courtyard.

'I forgot to ask you,' said Steiger, looking up at the stars, 'what part of the States you come from?'

'Charleston,' Basil said, remembering Lorena's advice that with his accent he should say, if asked, that he was from the south.

'Don't you miss it?'

'A bit,' said Basil. 'But we've been sent here on this mission. And I like this country. I'm becoming quite fond of it.'

That's true, he thought. It's silly, yet I am getting fond of this country. What an adventure . . . I'd love to tell someone about it, but this charming officer is certainly not the person to confide in.

'You went to a university?' asked Steiger.

'Yes.'

'Which one?'

Steiger stopped to light a small cigar. 'Dutch,' he said. 'Would you like one?'

'Thanks, but I don't smoke cigars.'

'You were saying that you went to the university of . . . ?' said Steiger as they strolled on again.

He was obviously a man who pursued whatever was on his mind.

'Harvard of course,' said Basil.

'Odd,' murmured Steiger.

In the silence that followed Basil could hear the distant grunting of ack-ack guns, mingling with the tinkling of the piano in the mess.

'That's odd,' said Steiger. 'I would have thought that you'd have gone to a Southern University. Isn't Harvard a long way from Charleston?'

'Quite right. But agronomy is taught much better at Harvard.'

'Really?' said Steiger. 'That's funny since the South is more agricultural.'

Basil made a dismissive gesture. 'Exactly—so they think they know all there is to know . . . Where did you learn English?'

'At Nuremberg.'

'You speak it very well.'

'Do I? It's not very difficult for a German.'

The two had almost reached the other side of the courtyard and the voices and laughter in the mess reached them as a confused jumble of sounds. The ack-ack firing had ceased.

'And it came in very useful during the fighting in France,' Steiger went on. 'After Dunkirk'—he glanced at Basil—'I was one of the officers present at the surrender of the 51st Highland Division, at St. Valéry-en-Caux.'

'In Normandy?'

'Not far from Dieppe.'

'Was there heavy fighting?'

'Very. We had to fight our way into the town street by street.'

Basil thought of his friend Al who was killed at St. Valéry.

'. . . The English are amateurs,' Steiger was saying. 'Brave, but hopeless amateurs. And there's no place for amateurism in war.'

'No.'

'Still, that's not your concern.'

'No.'

Basil felt both sad and furious.

'Do German students still fight duels with swords?' he asked, at a loss for anything else to say.

Steiger smiled. 'Very seldom, but it still does happen. The war, however, provides other ways of getting scarred.' He put a finger to his cheek. 'That's from a bursting grenade in the fighting around Amiens.'

'Indeed,' said Basil. He was thinking of Rupert Brooke's poem which Al had liked so much, but which he himself thought so terribly sentimental:

> 'If I should die, think only this of me:
> That there's some corner of a foreign field
> That is for ever England.'

'I had . . .' he began.

'Yes?'

'We have student traditions too.' (Al's freckled face rose up in front of him, with that deep dimple on his chin.)

'Not sword duels, I don't suppose.'

'No,' said Basil, 'nothing of that kind. No more than pranks, really. But sometimes they can be dangerous.'

He saw Al with his long white scarf draped around his neck and pointing up at the spire.

'I had a friend,' he said with effort. 'His name was Al Maclean' It did him good to say that. 'I remember once, we stole the dean's chamber-pot . . .'

Steiger laughed and puffed on his cigar.

'. . . and we went and stuck it on the spire of Christ Church . . .'

Steiger slowly turned towards him.

'Christ Church?' he asked softly.

Basil remained silent. 'Say something, answer at once,' he told himself. But he remained mute.

'Christ Church,' the German repeated. 'But that's at Oxford.'

This is the end, thought Basil. But he felt nothing. In the dark, he could not make out the German's expression.

'At Oxford, isn't it?' Steiger repeated calmly.

'You must do something, invent something,' Basil told himself. 'Say there's a Christ Church at Harvard, for instance. But your silence has condemned you and it's useless to pile more lies on those you've already told. You knew it would end like this. It's almost a relief.'

'At Oxford,' he said aloud. 'That's right.'

'In fact, you're English?'

'Yes.' Basil brought out a cigarette and calmly lit it.

'An escaped prisoner?'

'Yes.'

There, that's over, he thought.

'I'm very sorry,' said the German.

'Oh, you needn't be. What do you want to do?'

Steiger laughed. 'I'm not at all sure. It's a rather unusual situation, don't you agree?'

'I can well believe it.' Basil felt like he was repeating the lines in a play.

'I had my suspicions,' the German said.

'Really?'

'Nothing certain, though. In any case, I congratulate you on your coolness.'

'I've been expecting this for some days,' said Basil.

The German moved away and stood looking at him with his hands on his hips.

'The best thing to do, it seems to me, is for us to go back to the mess. And I'll have a word with the Italian major.'

'That seems like the proper thing to do,' said Basil. 'I should like the lady who's with me to be left out of all this. Will that be possible? She has nothing to do with it, and besides she really is an American.'

'That is possible.'

'There you are,' Basil said to himself, 'no unnecessary drama, just as you've always hoped. With a little luck, perhaps you'll end up in a monastic cell where you can write that book you've always been meaning to.'

'Will you walk in front?' said the German.

'Do you want me to put my hands up?' he asked as he saw his captor reach for his gun.

'As far as the mess, if you don't mind. I don't want to take any risks.'

'Do I look as if I want to escape?' Basil said.

'You've done so once before,' the German replied, stepping back a couple of paces. 'Go on ahead.'

Basil slowly raised his hands.

Just then he heard a noise behind the German and turning around he saw a figure spring from the shadows. He heard a thud and saw the German stagger and fall to his knees. Basil recognised Mattei as he raised his revolver and smashed the steel barrel into the German's skull. The officer moaned and slumped slowly to the ground.

Mattei grasped him under the shoulders. 'Give me a hand,' he gasped.

Basil took the man's legs. He was heavy and Basil was soon out of breath.

'This way,' breathed Mattei.

Basil could see the German's head dangling between Mattei's arms.

'In here,' said Mattei, nodding towards a tunnel under the rampart.

Then they stopped abruptly. Someone had coughed above them. Then Mattei saw the glow of a cigarette as the sentry walked slowly past. Soon the red glow disappeared.

They put the limp body on the straw strewn about the tunnel. 'Is he dead?' murmured Basil. Mattei felt for the neck artery.

'Yes. How did he corner you?'

'Just by chance.'

Mattei looked at him intensely. 'You realise what . . .'

'Lorena wouldn't have been brought into it,' Basil said quickly.

'To hell with Lorena. What about me?'

'I didn't ask you to step in. I was about to give myself up.'

'D'you want me to apologise for what I did?'

'Oh, there's no need to go that far,' said Basil wearily.

'Sorry to have dragged you back into things, but there's a boat waiting for me at Boueirat. So take your choice . . .'

'You call that a choice?'

'No, but you're the sort of guy who shouldn't be given choices. Are you going to fetch Lorena or am I? We'll go off through there . . .'

Mattei nodded towards the end of the tunnel which opened onto the desert. The archway was half-filled with sandbags and an old Vickers machine-gun—probably captured from the British—was propped against them.

'I'll go,' said Basil.

When he had disappeared into the night, Mattei went into the courtyard and picked up the German officer's Luger. Returning to the tunnel, he took the spare clip from the dead man. Searching further, he found a leather wallet containing a few German marks and a wad of Italian lire. He stuffed the money into his pocket.

As his eyes adjusted to the darkness, he stepped over the dead man's body and went to the low wall of sandbags and looked out. The moon had risen, and he could see a barbed-wire fence enclosing the empty space in front of him. To his right were parked cars.

He longed for a cigarette but had none left. He could hear the sentry walking above him, listened to the man's steps fading away, then returning, then fading away again, and suddenly Basil and Lorena were beside him.

'Basil told me that . . .' she began breathlessly.

'Quiet,' said Mattei.

'Look what I have.' She showed him the ignition-key. 'It belongs to an automobile with the number 17.707.'

Mattei could not help smiling. This woman was amazing. She seemed to find a way out of everything. Without her, he thought, they'd have been captured long ago.

'How did you get it?' he asked.

'Oh, I'll tell you later.'

The three of them, squatting on the damp sandbags, looked at the parked cars.

'Number 17.707,' Lorena reminded Mattei.

'And how do you expect me to find it? There's at least thirty cars over there—and certainly one sentry.'

'Haven't you ever stolen an automobile?'

'Several times.' Mattei smiled to himself. That's why I'm uneasy. Anyway, what the hell. 'Basil, you come with me.'

'Yes, all right,' he said.

'Give me the key,' Mattei said to Lorena. 'You never know, we might be lucky for once . . .'

She watched the two men clamber over the sandbags and follow the rampart along to the right. Then she thought of Svevo. As she was leaving the mess with Basil, she had glanced back. Svevo was watching her and then he had slowly lowered his eyelids. She would never forget him standing there with a cup of coffee in his hands, heels together as though at attention, and his eyes lowered in farewell.

She came to with a start. An engine had just coughed into life and grew into a loud, almost triumphant, roar. She clambered over the sandbags.

Then a dark shape emerged between two cars and shouted in Italian 'Halt!' Lorena heard the sound of hobnailed boots scurrying along the sentry-walk.

'What's up, Renaldo?' came a voice from above.

'Halt or I fire!' called the sentry in a sharper tone.

Lorena saw the flash as he fired. Then an automobile swerved towards her and slowed down with a door open.

'In the back!' shouted Basil, who was at the wheel.

She jumped onto the running-board, heard the whine of a bullet, and her fingers loosened their hold. But Mattei's arm shot out and hauled her in by the waist, and pushed her into the back.

Basil pressed the gas pedal to the floor and was driving like a madman, taking no notice of the bumping and jolting that seemed likely to shake the automobile—a Volkswagen—to pieces. He could see no more than five yards ahead and felt that at any moment they would crash into some obstacle left by the gods or a careless Italian. Once or twice the wheels slipped into the shallow ditch that bordered the track but each time he managed to pull out in time.

Then headlights appeared in the rear view mirror. 'They're after us,' he said.

'Press on!' Mattei roared. 'Boueirat must be straight ahead!'

Something white came rushing towards the Volks. Basil instinctively switched on his headlights.

'Put those bloody things out!' snapped Mattei.

Basil obeyed, but in that brief moment of light he had seen the white road-sign and an arrow pointing to the right: Sirte 60 Kms.

He stamped on the brake, the tyres screeched and gravel showered the mudguards.

'What the hell are you doing?' yelled Mattei. 'It's straight on! Straight on, I told you—to Boueirat!'

Some force had taken hold of Basil; a feeling he had never experienced before. It was partly a sensation of relief—a certainty that only one thing mattered now.

He changed gear, swung the wheel to the right, and took the turn to Sirte.

'Straight on!' Mattei shouted and tried to grab the wheel.

The Volks was gaining speed again. 'You'll turn us over,' Basil warned in an even tone.

'They're still following!' called Lorena.

Basil clung to the wheel. 'Mattei,' he said without raising his voice, 'Mattei, if you don't sit still, I'm going to stop. And,' he added as Mattei withdrew his hand, 'you know I wouldn't mind being a prisoner.'

'You're nuts,' said Mattei.

'Maybe.' They were now travelling smoothly along the Via Balbo. 'We're going towards Sirte.'

'I ought to shoot you.'

'You know you'll do nothing of the kind,' Basil replied without taking his eyes off the road. 'At least, not just now.'

The moon slid out from behind some clouds and he had a better view of the dark stretch of road running between the light expanse of sand.

'I'll shoot you one of these days,' said Mattei in a tone that chilled.

'That's right. One of these days,' said Basil offhandedly.

37

Basil was doing over seventy. The desert looked like a milky lake under the moon. He glanced up at the mirror and saw that the headlights were farther behind now.

'In any case,' he said, 'it's too late to turn back.'

Mattei broke his sullen silence. 'You're a stupid bastard.'

Basil shrugged.

'What's got into you?' Mattei went on.

'Let's call it strategic awareness. I want to warn our chaps of those tanks.'

'You've chosen a fine time,' snapped Mattei. He turned to Lorena. 'I suppose it was you who put this blasted idea into his head? Strategy!'

'I don't think so,' she said.

'And I was stupid enough to come back for you . . .'

'For me?' exclaimed Lorena.

'Oh, Christ!'

No one said anything for a minute or two, then Lorena announced, 'I can't see their lights now.'

'They're not stupid,' growled Mattei. 'What's the point of chasing us through the night? The units ahead of us will be warned. We'll meet with a hot reception before long.'

'We'll see,' said Basil.

'I'd love to kill you. Remind me to shoot you if we're ever in a peaceful spot some day.'

'That's a promise.'

Basil knew there was no turning back now and everything seemed so clear and simple.

Mattei gazed at the road unfurling ahead of them. 'The trouble is, we'll have to fight our way through,' he said. 'Strategy, hell, it's plain suicide. So slow down a bit. We need time to think.'

When they were about fifteen miles from Sirte, Basil saw a rough track going off to the south-east. He stopped the automobile. 'What do you think?'

'You talking to me?' said Mattei.

'If you're still with us, yes.'

'Right now, I could have been well out to sea. What d'you want to know?'

'Shall I take this track?'

'Take it by all means,' Mattei said mockingly. 'All the tracks we've taken have led somewhere. No reason why this one shouldn't. It'll come to the same thing, whatever we do.'

'Why?' Lorena asked.

Mattei put on his patient look which came when he felt despair. 'Near Sirte, we'll run into troop concentrations and won't get through. If we take that track, we'll run into patrols or supporting units that have been informed about us. They must know we're trying to reach the British lines. It's all up to you now to decide what to do.'

'I'm not stopping you from getting out,' Basil said calmly.

'Nothing doing. I want to see your face in the end. They won't make any mistakes this time. Well, get going, we're wasting time sitting here.'

Lorena thought back to what Svevo had said when he gave her the key to his car: 'It's number 17.707. A lucky number, don't you think?' But they had not taken his automobile.

Basil looked at the rough track and it came to him again that the choices in his life were becoming fewer and fewer, as if at some point in the near future there would be only one possible road to take.

'All right,' he said.

Mattei picked up the Schmeisser and rammed in a magazine. Then he fingered the four hand-grenades which lay next to him on the back seat.

'Let's go,' he said.

Just before dawn the track became so treacherous that their speed was reduced to ten miles an hour. The flat sandy landscape was now giving way to rolling hills strewn with boulders. Frequently the track wound around one of these rocky hills, slowing the Volks even more. In the distance, a higher rocky range stretched across the horizon but in the dim light it was difficult to judge how far away it was.

'You're sure we're headed the right way?' said Lorena.

'We're bound to bump into something somewhere or other,' Mattei replied.

Basil said nothing. He knew that Mattei was right—they were bound to end up somewhere and he was determined to follow this track. He thought back to when he had stopped along the roadside, taken off his shoes and waited for the first Italian to come along. He didn't feel like taking the easiest way out anymore. Something was propelling him along which left no room for indecision. He almost felt like a stranger to himself without the comfort of his usual passivity. Suddenly he said: 'Look over there!'

A hundred yards or so to their left, they saw a shower of reddish sparks accompanied by a heavy thudding, like the regular beat of a hammer on an anvil.

'Artillery fire,' said Mattei.

Small shells were now exploding on their right, sending chips flying off the boulders.

'Step on it!' shouted Mattei. 'They're firing too high. We might just get through!'

Basil accelerated as the firing came nearer. 'We've had it this time,' he thought. Then he realised they were beyond the danger zone.

'They know where we are now,' said Mattei. 'Press on . . .'

Two miles further on, the chase began. It was probably a patrol or a detachment which had received orders to intercept the fugitives. There were five motor-cyclists and one with a sidecar on which a light machine-gun was mounted, followed by a Borgward truck carrying a group of soldiers.

Basil reached a junction with the leading cyclist about two hundred yards behind and as he turned left he saw the man raise his arm and heard the motor-cycles accelerate. Mattei clambered over to the back seat—'Move, Lorena, this is my affair'—and knelt on the seat with the tommy-gun pointed at the back window. The Volks had little difficulty in out-distancing the heavy truck, but the cyclists were steadily gaining ground.

Mattei handed Lorena the Webley. 'Don't shoot until I tell you to,' he said. 'What matters is not so much to hit them as to discourage them.'

'You think they can be discouraged?' she said with a weak smile.

'No,' Mattei replied softly. Then added, 'Aim low and hold it with both hands.'

The surface of the track became more uneven as they approached the inky range and it wound continually around large boulders.

'It prevents them from getting a good aim at us, anyway,' said Mattei. 'What's it like ahead?'

'Beginning to climb a bit,' Basil said over his shoulder. The track curved around a rocky spur to a straight stretch. Basil slammed his foot down on the accelerator to reach the next bend as soon as possible. It seemed an endless distance.

'Here they come,' said Mattei. Three cyclists appeared at the beginning of the straight stretch less than one hundred yards away. 'Step on it. We're like sitting ducks.'

'I'm doing my best,' said Basil. A tightness took hold across his shoulders as he caught sight of the three jolting figures in the mirror. I'll never make it, he thought.

Mattei picked up one of the grenades. 'We'll see what this does.'

Mattei calmly released the pin, put his arm out of the window and dropped the grenade as if disposing of an apple-core. The grenade tumbled along the track and rolled to a stop near a shallow ditch.

Mattei counted to four. The grenade exploded and threw up a cloud of sand just before the cyclists reached the spot. One of them swerved, struck the front wheel of the man behind, and both toppled to the ground. The third braked and skidded to avoid them.

'It worked!' exclaimed Mattei. 'Make the most of it.'

As they reached the next bend, Mattei and Lorena saw the Germans picking up their bikes. Then another rocky spur hid them from sight.

They were now travelling across flat ground strewn with pebbles and boulders but devoid of any vegetation.

'We've left them behind!' shouted Mattei, looking at the empty track behind them.

Basil changed gears as he reached a slope leading to a gap in the rocks. He caught sight of a notice which had been blown sideways by the wind. On it was scrawled in big black letters: *Hai fatto il tuo testamento?*

'What's all that about making your Will?' grunted Mattei. 'Are they trying to tell us we're crazy?'

'No,' Basil replied, 'it's to let us know we're entering No Man's Land. Lorena, perhaps Shepheard's Bar isn't so far away.'

A few seconds later one of the front wheels ran over a mine.

He felt a violent twist on his wrists and saw the hood of the car crumple up like paper. A wheel flew into the air and bounded off some rocks, while at the same time a great shower of earth and pebbles erupted around him. He was stifled by the acrid smell of cordite. The Volks sagged sideways like a wounded animal, and Basil pushed open the door with his shoulder and slid to the ground.

The explosion had made a shallow crater and smoke hung around the edges.

'You hurt?' came Mattei's voice.

'I don't think so,' said Basil.

All strength seemed to have been drained from him. He stared at the hood which curled back like a peeled banana.

Lorena was lying near him, her face pallid in the grey light of dawn. She opened her mouth as if to say something, but no sound emerged.

Mattei got to his feet and staggered around the automobile to the other two. A streak of blood lined his cheek; his face and shirt were smeared with earth.

'We can't stay here,' he gasped, bending over Lorena. 'They'll be here in a few minutes.'

Basil looked back down the slope. The cyclists were about three hundred yards away, followed by the truck. They seemed to have slowed down, as if secure that the chase had reached its conclusion. A few soldiers stood in the truck looking over the driver's cabin, their arms resting on the top. Then the leading cyclist came to a halt.

Basil realised that they were frightened of mines.

'They only need a little patience,' he said.

'Yes,' Mattei agreed, looking about him. 'We can make things a bit difficult for them, but that's about all . . .'

I knew all along, Basil thought, that there comes a time when there is only one way to go. All this confused wandering seems to have been part of some subtle plan. Was it designed to end at this parched spot?

About twenty yards ahead the track disappeared through the narrow gap in the rocks; on the other side of the ridge a plain stretched into the distance.

'I'll stay here,' Basil suddenly said, his voice echoing in his ears.

That was you who spoke, he thought vaguely to himself.

Mattei looked across at him.

'I'll stay and try to hold them up,' said Basil. 'It's the only way.'

Lorena's face was calm. She didn't seem to be seeing or hearing the two men. She sat immobile except for her trembling hands that were clasped in her lap.

Basil looked hard into Mattei's dark eyes.

'You must let the British know . . . about the tanks . . .'

'You and your blasted tanks,' growled Mattei.

'You must do that, Mattei.'

'I will, I will. If I get that far, I will.' Then he added in a tone that was almost affectionate: 'Whatever put this idea into your head, you bloody fool?'

'I don't know. That's just what I'm wondering myself. Promise me about those tanks . . .'

'It's a promise,' Mattei assured him.

'Now get going,' Basil said, lowering his head so that Mattei could not see his lips twitching uncontrollably.

'If you think I'm going to stay here . . . !' Mattei fetched the Schmeisser and gave it to Basil. 'Here, you'll need this.'

Mattei glanced at the Germans who were now gathered around the truck at the bottom of the slope, about two hundred yards away.

Basil moved the bolt of the Schmeisser up and down. Mattei clamped the loaded magazine on for him. 'You'll get slaughtered, old feller.'

'Maybe not,' said Basil. 'The pleasant side of things, remember? One never knows.'

Mattei took Lorena by the wrist. 'Come on . . .'

She looked at him as if not fully understanding what was happening.

'I want to stay here,' she said in a voice that the other two did not recognise.

'Are you hurt?' Basil asked her.

She shook her head.

'Then stop acting the bloody fool and listen to me,' said Mattei. 'You see that gap in the rocks? We'll be safe from their fire once we're through there. But to get there, we've got to crawl.'

Lorena nodded, her eyes still blank.

Mattei turned to Basil. 'Don't waste your bullets. You've got two more full magazines.'

'All right. Now get going.'

Basil looked up at Mattei who was gazing at him through narrowed eyelids, his lips pressed together.

'Don't forget about the tanks,' said Basil. 'Please don't forget.'

'No, I won't. I'll never forget them.'

He patted Basil on the back. ' 'Bye, feller.'

'So long, Mattei . . . I'll cover you.'

Basil pointed the Schmeisser down the slope and was surprised at the weight of the weapon. He could see the Germans' cycles lying on the ground but the men were now concealed in the folds of the ground.

He looked around and watched Mattei and Lorena crawling up the slope. I didn't say good-bye to Lorena, he thought. And at that very moment bullets whizzed over his head. The Germans were not shooting at him but at the two figures near the top of the ridge.

He fired the Schmeisser and was shaken by the noise and violence of his weapon. His ears rang as the empty cases spurted out to his right. Then he began to shoot singly and felt pleased at the bullets kicking up the earth around the recumbent motor-cycles.

When he had emptied the magazine he turned on his side to look behind him. There was no one in sight.

38

He was alone now.

The Germans had stopped firing. The silence made his solitude a reality. It was the beginning of an end he had never dared imagine.

The grey dawn spreading over the rocky track was the dawn of his death. The bleak sterile landscape was the landscape of his death. The oil and gas trickling out of the shattered automobile, the water seeping into the ground, the smell of burnt rubber, these were the accessories to his death.

He was lying flat behind the sagging Volks. He looked at his watch—in another ten or fifteen minutes Mattei and Lorena ought to be safe, perhaps within sight of a British patrol.

He crawled to the open door of the Volks and dragged out all his means of defence—the two full magazines and three hand-grenades. A bullet struck the side of the automobile and he rolled into the shallow crater made by the mine. It provided little protection, but from it he could fire under the automobile between the front and back wheels. He clipped a fresh magazine on the Schmeisser, as Mattei had shown him, then stretched out to wait.

Another bullet struck the car and ricocheted off with a long-drawn-out whine. Then he caught sight of a movement near the truck.

He had no feeling of danger. The firing didn't seem to be aimed at him personally. It was rather like watching a film in which the excellence of the sound conveys the human tragedy.

He gripped the Schmeisser, badly wanting to fire it, but knew he should preserve his ammunition. The more time that passed, the better the chances would be for Mattei and Lorena.

Yet he had a vague, confused feeling that what was happening had little relation to the other two, the tanks or the British. It was another contest. One between himself and the soldiers down the slope. An important, even decisive, contest.

Decisive, he thought, or rather tried to think with sufficient conviction. He felt his heart pounding and looked around the shallow crater which gave him a false impression of security. The mine had been deeply buried, which was probably why they had not been wounded. Maybe that would have been better, he thought, for them, if they had been unable to crawl away from the wreckage. Was it by chance that he was here alone? Or was it really his own decision?

Something warm trickled down his forehead. I've been hit, he thought. He passed a trembling hand over his eyes. It was only sweat. He was afraid now. He wasn't wounded but calmness had given way to stark fear.

'You'd like to believe that your death was foreordained,' he said to himself. He thought of Mattei informing the British of the German concentration of tanks, the RAF breaking it up and the British advance continuing to Tripoli, then to Tunis, the whole of North Africa in our hands and serving as a base for the liberation of Europe . . . and he would have been the one to . . .

'But even if that happens, you'll never know it—unless (keep hoping) you're still alive. And even then, who'd believe your story? The living always meet with suspicion and would you really want to be believed? You'd find the whole thing ridiculous. How often had Julia said : "Basil, you'll never be a hero, a financial wizard or a famous lover, nothing like that. You don't take life seriously." '

Once he had answered this remark by asking her to marry him. 'Basil,' she exclaimed, 'you're quite indecent!' So, having a sense of the ridiculous, he had not pursued the matter. But now, if he ever got back to England—he would marry her no matter what she said.

But a second later he knew that light-hearted world of his past was gone forever.

Professionals, he thought, as the well-directed burst of firing began again.

The ground in front of him was whipped and torn by a hail of lead, and all he could do was to crouch down and try to bury himself in the earth, a sickening fear in his stomach and the hammering of automatic weapons resounding in his head. The vision of Skinny's bloody throat and the gunner's body slumped in the seat passed before his eyes. Men will see my mutilated body, he thought angrily, and raised his head. He saw them advancing up the slope—three soldiers bent double and trailing their guns, peering up from under their long peaked caps, tight-lipped, converging on him as the covering fire whined and pinged around him. He fitted the butt of the Schmeisser into his shoulder and aimed it at the leading German—a burly man with his mouth half open, gasping and sweating despite the chilly dawn.

Basil squeezed the trigger, the butt kicked, and the German fell forward, raising a cloud of dust as he dropped heavily to the ground. Then Basil directed his fire on the soldier who was bounding back down the slope, and aimed at his legs. The man plunged sideways, flinging up sand and pebbles. The slope was barren except for two yellow heaps, one inert and the other writhing feebly.

A pause, he thought, and next time they will be more prudent, leaving him with a minimum of opportunity, the unavoidable minimum which depended more on intangibles than on himself.

The wounded soldier had turned on his stomach and was crawling away. Blood covered one leg which he dragged behind him like a dead object. Basil was astonished at having inflicted so much pain. It was the only thing he feared—some hideous wound, the suffering and the humiliation.

You could surrender now, he told himself. He had only to strip off his shirt, tie it to the Schmeisser and hold it up. Easy, in fact. A simple decision to make. Then he would be able to see Julia again. He pictured her standing in the rain in Duke Street, waiting to cross the road, wearing a black raincoat and a red beret, as he drew up in his M.G. sportscar.

The wounded man had reached a fold in the ground, and dragged himself out of sight, the foot on his stiff leg scraping the earth.

Hardly had he disappeared from sight when the firing started again, splintering the automobile and smacking into boulders. He buried his face in the ground. One of the tyres collapsed, a door burst open and broken glass flew through the air. Suddenly he felt a hammer-blow on his hip and he cried out.

Like the yapping of a dog run over by a car, he thought with horror. But he realised that surprise more than pain had made him cry out. His hand hesitated at touching his wound, a round hole oozing blood that was running towards his waist. Then he felt where the bullet had come out (shot through the body, he thought) near his back.

He propped himself on his elbows, and felt something move inside him, some heavy mass of liquid weighing on his stomach. Like mercury.

He seized a grenade as he heard the soldiers drawing near, tossed it haphazardly over to his right, saw it spinning through the air and then vanish from sight.

'*Achtung!*' someone shouted.

An instant later, the explosion rent the air.

Basil threw himself forward and, although his legs gave way under him, reached the back of the automobile. The Germans were crouching on the ground (four, he counted, four against one) but none of them appeared to have been hit by the blast. Before the smoke died away, they were on their feet and advancing again. They were no more than fifty yards from him. The covering fire was directed to his left, at the spot he had just left.

He felt an ankle give way, and realised that a bullet had glanced off his shoe. The Schmeisser seemed to empty itself; none of the enemy was hit, but the burst brought them up short. One man fell forward and with the same movement lobbed a grenade up the slope.

'Oh God, don't let it be this,' he prayed as he saw the grenade rolling towards him.

It exploded five yards in front of him and the white flash blinded him for a moment. He fired again, realised he had emptied the magazine, and pulled the pin from another grenade and sent it rolling down the slope. (You can still get out of this, he thought, if you pretend to be dead.) The grenade burst at the feet of the leading man. He was flung backwards, his gun and helmet spun through the air, his ripped clothing flapped wildly and he crumpled to the ground like a sack. The other three scurried back down the slope.

'They're fleeing from me,' Basil thought ironically. But at the same time he knew there was nothing left for him but to meet his death proudly.

It was as if he had made a pact with these Germans—with the men he had killed and wounded and with their comrades. As if he had accepted the rules of this game of death.

Nothing of the past was in his mind now; that was over and done with. He was sitting where he had fallen, from fear more than lack of strength. Sitting with his back against one of the rear wheels and staring down the slope at the wounded soldier whose face was contorted as his bloody hands tried to push his intestines back in his body. I must, Basil thought to himself, summon up enough strength to make a good end. That's all that matters now.

He got to his knees, the Webley in his left hand. A bullet smacked into the automobile. He crawled to the crater and picked up the last magazine. His hip throbbed with pain but at least he could still move around. This was a good sign, he told himself.

He clipped on the magazine and then rose slowly to his feet by supporting himself against the side of the car, heedful of the weight dragging at his hip. Blood made his pants stick to his thigh, but his legs held him upright and he was able to walk.

'Ferguson goes to war,' said an inner voice mockingly.

A burst of ragged firing came from below.

Not now, he thought, not yet.

He saw a face staring at him from the window of the open car door—an unshaven face streaked with black (your war-paint) and eyes glaring, very bright in the blackened mask.

He clutched the Schmeisser against his side.

'*Alle heraus!*' came a harsh shout.

The final assault, he thought. First he saw the cyclists advance in their round helmets, then six or seven soldiers in long peaked caps—walking very slowly, it seemed to him—bent forward ready to throw themselves to the ground if necessary, their gaze anxious and uneasy. In the centre an officer, holding himself very upright, urged his men on with voice and gesture.

Then Basil took a step forward, leaving the protection of the automobile, and stood clearly outlined at the top of the slope.

The Germans wavered and almost halted, astonished at the sight. And Basil saw, with a sort of fearful joy, a look of incredulity spread over the officer's face. There was less than a hundred yards between them. A duel, he thought.

'Come on, you bloody bastards!' he heard himself shout.

He started walking slowly down the slope, firing short bursts, spraying the ground ahead of him. The Germans scattered. He had no idea what he was doing. He put one foot in front of the other, felt his right leg give way every now and then, and watched the empty cartridges bouncing before his eyes. He had just come level with the soldier whose entrails were hanging out when he was hit in the shoulder and the Schmeisser fell to the ground. He bent to pick it up and a hard blow on the side of his head, as though from a stick, sent him to his knees. He clutched the Webley in his right hand.

'Surrender!' shouted the German officer in Italian.

Basil straightened up and thrust out his right arm as at shooting practice. But a great weight was dragging him down, and he was too weak to press the trigger.

'Surrender!' The voice was quite near now.

I want to, I still can, he thought confusedly, I've only to . . .

He tried to raise his hands, but only one responded—the one holding the Webley.

He saw them standing in a semi-circle about ten yards from him with their weapons lowered.

A powerful force dragged him to the ground, and his gaze fell on his bloodstained pants. I've never worn these trousers before, he thought. And the next moment came the pain, worse than he had ever imagined. It reached its paroxysm and erased all other feeling, all thought. His face touched the rocky ground.

He saw the sky above him and the clouds racing unconcernedly across it as though being drawn to the ends of space. Then his vision narrowed and the sky began to swim into darkness. The utter futility of it all, he thought.

39

They met a British patrol just before six that morning. They were quite close before the second-lieutenant who was in command of the patrol spotted them and walked slowly towards them. He was short but sturdy and wore a khaki jacket that came down low over his dirty pants.

'Hello,' he said.

'Hello,' Lorena replied. She was completely exhausted.

'We've come from the Italian lines,' she said.

'Are you Italian?'

'No, American.'

'Ah, I see.'

'And you too?' added the officer, addressing Mattei.

'No, he's French,' said Lorena. 'We were with a British officer ... We helped him to escape,' she added.

'Where is he?' the officer asked, as though expecting him to appear from behind a sand-dune.

'We were being chased by Germans. He stayed behind to hold them up.'

Lorena thought of Basil's face as they left him—the face of a man already withdrawn from the world.

'He's probably . . .' She felt she was going to be sick.

'Germans, you say?' the officer asked in a tone of some disbelief. 'Are you sure?'

'They landed three days ago,' said Lorena.

'Yes, we know about that. But are some of them so far east already?'

'That's what we wanted to tell you,' Lorena said, looking

longingly at the mugs of tea held by the soldiers who had gathered around them.

'There's a large concentration of German tanks at Fort Cadorna,' she went on. 'Basil . . . this British officer wanted to let you know. Mattei, you tell him . . .'

'Where's Fort Cadorna?' the officer asked.

'South of Boueirat, sir,' said his sergeant, who had been listening attentively.

'It's ten kilometers south-east of Boueirat,' Mattei told them in French. 'The tanks are Panzers, Mark Threes,' he added

The officer raised his eyebrows. 'Are you sure of all this?'

'Yes, we saw them.'

'This is important information. What do you think, sergeant?'

'I agree, sir. Shall I get on to Brigade H.Q.?'

'Yes, try and send a message to the I.O.' The officer turned back to Lorena. 'What's the name of the British officer you were with?'

'Ferguson,' she said. 'Lieutenant Basil Ferguson.'

'What was his unit?'

'I don't know.' It suddenly occurred to her that Basil had never really explained what he did in the army.

'I haven't heard of him.' Then he smiled. 'Would you like some tea?'

Lorena and Mattei were riding in the bren-carrier, next to the officer. The light tank was following, raising clouds of sand. There was just room for the two extra passengers in the carrier, which was loaded with jerricans and spare parts, boxes of ammunition and tinned rations, all clinking and clanging at every bump in the desert track. Lorena was thinking of Basil, that she would give anything to see him again but that she would probably never know what had happened to him; there would always be a doubt in her mind, and this would form part of her life, like Amedée-Jean and Svevo and this man who had made love to her and who was sitting here by her side, his eyes half closed with that air of ease which she had come to know so well.

'Maybe,' she said in French, 'maybe he was able to surrender.'

Mattei turned his weary face towards her. His eyes shone in the dark stubble on his face.

'I hope so,' he said.

'You think he might have?'

'I hope so,' he said again. 'In any case, we'll never know.'

'I'll try to find out. I . . .'

'Did you put the idea into his head?'

'About the tanks?'

'Yes.'

'I don't know,' she said. 'I might have, just a bit. I really don't know.'

'We might know what happened one day,' Mattei said with a weary gesture. 'Two out of three have come through, that's not too bad . . . No, out of five,' he added, then in answer to her questioning look said, 'Renata and Skoda.'

'Two out of five, that's not good at all.'

No one spoke for a moment. Then the officer said to Mattei : 'I've just thought—I suppose you've come to join the Free French?'

'The what?'

'Didn't you know there's some French fighting with us again?'

'No,' said Mattei. 'No, I didn't know that.'

He deliberately avoided meeting Lorena's eyes.

The information given by Lorena and Mattei eventually reached British Army H.Q., which already knew about the German build-up at Boueirat and Sirte. But no attempt was made to break up these enemy concentrations. The Allies, after their brilliant victory over the Italians, had only just begun to regroup; Wavell was preparing to withdraw several Divisions to send them to help in the defence of Greece; there were no air or armoured forces available to attack the Germans, whose offensive was in any case not expected for several weeks.

Rommel caught the British on the move when he attacked in force in March. He recaptured El Agheila on 24 March and then swept forward, reached Bardia on 12 April, and three days later his armour was nosing into Egypt. He had cleared the Allies out of Cyrenaica in less than six weeks.

But the desert war was to continue for another two years before the Allies finally succeeded in clearing the Germans out of North Africa.

1943

Mattei focused his field glasses on the brown walls of the distant town.

'What's that place?' asked Colson.

'Tarhouna,' Mattei replied.

'D'you know it?'

'I've been through it,' Mattei said, getting back into the jeep. The constant moaning of artillery filled the air and over towards Tripoli the sky was blackened by huge columns of smoke. By the roadside, just ahead of them, two bodies covered with flies lay near an overturned Volks.

'They stink,' said Colson. 'Do we beat it?'

Mattei nodded. 'On your way.'

'What are we going to do?' asked Bonnard from the back.

'We're going to occupy Tarhouna, just the three of us,' Mattei answered.

Colson shrugged his shoulders and looked at Mattei in disbelief. As they passed the Volks, the flies on the corpses buzzed and rose in a frenzy.

'Bonnard,' said Mattei, 'be ready to fire, just in case.'

As they drew nearer Tarhouna, the road became increasingly littered with empty tins and haversacks, jerricans and webbing equipment.

'I think we're nuts to go into this town like this,' Colson said, steering the jeep slowly through the rubble. 'We could easily wait for the others.'

'I thought you wanted to win a medal,' retorted Mattei.

'I'd rather do it like Montagnac. He got his by knowing someone on the Staff,' said Colson dryly.

'Well, we're not going to wait. We'll take Tarhouna and then sit back and wait until the others arrive. Carry on.'

'Some people think they can win a war by themselves,' Colson muttered. 'You make me sick.'

Mattei said nothing. They were close to the town now and he recognised the north gate and remembered the stifling tarpaulin and Lorena's calm voice. 'Go on,' he said. 'Through the gate.'

The jeep rolled into the square where a dozen Arabs lounged and stared in silence. Colson, feeling more confident, raised a hand in greeting but the Arabs sat motionless.

'Talk about a welcome . . .'

'We'll make up for it when we get to Paris,' said Bonnard.

'It's taken two years to come eight hundred miles,' grunted Colson. 'At that rate, it'll be 1947 before you see Clichy again. And there's a sea to cross.'

Two years already, Mattei thought. Two years since I've seen Lorena. It had been in Cairo. He had been on a twenty-four-hour pass and they had met at Groppi's, the Greek teashop. Lorena had arrived before him and he remembered her amused look as he approached her table. Mattei, the fisherman, was now dressed in British battle-dress with the badge of the Free French and a blue cap of the French Colonial Army.

'You look swell,' she had said. 'Very warlike.'

Mattei had smiled warmly. 'How are you?' he asked, sitting down.

Lorena was wearing a light printed dress that suited her very well. In the course of their conversation, she explained that she was staying at the American Consulate in Cairo while awaiting passage.

'To the States?' he had asked.

'Yes,' she said. 'But the long way around. A Greek ship will take me to Cape Town and then I hope to get a plane from there, or another ship.'

She was obviously happy and he wanted to make love to her. But he did not know how to approach her. They parted late that night with only a kiss. After the door to the Consulate had closed behind her, Mattei went to the Ezbequieh district and got blind drunk. He knew that they had always been worlds apart but the inability to communicate on any level now hurt him deeply. When she had said good-bye and told him not to forget to write, he had repressed the urge to slap her in the face. The long night ended with him getting into a fight and dragged back to camp by three Military Policemen. His commanding officer had given him a lecture but did not punish him. Mattei was indispensable; he was the specialist in weapon training.

All that seemed so long ago as he sat in the hot sun looking at the flat roofs and narrow windows of the buildings surrounding the square in Tarhouna.

'Stop here,' he said.

Colson put his foot on the brake. 'Ah, you're beginning to make sense,' he said. 'Want to turn back?'

'No.' Mattei handed him his gun. 'Look after that for me.'

'You going to piss?'

Mattei said nothing. I'm acting like an idiot, he thought. There'll be no one there, and even if there is . . .

'What do you want us to do?' asked Bonnard.

'Stay here. I won't be long.'

Mattei got out of the jeep and started down a narrow street. He walked slowly and could feel Bonnard and Colson's eyes boring into his back. He turned a corner and met silence. The street ahead of him was deserted; so different from the streets teeming with Arabs and carts of a few years ago.

You're being stupid, he said again to himself. Suddenly he stopped. His heart began to pound as he recognised the house and the flag, a white cross on a red background. He lit a cigarette and then walked towards the Consulate. He pushed open the door to the garden. The gravel under his heavy boots resounded in the silence. Then a woman appeared at the top of the steps.

'You are English?' she called, touching the dark hair which was coiled around her head.

'No,' Mattei replied. 'I'm French. But it's the same thing . . . we belong to the First French Division.'

She looked past him.

'The others are waiting outside,' he said in answer to her questioning look.

'We were expecting your arrival, but we didn't think you'd be French. I'll call my husband, he'll be delighted to see you.'

She turned and called. 'Amedée-Jean.'

It can't be, thought Mattei. I must be dreaming.

'Yes, what is it?' came a voice from inside.

'The English are here!' She smiled at Mattei. 'Well, almost . . .'

Amedée-Jean came to the door leading a small girl by the hand.

He was dressed in the blue blazer and grey pants of a few years ago. He walked slowly down the steps, helping the girl jump from one step to another.

'Amedée-Jean Dalloz,' he said, holding out his hand to Mattei. 'I am the Swiss *chargé d'affaires.*'

'Sergeant Mattei, First Free French Division.'

'Mattei?' repeated Amedée-Jean with a frown. But his face cleared immediately and he went on warmly, 'We're glad to see you.' He bent down to the girl. 'Say hello to the gentleman.'

'He's a soldier,' said the girl shyly.

'He's a French soldier,' Amedée-Jean told her with an open smile. 'Anita, get us something to drink.' He turned to Mattei. 'You will have a drink with us, won't you?'

'Not now. Thanks all the same. I must get back to my jeep.'

'Is that artillery we hear?' asked Amedée-Jean.

'Yes. There's still a few units holding out along the coast road.'

'Well, there's no danger here anymore. The last of the Germans withdrew yesterday. Did you see any people in the streets?'

'A few Arabs.'

'The Italians are hiding. They're scared.' Amedée-Jean looked at Mattei. 'I think I've seen you somewhere before.'

'There are lots of Matteis.'

'Yes, I suppose so.'

'I want to go in, Daddy,' said the little girl. 'I'm hot.'

'We're going in now, darling,' said her mother. Turning to Mattei she said, 'Please excuse us.'

'Of course,' he nodded. 'Mr. Dalloz, I'll be off now.' Stepping forward with his hand extended, he spotted what looked like an unfinished mask near the steps.

'That's an odd sort of thing,' he said.

'Oh,' Amedée-Jean replied, following Mattei's gaze, 'there were a whole lot of those masks here when I first came.'

'Give it to me,' Mattei commanded.

Mattei walked back to the jeep, the mask held tightly in his hand. Bonnard and Colson were talking with some Italian civilians.

'What have you been up to?' Colson asked.

'Nothing. Just strolling around.'

Bonnard looked at the mask. 'Where did you get that thing?'

'Someone gave it to me.'

Colson shrugged his shoulders. 'He'd have done better to have given you a bottle of wine.'

Then he thrust aside the civilians who had crowded around the jeep. 'We're moving on now?' he asked as he heaved himself into the driver's seat.

'Yes,' said Mattei.

'Where to?'

Mattei put the mask down on the seat and then climbed into the jeep.

'To Djerba,' he said, and began laughing softly.